THE CRUSH CONTEST

"Hmm." She tapped her finger on her lips. "Everyone's had a crush on someone, right? It wouldn't be the most embarrassing revelation in the world. Could you find something like that?"

I thought about it. I really did not want to stand up in front of total strangers—or worse, former classmates—and get laughed at, but Aida was right that an admission of a decade-old crush on a boy in a college class wasn't the worst thing I might reveal. Besides, everyone had a crush on pretty boy Tristan back in the day. That might work well for this kind of contest.

"Would that be enough to win the prize?" And a guaranteed trip to Germany.

"Why don't we forget about the prize, okay? I'm more interested in helping you work through your anxiety."

Right. My forced therapy. "I just don't see how muscling through one reading will achieve that."

She bit her lip. "Okay, so here's the deal. It's not a one-night contest. It's an elimination-style competition. Like *American Idol*."

"Oh." That changed things considerably. I just wanted the money, but I couldn't imagine doing this week after week. Staying home and playing *Undertale* on the genocide route was sounding better and better.

Aida stood, one hand bracing her back. "Look. It's right up the street. Let's just go check it out."

When she left, I skimmed the journal, hunting for something safe and boring. I didn't believe reading something embarrassing was going to magically cure me. Nor was I going to win a weeks-long contest. But as Mr. Shepherd, my cross-country coach, used to say, *"Running begins, not with the feet, but with the mind."* Maybe just preparing to do the contest, imagining myself succeeding, would be therapeutic on its own.

I took a deep breath and pretended I was actually going to go through with it.

CRUSHING IT

Lorelei Parker

KENSINGTON BOOKS
www.kensingtonbooks.com

KENSINGTON BOOKS are published by

Kensington Publishing Corp.
119 West 40th Street
New York, NY 10018

All Kensington titles, imprints, and distributed lines are available at special quantity discounts for bulk purchases for sales promotion, premiums, fundraising, educational, or institutional use.

Special book excerpts or customized printings can also be created to fit specific needs. For details, write or phone the office of the Kensington Sales Manager: Kensington Publishing Corp., 119 West 40th Street, New York, NY 10018. Attn. Sales Department. Phone: 1-800-221-2647.

Kensington and the K logo Reg. U.S. Pat. & TM Off.

ISBN-13: 978-1-4967-2571-4 (ebook)
ISBN-10: 1-4967-2571-9 (ebook)

ISBN-13: 978-1-4967-2570-7
ISBN-10: 1-4967-2570-0
First Kensington Trade Paperback Printing: July 2020

10 9 8 7 6 5 4 3 2 1

Printed in the United States of America

To my gamer kids,
Eve and Zoe,
for the extra hearts

Acknowledgments

This book owes its existence to Wendy McCurdy and her continued faith for which I am deeply grateful. Together, we strategized on a game plan and the basic rules of combat, but then she trusted me to go off alone into the battlefield.

I died several times as I trained up during the initial drafting, but my faithful friends kept me supplied with free lives to power through to level one. As I finished each round, I enlisted the help of Kelli Newby, Kristin Wright, and Elly Blake, very special people who are always ready to read for me, like the bosses they are. They challenged me with firepower, identifying weaknesses and forcing the book to grow stronger.

I'm so lucky to have an amazing support group, including Ron, Summer, Jen, and Kelly, who are willing to give me all they've got. To all of you, thanks for always being there when I need to take a break and recharge or when I'm doubting my skills. You guys always have my back in the end.

I'm constantly awed by the team at Kensington for everything they do to bring books to life and shepherd them into the world. Thanks especially to Carly Sommerstein, Jane Nutter, and Lauren Jernigan.

Thanks also to my agent, Mike Hoogland, for all you do.

And to my kids, Eve and Zoe, who constantly show me how the game is played.

Chapter 1

I didn't want to die. Not today. Especially not in front of my coworkers.

Dying would only make this ordeal more embarrassing than it already was.

The earth could swallow me up, but that would also be too conspicuous.

And curling into a fetal position at the foot of the podium would only prolong my shame.

Nope, I wanted to disappear as if I'd never existed. Game over.

I risked a glance at Aida whose eyes were frozen in wide-open horror before she blinked her expression back to normal, polite for once in her life.

But while she wasn't laughing at me, her husband, Marco, sat behind her, one finger strategically draped across lips, biting back a smile by supreme force of will.

Reynold Kent, the only one whose opinion mattered, sat at the back of the room, giving nothing away, arms crossed, stone-faced.

"Guys, it's just my stomach." I lifted the mic attached to the placket of my shirt to prove it was my gut not my butt. I knew what it had sounded like, the gurgle of nerves churning in my bowels—like a strip of bubble wrap being popped in rapid succession followed by a balloon losing air. Those dulcet tones ended in a high-pitched curlicue, as if my stomach had asked a question. *Pffft?* The rumbling hadn't been enough to register on the Richter scale, but it had most certainly imitated a fart.

I shouldn't have been surprised. Every single time I spoke in front of people, something awful befell me, which only made my stomach twist into knots of self-fulfilling prophecy.

I didn't want to be here, but I *needed* to be here.

Aida rolled her hand to urge me to continue with the presentation, and so I shuffled the index cards. Reynold checked his phone.

I squeaked out the words on the next card. "The mage can command a variety of mystical weapons."

Like an amateur actor on a local car commercial, I gestured to the video playing on the screen behind me where a badass staff-wielding mage cast balls of flame that erupted, *boom-boom-boom.*

"Among her arsenal, the mage possesses the power to detonate her enemies with explosions of magical gas."

Marco snickered, and my courage crumbled.

I pulled the microphone off and dropped it on the table.

Reynold said, "Thank you, Sierra. That was . . ." He winced. "That was not great."

I didn't know what to say. I was blowing my one chance to prove I could demo our new video game at Gamescon in a couple of months. As lead developer of Extinction Level Event Game Designs, I should have been a shoo-in. Nobody knew the game like me. But the prospect of presenting to a room full of strangers made me sick with dread. I'd barely made it through this practice run, and I knew all three people present.

Aida ran a hand over her round belly. "Sierra, why don't you try again?"

If she weren't due to drop her spawn at the end of June, she'd be the one going to the trade show. She had a face made for showbiz and the charisma to charm the pants off reviewers and investors. With her out of the picture, the company needed someone to replace her, and that opening ought to have given me a chance to get a free trip to Cologne, Germany, to geek out on everything I loved, surrounded by other nerds. But like a hero in an adventure game, I first had to prove my mettle.

Sadly, my mettle had long ago abandoned me.

Reynold stood. "Look, if you can't do this, we'll have to find someone else who can."

No other developer was ready for prime time, and the sales staff wasn't yet well versed in the game. Yes, I sucked, but so did everyone else in some way or other. I'd have to pray for an extra life.

I picked up my things and left the conference room, defeated.

In the hallway, Wyatt from customer service emerged from the coffee nook carrying a mug in both hands, like an offering. The scent of cheap French roast mingled with his Drakkar Noir. One of those two things tempted me. I needed some caffeine.

"How'd it go?" he asked.

He wore khakis and a crisp pink Oxford that might have flattered him if he had a little more skin color. His styled blond hair had benefited from a decent salon cut and expensive products. He looked like every guy who worked in the office: unoffensive but unremarkable. Only his crooked front teeth set him apart. I'd once found his imperfect smile charming.

I shrugged. "Same as always. Epic fail."

"You'll get it right." Working the help desk had taught him optimistic ways to rephrase failure.

"Thanks?" Everyone else had more confidence than I did that I'd conquer this hurdle.

"So maybe we could go get a drink after work?" His expression left no doubt that a drink meant more than a drink. He had some nerve.

"And after?"

"Who knows?" Now his expression read full-on lech. My stomach hadn't quite recovered from the earlier presentation, and it churned at his implication.

"Wyatt, you have a girlfriend."

He tilted his head. "She's out of town."

Gross. A few months ago, I'd hooked up with him after one too many drinks but before he'd met Karen. Ever since, he thought he could coax me back for a booty call. Yeah, no. I didn't do cheating. Or cheaters.

Why did these jerks act like I owed them anything?

"Go home, Wyatt."

"Come on, Sierra. You didn't play so hard to get St. Patrick's Day."

True. I never played hard to get. I might balk at hooking up with a guy who was off the market, but my standards had fallen despairingly low when it came to emotional availability. I had a tendency to climb into bed with guys who weren't offering anything longer than a night, at least not to me. Maybe that was why I only got the sex while people like Karen got the boyfriend. Not that I'd want a Wyatt for a boyfriend.

Sadly, I was surrounded by Wyatts. At least, I wouldn't knowingly be a part of his philandering.

"You don't deserve Karen." I turned and walked away.

He called after. "You're a four, Sierra. You should take what you can get."

Despite his insult, I expected he'd send me a dick pic any minute now.

Asshole.

Back in my own office, my tension unwound. I made a beeline for my comfort zone—my Alienware gaming laptop, docked beside a pair of widescreen monitors. Before Aida invited me to the meeting room, I'd been in the middle of resolving a fascinating defect where a character's inventory suddenly blipped out. I unpaused the action and entered my world.

Inside the game, I was a goddess, even if I had to fight off an armored giant carrying a flaming mace. Inside the game, I had control and power. It didn't matter if my enemies were CGI or avatars played by real live opponents in some far-flung living room. It didn't matter if they were men or women, tall or short, rich or poor. We were all as powerful as our gaming skills allowed.

In virtual space, no one could hear my stomach scream.

I longed to meet the actual players on the other side of the monitor. My people. Ever since I'd first learned about gaming conventions, I'd wanted to attend one for myself, but I could never justify the expense. And here I was blowing a free trip to one of the biggest cons in the world because my head and my body couldn't make peace with each other long enough to allow me to overcome my nerves.

Short of Xanax, there was no way I'd shake the crushing performance anxiety that had plagued me for nearly ten years.

The knock came on the doorframe sooner than I'd expected.

"Beware of dragons," I hollered over my shoulder.

"Can we talk?"

I paused the game and spun around without getting up. I pulled my feet up and rested my elbows on my knees, chin on fists.

Aida ventured in, grabbing a rolling chair from beside the unused desk, sighing as she sat. "My God. I'm going to pop if I get any bigger."

"Do you want to ask me not to kill the messenger?"

"Reynold says you're just not ready yet. But he's open to changing his mind."

I chortled. "Oh, and how am I supposed to do that? Finger puppets?"

She didn't laugh. "You know he's considering Gerry."

"Old Man Morris?" Things must be bad if he'd rather send the resident network guy instead of a scrappy young developer. "How? He doesn't even program."

"Neither do I." She raised a brow, chiding. "Gerry has a pleasant demeanor." Somehow I knew she was quoting Reynold, not stating her own opinion.

"I should find a way to knock him out of the running. I'll switch his coffee with decaf, and he'll fall asleep while Reynold's auditioning him for the spot."

"You of all people would never do that."

She was right. Not just because coffee was a sacred and untouchable source of joy and I'd never mess with anyone else's elixir. But also because I'd once been the victim of a sabotage that had left me with this crippling fear of public speaking.

Aida used her heels to roll her chair closer. "Besides, I think you'd rather get that spot on your own, right?"

"That was what I was trying to do earlier. You saw how that went. How am I supposed to overcome my own body turning on me?"

"I had an idea." She unlocked her phone, and her thumbs clicked and scrolled. "I saw a post on Facebook the other day that caught my attention at the time because it was so . . . weird, I guess. But I got to thinking—"

"What? Is someone selling healing crystals this time?"

Her maroon lips pressed together in judgment of my quippy sarcasm. I coveted whatever brand of lipstick she had on—something more practical to my everyday life than this conversation.

Aida persisted in the belief that there had to be a magic cure to this mental block. When therapy went nowhere, we'd tried guided meditation videos, herbal teas, and a workshop on using imagination to boost confidence. But I wasn't lacking confidence exactly. It was more that I could picture every kind of humiliation that awaited me if I stood in front of a group of people, with all eyes on me, and attempted to speak on any topic upon which I was supposed to be an expert. I could lead a yoga class at the local YMCA, but ask me to stand behind a microphone and I froze.

If I somehow overcame my resistance, calamity—or unusually loud gas—struck.

She sighed. "Hey, the aromatherapy might not have worked, but you have to admit our town house smells great."

"Sure." I picked up a *Sonic the Hedgehog* Funko that had fallen on the floor and stood to place it back on the credenza.

"It's like strolling through a cool forest meadow at sunset in our bathroom."

She angled her phone toward me. "Do you remember Alfred Jordan?"

I squinted, trying to place the name. "Alfred? No."

"He's in this Facebook group I joined for Auburn alums who live here in Atlanta now. Anyway, listen to this." She read the post on-screen. " 'The Vibes Taphouse presents its first annual Chagrin Challenge. Bring your embarrassing anecdotes, diary entries, poetry, or other past shames for a chance to win prizes, up to the grand prize of one thousand dollars. All participants will receive a free drink and all the chiding.' "

"Uh-huh?" She couldn't have been suggesting I volunteer as tribute. I could only assume she was thinking of winning herself an extra grand. "So what? You're going to reveal your most mortifying secrets to a roomful of strangers?"

She'd do it, too. Aida had gumption to spare, not to mention an unending supply of stories that would have an audience clutching their guts. She wouldn't hesitate to expose her embarrassment, especially if there was a competition involved. They might as well write the check out to her right now.

"*I'm* not going to do it." Her eyes bored into mine, begging me to get a clue.

My heart sank. "No way."

"Sierra, we've tried every gentle option we could think of. We haven't tried trial by fire."

"You mean death by a hundred snickers." I crossed my arms.

"No. What you're describing isn't just humiliation, it's humiliation squared." I combed through the possible anecdotes I might share and heard a record scratch. "What am I supposed to tell them? About the time I neglected to wear a bra under a white shirt on a day of a heavy downpour?"

Aida snorted. "Don't you have a diary?"

"My journal?" My stomach cramped. I visualized myself standing in front of a room filled with mean drunks, heckling me. Or worse, a bunch of bored drunks, yawning as I revealed myself. I balked. "There's no possible way I can share whatever I've written in public. I would rather die."

She grabbed a pen from my Power-Up Mushroom mug and scribbled a note onto a Post-it. "Here's the website for the event. Check it out."

"Fine." I swiped the sticky note. "But no promises."

Chapter 2

Aida, Marco, and I carpooled home from the Midtown Atlanta office to Virginia-Highland, a hip little neighborhood a
ten-minute drive away, where Aida and I had rented a town
house together right out of college. She'd started work at Coca-
Cola, and I'd gotten a job at a startup software company that
went belly-up a few years later. It was an expensive area, but
we'd been hired with strong opening salaries and figured they'd
only go up with time.

We were wrong.

Neither of us anticipated we'd put our financial security on
the line by starting our own company, but after I lost my job, we
took a serious look at the games Marco and I had been developing and decided it was time to find an investor.

Enter Reynold and his venture capital.

Our company blossomed along with Aida's budding romance
with Marco. I probably should have moved out when Marco
moved in, but where would I have gone? Instead, I relocated to
my lair in the basement, at a fair discount in my rent, but they
were progressively squeezing me out. Once their baby came, we
might need to reassess the arrangement.

If this next game sold well, maybe I'd get my own town
house. Maybe even one of the cute cottages down the street.

Aida tossed her purse on the table and followed me to my

home sweet home in the cave below. While I tugged off my shoes, she took a seat on my futon. "So I was reading the comments on that Facebook post I showed you."

"Uuugh." I dropped down on the floor cross-legged and unlocked my spare laptop to unpause a game of *Undertale*.

"Look. There seemed to be a lot of interest from alumni around the area. You might reconnect with someone you knew at Auburn or meet some new friends."

"Mmm-hmm." I was paying attention, but my focus was on the screen where my character entered a room and . . . yes! I found Papyrus guarding a door, saying, "*Oho! The human arrives!*"

"Or a nice guy."

I paused the game. "Sure. I'll have no problem meeting some random guy at a bar who's single, attractive, roughly my age, and who isn't put off by a nerd girl like me."

Aida crossed her arms as well as she could over an eight-month pregnant belly. "Come on. You never have trouble attracting cute guys, Sierra. You just need higher standards. And you need to vet them a little better before you bump uglies."

"Sex is the easy part, though."

She gave me the *bullshit* eyes. "It's not easy forever. You're going to have to make small talk with them at some point. Maybe next time you meet a guy, kiss him good night and wait for him to call. It might cut down on your Wyatt ratio."

"Yeah. But when they don't call, I'll have missed a chance to get laid."

"Did it ever occur to you you could call *them*?"

God forbid I chase after a guy. "What? To get a verbal rejection instead of the silent one?"

She threw up her hands, and then she got that coy smile I hated. It meant she had an idea. "Maybe . . ." She looked altogether too confident for a maybe. "Maybe it's all interrelated."

"What?"

"Look, you're really great at what you do. You drive your developers to get huge projects done. You're super confident about your own work. But then you freeze up when you have to do anything resembling public speaking. And you shy away from intimacy with guys. Maybe it's the same issue."

"Well, I don't like to speak in public because I don't want to make an ass of myself."

"You're afraid that people will see the real you and not like you."

"Okay, armchair psychologist." I was ready for this interrogation to end.

"No really. I think I'm on to something."

"And the solution is to do what? Read my horrifying diary to strangers?"

"Don't you have something old? Like from high school? I'm pretty sure this event is supposed to be as funny for you as it is for the audience. Like reading confessions from the past that no longer relate to you now."

"Hmm." I did have high school diaries, but they were boxed up in the basement at my parents' house out in Norcross.

"What about that one class you took sophomore year at Auburn? Didn't you keep a daily journal?"

Even though it had been a decade ago, I had a good reason to remember. "Um, yeah. That was that public-speaking class."

Her eyes lit with a sudden recognition. "No, seriously? The one with the contest?"

"Yeah." Even ten years later, my heart beat faster at the memory of the ordeal that had paralyzed me so completely. Aida had been there to pick up the pieces, like always. And here she was pushing me into another. "We had to do morning pages for that class. I kept a notebook."

"So what did you write in it?"

I held up my hands. "I dunno. We were supposed to empty our minds of the concerns of the day and flex our creative muscles. I probably kept it fairly light, worried the teacher might collect them at any moment."

"Do you still have it?"

"Maybe."

I cast about my room until I located a box of junk from college that had become a makeshift base for a stack of miscellaneous crap. I removed the shoebox filled with birthday cards, cross-country medals from high school, and other nostalgia I didn't want but couldn't bring myself to throw away. The cardboard lid of the storage box had collapsed from the weight. I sat on my haunches and rifled through archaic term papers, copies of student loan applications, housing agreements, and various certificates and awards. Underneath it all, I dug out several spiral-bound notebooks labeled with the names of the classes they'd belonged to.

The bright red one had *Comm 1000* written in black Sharpie and other doodles of flowers and geometric shapes. One drawing stood out among the others, mainly because it was too artistic to be the chicken scratches of someone killing time. More intriguing, it appeared to be a rendition of my face, or how I might have looked ten years ago.

I ran my thumb over the drawing, trying to remember how it got there. Ten years was a long time, and my brain only held on to flashes of memories, images that had seared in permanently, and even those had eroded over time or coalesced with other memories to form new beliefs about my past. The details were lost. Or perhaps they were captured in the notebook I held before me.

I sat on the edge of the bed with the journal in my lap and flipped open to the first page.

My handwriting had been so neat, so confident ten years ago. But holy cow, the sheer number of words shocked me. How had I had so much to say?

I scanned the opening entry.

This is my writing journal. I have to write in my journal for fifteen minutes every day. I am now writing in my journal.

Oh, that was how. I went from worrying my journal might reveal too many deep dark secrets to thinking it might be one long obvious attempt to cheat the assignment. Further down, the bullshit fell away, and what I'd written began to show a peek into my nineteen-year-old brain.

"Listen to this."

Aida propped a pillow behind her and leaned against the wall, where a headboard ought to be, and I read the last few lines on the page.

" 'I don't know anybody in my smaller classes, and in the auditorium classes, I feel invisible. I hope I make a friend soon.' "

I glanced up at her and smiled because I'd met Aida in an auditorium class when she'd plopped down next to me after missing the first week and said, "*You look like you take good notes.*"

The very last line read: *This daily journal is going to suck.*

Maybe farther back, I'd find more interesting tidbits, but it would take me forever to read the journal cover to cover. I held the makings of a novella in my hands. Plus, there was the more pressing question . . .

"How will reading this in public make me feel less anxious?"

"Think about it. You're worried you'll be embarrassed when you get up to speak. But if the entire aim is to be humiliated, and if everybody there is hoping to be the most humiliated, then your fear becomes your secret weapon. You'd be swimming in your element."

It made a weird kind of sense. And the grand prize, if I could win it, would cover the entire expense of a trip to Gamescon whether or not I got picked for the presentation.

"I doubt I wrote anything worthwhile, though." I flipped through a few more pages, and a name I'd tried to forget jumped out at me. My eyes shot wide open. "Or I might have confessed I was in love with Tristan Spencer."

Yummy Tristan Spencer.

Tristan had been the classic skater boy, with long blond locks and smooth soft-looking cheeks, often dusted with the sunlight of his golden scruff. Yeah, I'd etched him in my memory with all the poetic imagery of a love song. He'd worn one earring in his left ear, and his unconventional style stood out on the conservative campus, like a rebel, like a rogue. And his lips—

Aida broke my trance. "Tristan Spencer? There's a revolting blast from the past."

"Speaking of mortifying moments."

"Speaking of your terrible taste in men." She gave me the maternal smile that seemed to have developed along with her child within.

My obsession with Tristan had been legendary, but Aida only remembered his role in my public disgrace. Sure he'd pulled a nasty trick on me that destroyed my confidence for the past ten years, and I hated him in theory. After all, Tristan's prank was the whole reason I was sitting here digging through my old journal, chasing another cockamamie scheme to overcome a panic that lived in my bones.

But it was hard to hold a grudge that long, especially one I'd been trying to forget.

"I know, but Aida, he was so beautiful. I probably filled pages of this journal with confessions of longing. "

"Hmm." She tapped her finger on her lips. "Everyone's had a crush on someone, right? It wouldn't be the most embarrassing revelation in the world. Could you find something like that?"

I thought about it. I really did not want to stand up in front of total strangers—or worse, former classmates—and get laughed at, but Aida was right that an admission of a decade-old crush on a boy in a college class wasn't the worst thing I might reveal. Besides, everyone had a crush on pretty-boy Tristan back in the day. That might work well for this kind of contest.

"Would that be enough to win the prize?" And a guaranteed trip to Germany.

"Why don't we forget about the prize, okay? I'm more interested in helping you work through your anxiety."

Right. My forced therapy. "I just don't see how muscling through one reading will achieve that."

She bit her lip. "Okay, so here's the deal. It's not a one-night contest. It's an elimination-style competition. Like *American Idol.*"

"Oh." That changed things considerably. I just wanted the money, but I couldn't imagine doing this week after week. Staying home and playing *Undertale* on the genocide route was sounding better and better.

Aida stood, one hand bracing her back. "Look. It's right up the street. Let's just go check it out."

When she left, I skimmed the journal, hunting for something safe and boring. I didn't believe reading something embarrassing was going to magically cure me. Nor was I going to win a weeks-long contest. But as Mr. Shepherd, my cross-country coach, used to say, *"Running begins not with the feet, but with the mind."* Maybe just preparing to do the contest, imagining myself succeeding, would be therapeutic on its own.

I took a deep breath and pretended I was actually going to go through with it.

Chapter 3

As a programmer, I spent my work hours holed up in my dark office or working remote from my equally pitch-black basement. I was slowly becoming a vampire, and since I loved makeup, I'd become a vampire of the glittery variety. I liked to experiment with hair color, and I had a fairly idiosyncratic wardrobe that showed off my specific interests and fandoms. Starting in high school, my parents fed my addiction for pop-themed T-shirts and dresses. If it had anything to do with *The Legend of Zelda* or *Mario Brothers*, I needed it. I had four IKEA dressers and a closet overstuffed with the clothes I'd amassed. For cosplay, I even had Asuna's battle cloak from my favorite anime *Sword Art Online*, a story set entirely inside a virtual reality video game. Totally my jam.

Getting ready to be ordinary in public took a little extra thought. When I went to yoga, I twisted my hair up to minimize the shock of the colors and donned plain yoga pants and a fun T-shirt. Most people were cool about my style, but I knew there were times to tone it down.

Like tonight when I'd have the added stress of a potential spotlight on me. Knowing strangers would be picking me apart ratcheted up my need for maximum camouflage.

First, my hair. A few months back, I'd gone to the trouble of oil-slicking my normally light brown hair. It looked cool—a mess of purple, blue, hot pink, and green—but it made me stick out in a way I wanted to mitigate when I was already outside my element. Fortunately, it had grown out enough I could almost completely hide the colorful ends in a pair of space buns.

Next came my makeup. Many visits to the consultation chair at Sephora had netted me an extensive collection of foundations, blushes, lip tints, eye shadows, and liners. I'd become an expert at concealing all my blemishes, hiding red patches, enhancing my cheekbones, drawing a perfect cat eye beyond my lashes, and accentuating all the colors and gold flecks in my hazel eyes. Nature might not have blessed me with beauty, but science helped.

Finally, clothes. For tonight, low-key was the idea, so I dug out my navy *Zelda* MAKE IT RAIN T-shirt and a flared plaid miniskirt. I threw on a pair of knee-high socks and my black Converse high-tops. Comfortable. Cool girl.

By seven, I was sitting in the living room, playing a little *Mario Kart* while waiting for Aida to finish getting ready. *Mario Kart* was my relaxation game. I loved to race against whoever might be connected locally, especially against one specific player who never played this early in the evening. My late-night nemesis often beat me, but that was exactly why I'd added him to my list of favorites. Losing only served to galvanize my competitive streak.

I'd won four races against unchallenging players when I heard Aida making her slow descent. I powered down mid-race, grabbed my backpack, and stuffed in the journal I was most probably *not* going to need. Aida would have to understand if I bailed on her. This was a kamikaze mission.

As we headed out the front door, she gave me a once-over. "You look super cute. I wish I could wear anything resembling a miniskirt."

"You are rocking the elastic black maternity ensemble."

"Coincidentally, the name of my band."

She really did look amazing. She'd always had a killer body, toned and tanned, but pregnancy had softened her in a way that suited her. Her black hair shone, and when she wasn't grumbling about the alien invading her, she seemed legitimately happy. I tried not to envy her.

I waited on the front porch while she locked up. The sun had begun to set, and a mild summer breeze promised a nice stroll up Virginia Street, past the distinct and beautiful homes I wished I could afford.

Within ten minutes, we found ourselves at the edge of the cute strip of restaurants and stores that drew people our age to this neighborhood. Enough light lingered on the main drag that the streetlamps hadn't yet kicked in. Aida pointed out the entrance to the bar that hadn't been there a year ago. I'd never even stopped in since it had replaced whatever clothing store I'd never shopped at. The facade blended in well with the rest of the neighborhood, with the exception of the vertical marquee sign that read *VIBES* in lights and the fact that the building had two floors when most of the others were single story.

Aida pressed on ahead of me. "Come on. There's no harm in checking it out."

I followed her through the door, moving out of the way of a couple exiting. I caught up as Aida was taking a stool at the bar. I slid in next to her as a man's voice thundered, "Sierra Reid?"

This was not an uncommon occurrence. For one thing, Atlanta was a magnet, and a lot of people I'd gone to school with had gravitated nearby. I'd go to Piedmont Park and run into someone from my high school cross-country team or my college dorm. For another, I'd dated any number of Atlanta's not-so-finest via dating apps. I hoped this wasn't one of those.

I turned toward the speaker and discovered a rather attractive bartender with the barest hint of a beard smiling like he'd been expecting me. I gave him a quizzical look. "Hi?"

Aida held out her hand. "I'm Aida Vargas. You must be Alfred."

Aha. He was obviously the Alfred who'd advertised the contest. She must have called ahead to make sure I'd go through with this charade and dropped my name.

He shook her hand. "Call me Alfie." He reached over to me, and we clasped hands. "You probably don't remember, but we were in school together."

I narrowed an eye and processed him with this new knowledge. Surely I would have remembered someone as cute as him. He had a low-key Harry Styles vibe going on with the kind of floppy brown hair parents would say needed a trim, but that in reality needed a good ruffling. His friendly eyes were framed by long dark lashes. And he wore a crooked half smile that made me want to lie.

"Alfie! Of course." Had we shared a class together? "How are you?"

"Great." He spread his arms out as if to showcase everything around him. "I bought this bar a year ago. Dream come true."

He was the owner? Maybe he could clue me in on the expectations for this contest. "So Aida dragged me here for some kind of humiliation festival?"

"Chagrin Challenge." He reached under the counter and retrieved a light-blue flyer. "I'm hoping more Auburn alums show up. It's good to see you both!" He glanced at Aida, but his eyes came back to mine. "It's been way too long."

"Yeah. I—"

Aida slid off the stool. "I'm just gonna go see about signing you up." She reached into her purse and dropped a twenty on the bar. "Could I get a Sprite and whatever she's drinking."

Before I could body slam her, she was away. As she headed toward the small stage on the far side of the room, Alfie reached up and grabbed a glass. "What'll you have?"

Good question. Alcohol might calm my nerves, but it could also blunt my natural inhibitions. I might confidently make an ass of myself fueled by liquid courage. "Club soda with lime. On the rocks."

He busied himself with the drinks and laid down two cocktail napkins before setting the drinks before me. I expected him to get back to tending to other customers, but he didn't move. "That's a great shirt."

I glanced down as if I didn't remember what I was wearing. "Oh, yeah. You know the game?"

"Sure. I used to play it with my dad." He started humming the tune to the "Song of Storms"—the notes on my shirt—and I grinned.

I remembered hanging in my dad's man cave on the grungy sofa watching him play before he handed over the controller so I could sneak in a half hour before bedtime. "My dad was big into *Mario Sunshine*. That was my intro to Nintendo."

He leaned forward, elbows on the counter. "Your intro? Besides *Mario* and *Zelda*, what else do you play?"

"Mostly MMORPG games."

His forehead creased. "I know RPG stands for role-playing games. But what's MMO?"

"Massively multiplayer online games. Like *Skyforge*, *World of Warcraft*, and oh my God, have you ever seen *Age of Wushu*?"

He chuckled. "No. It's good?"

"It's beautiful. Plus martial arts? What's not to love?"

A tall blond woman squeezed in behind Alfie, laid a hand on his shoulder, and whispered in his ear. He leaned closer to speak to her for a moment, long enough for me to catch the way they communicated in shorthand, like people who have spent a lot of time together. They were probably more than just coworkers. When she moved to take the order of a neglected customer at the other end of the bar and Alfie turned his attention back to me, I realized I'd been flirting, taken in by his pleasant demeanor. He was clearly a good bartender, getting me to geek out about stuff I liked without making me feel like a giant dork. And his eyes hadn't once drifted below my own. Bonus points.

"Sorry. I'm sure you're not interested." I touched my buns to make sure no strands of hair had come loose.

"Why do you say that?"

"It's shop talk. Do you even game anymore?"

"A little, though I'm beginning to think I've been missing out on a whole world. You'd be bored with my collection of worn-out old games."

"Nothing wrong with the classics."

"So did Aida say she's signing you up for the contest tonight?"

I shrugged. "She thinks she can drag me to poison, but I dunno."

"Do you have something to read? A diary maybe?"

I reached into my bag and slid out the notebook. "It might be lame, but—"

"Yes! Comm!"

"Yeah. Did you take that class?"

He tilted his head for a second like I'd said something confusing, but he only said, "It was a requirement."

"Oh, right." I ran a hand over the notebook. "I figured it's probably more embarrassing to me than funny for anyone else."

"I wonder if only our class had to do those morning pages."

I heard the "our class" and another piece of information clinked into place. "You were in my comm class."

"Yeah. I thought more people might have those notebooks lying around, but when I brought it up, I only got one comment from someone who might bring his. Meanwhile, I'm planning to humiliate myself with a piece of poetry."

Without meaning to, I laughed. "Oh, God. Sorry. It's not funny."

His eyes crinkled at the corners when he smiled. "Tell me that after you hear it. I wrote it a long time ago." He stage whispered, "I'm kind of nervous."

"You're going to read it anyway?" He didn't look nervous, but maybe he was hiding it. Like me.

The lights flashed, briefly, and Aida returned to her stool with a wink and a nudge. "You're all signed up."

A microphone switched on, followed by feedback. Alfie nodded. "That's my signal. Wish me luck!"

He skipped backward, then spun around and jogged up to the mic, exactly unlike someone nervous to perform.

Chapter 4

"Hello everyone! And welcome to the first annual Chagrin Challenge." Alfie wrapped his hand around the mic and yanked it from the stand. "Thanks to the fifteen of you who volunteered to share your experiences for our entertainment. Please stop by the bar after your humiliation for a glass of house wine or tap beer of your choice."

The crowd laughed, and I smiled even though he was talking about me and my humiliation.

"Okay, so I need to run through the ground rules before we get started. First, if your content is deemed offensive, you'll be disqualified and possibly asked to leave. Swearing and R-rated sexual content is permissible. Intolerant hate speech is not. Got it? Second, please stay until the end of the contest to find out who is moving on to next week. We'll be cutting three people per round, which means culling down to twelve of you tonight, so bring your A game! Mind you, there are some twists to come! Oh, and as you probably know, the grand prize is one thousand dollars. Are you ready?"

Applause erupted along with a few hoots. The bar had gotten progressively more crowded since we'd arrived. I scanned the people sitting at tables or gathered along the wall in the back, wondering how Aida expected me to stand in front of total strangers and recite the alphabet, let alone read from my journal. My pulse throbbed in my fingertips and blood roared in my ears.

"We're going alphabetically, so we'll be starting with A. Coincidentally, I'm first. Don't worry, I'm not competing, just showing solidarity."

The lights dimmed, and a spotlight lit him so he seemed to be the only person in the room. He cleared his throat. "Okay, I am already having second thoughts, but I promised someone I'd do this." He lifted his eyes and looked in the direction of the bar, where I was sitting. He took a breath and blew it out roughly through rounded lips. "My only excuse here is that I wrote this a long time ago. It's called 'Raging.' "

He dropped his head for a moment, and everyone in the room quieted, anticipating, encouraging maybe. Alfie straightened and put the mic back on the stand before holding out a piece of paper that wavered, giving away a tremor of nerves. My heart went out to him.

Then he began to read in a clear, confident voice.

> "She reaches her hand across the never-ending sea
> Toward mine extended
> But a storm rages within, without
> And with a touch she's apprehended
> The damp of my palm, the tremor of my fingers
> She's heard the unintended
> Thunder in my heart
> The lightning that sparks between us
> And as the rain hits my face
> She turns toward the sun."

For longer than a heartbeat, the room remained utterly silent. My chest grew tight from the breath I'd been holding. I exhaled at last with a whispered *wow*. Then the crowd seemed to realize he was done and clapped appreciatively.

Alfie took a small bow and said, "Miranda, take it away."

Nobody laughed at him, but as he stepped away from the mic, several people elbowed him, chided him. Had they failed to hear what I heard?

I blinked away tears that had welled up. How silly.

The woman who'd been working with Alfie behind the bar stepped up to the mic and said, "Big round of applause for our fearless leader. My name is Miranda, and I'll be taking over moderation duties for the rest of the evening. I hope you're ready to go as I'll be calling your names without much fanfare. Our very first casualty is Bryce Lieberman. Let's give him a warm welcome."

Alfie slid behind the bar and began quietly taking orders from the people holding their money out, waiting. I didn't know I was staring until he flashed me a smile and asked, "How bad was that?"

I wanted to tell him it was beautiful, but would he think I was dumb for appreciating his words when he found them so lacking? "You did great."

He filled my glass with club soda. "Promise me you'll take your turn. Please?"

My mouth went dry at the thought, but the club soda helped settle my stomach. "I'm thinking about it."

Aida nudged me. "Shhh."

People were laughing, and I tuned in to Bryce, who was midway through his performance. He held the mic, like a stand-up comic, journal in the other hand.

"I already said yes to Jodie. I don't like Jodie, but Tobin does, so I knew he'd be mad if I took her to Homecoming."

Bryce performed with all the sullen attitude of a petulant teenager. A little whine, a lot of entitlement.

"But now I can't ask Patrick, and what if he goes with someone else and then they fall in love and get married and I never had a chance to let Patrick know I liked him?"

Bryce played up the dramatics of his dilemma, and he was rewarded by snickers. I suddenly worried my journal was going to be too boring. I opened it up to the marked page and read it, looking for anything that might generate laughter. But my writing was flat and cowardly. I scanned the next page, then the next. By the end of the first week of class, I'd started actually journaling. It was there I found pay dirt. A real confession of late-teen infatuation. And it was actually pretty funny, or so I thought. It might do.

A girl named Dana followed Bryce and read a passage about how thrilled her thirteen-year-old self was to get her first period. I began to understand how everything was funnier because the author of the diary was *Dana*, but not current-day Dana. She was able to poke fun at herself because there'd been time to gain perspective, and although what she was reading wasn't exactly funny, everyone laughed along because her adolescent struggle felt somehow universal. At least all the women could relate.

Suddenly the phrase *tragedy plus time equals comedy* made perfect sense.

A guy named Gary told a story about attempting to have sex in a train bathroom that was so outlandish, I had to wonder if it was even true. But I was crying with laughter when he said, "That's when the train conductor knocked on the door and said, 'Ticket, please.' "

When Heather was called up, I excused myself to go to the bathroom. All that club soda wasn't playing well with my growing nerves. I took my notebook into the stall and whisper-read my entry aloud, wondering what I'd gotten myself into.

When I came back, another girl was up on stage. I asked Aida what I'd missed. "Nothing. That's Hillary."

I was counting as each contestant went up. The sixth person's name was Mike. I tried to anticipate when I'd be called, but there was simply no way to extrapolate from the names. I could be last if the rest of the contestants all had names beginning with R. Or there could be eight guys named Steve, waiting their turn.

But seven and eight were Porter and Quinn. I spaced out completely on their readings, scanning my page again. What if I offended someone?

Nine was a Ray. Ten was Rosemary. I shot a glance at the door, wondering if I could bolt before they called me. Aida laid a hand on my knee. Maybe I should go back to my bland original selection.

Eleven was Shannon. I had to be next. I shook out my hands because I could no longer feel them.

When Shannon left the stage, I grasped my journal, knowing what was coming as Miranda said, "Remember Shannon was contestant number eleven. Please vote for contestant number eleven." I was going to throw up. "Next up, please welcome Shawn."

That was the moment of reprieve I needed. I shot off my stool and took two steps toward the exit.

"Hey." Alfie's voice caught my attention. "Sierra."

I stopped dead, as my fight-or-flight impulses warred with each other. Alfie came around the end of the bar and faced me.

My adrenaline surged, and I wanted to cry. He'd made me promise I'd perform, but everything was closing in, and I needed to be outside.

Alfie laid a hand on my arm. "Take a breath. Now let it out."

I did as he said.

"And again."

I inhaled. I exhaled.

"Good." He cocked his head. "I wanted to bail, too, before. I find talking in front of people to be the scariest thing in the world."

"You?" He seemed to have it all together. He had to be lying to make me feel better.

"Fake it till you make it."

I'd heard that one way too often. "That's what my cross-country coach used to say." He'd also said, "*By failing to prepare, you are preparing to fail.*" Words of advice that cemented my desire to flee before I fell flat on my face publicly.

Alfie inched a little closer and made direct eye contact. "Look, you don't have to go up there. No obligation. But don't leave, okay? I'll still give you the free drink."

His words uncoiled the tightly wound tension in my neck, and the jittery belly nerves I'd been fighting effervesced into a different kind of falling sensation. I instinctively glanced around for Miranda, not wanting to get him in trouble with his girl-friend. Or wife?

I nodded. "Okay."

Once the pressure to perform had ebbed, I felt a bit silly for my overreaction. After all, Alfie had managed to read poetry, which I'd never have the courage to do. I wanted to make him proud of me.

Which is why, when I heard Miranda say, "Next up, please welcome Sierra," I turned and walked toward the stage before I could lose my nerve again.

The spotlight was soft, not blinding, but beyond the golden radius I could only make out the edges of the tables closest to the stage and the distant bar, an island of its own light. It gave me the impression I was only speaking to a couple of people. I found a friendly face subdued by shadows and opened my journal.

My stomach knotted, and I breathed in and out like Alfie had advised.

"This is from a writing class I took about ten years ago." A frog caught firmly in my throat.

"Speak up." The disembodied voice came from out in the blackness. I squinted as if I'd be able to see who'd spoken.

I leaned into the microphone and apologized. The speakers emitted a high-pitched squeal like an external representation of my mounting panic.

I coughed. Miranda handed me a glass of water, and I grate-fully took a sip.

The water soothed my throat, but it couldn't overcome the cramp in my lower intestines. If I made fart sounds, I would die. That thought made the water churn, fueling new worries it might come right back up. I could live out in real time a leg-endary urban myth about some poor soul whose bodily fluids flew from both ends at once.

Aida called out, "You've got this, Sierra!" and my cheeks flamed. It was bad enough I was bombing. I didn't need her shouting out pathetic encouragements. But the surge of irrita-tion at her had the unexpected effect of taking the edge off my nerves enough to allow me to regain control of impending hysteria.

I took another calming breath, then repeated my opening statement, louder now.

"This is a journal from a writing class ten years ago." I continued.

"The question I asked myself today was this: In the event of an apocalyptic catastrophe that wiped out humankind while somehow sparing my comm class, would we be able to repopulate the earth?"

A burst of laughter surprised me, and I smiled. Maybe I could do this.

"I mean, biologically, it would be feasible. The ratio of boys to girls in our class might be low, but if we're only talking numbers, the men could spread their seed widely. It only takes one stallion. But that assumes these guys are studly enough to attract even a single woman."

I swallowed and shot a glance over at Alfie, lit from behind at the bar. He leaned forward on his elbows, listening intently. He raised a hand and flashed a thumbs-up. Relieved, I soldiered on.

"Granted, the women might be willing to sacrifice for the salvation of humanity, but would it be a stick-and-carrot situation? Or would there be a possibility of some voluntary coupling? Could we ensure the survival of the species without resorting to drawing straws?

"And what if the stallions balk at procreating with the women available to them? Though who are we kidding? Unless all the stallions are gay, the studs will be down—or should I say *up*—for the effort. So, it's a simple question of physical attraction. How many people in the class are instantly doable?"

I stole a glance at the lady I'd picked as my friendly face earlier. She had a smile plastered on, so I took that as a good sign. My mouth was beginning to feel like cotton, so I gulped more water.

"As it turns out, a large class filled with college kids would be the ideal resource for repopulating the earth. My comm class is packed with so many pretty girls, I have to wonder if my participation would be required at all. Maybe the boys in the class would have such a luxury of options that I'd manage to remain single even when I was practically the last girl on Earth."

This might have pushed past funny into pathetic, but they hadn't kicked me off the stage. And pathetic was the name of the game, after all. Still, my hands shook a bit as I reached for the glass of water and took another sip. My time was probably running out, and I wanted to get to the gushy schoolgirl crush since that seemed to be the money shot.

"In my hunt for my postapocalyptic fuck buddy, I returned time and again to the one boy in the room who could probably single-handedly repopulate the planet. With or without the apocalypse.

"Tristan Spencer is the prettiest boy I've ever seen. I'd have Tristan Spencer's postapocalyptic babies, and he wouldn't have to ask twice.

"We've been in classes together before, but I've never had the nerve to talk to him.

"Maybe tomorrow.

"Maybe the world will end tomorrow."

I closed my notebook and stepped away from the mic with a sigh of relief.

The speaker popped once, and then for a moment silence descended. I'd done it. My mouth had gone completely dry, I needed to pee, and my hands still trembled, but I'd stood in front of a roomful of strangers and shared a personal anecdote. My heart hadn't exploded. I hadn't vomited. I bit my lip and risked a small smile, satisfied with myself.

The audience clapped. I hadn't fallen flat on my face or somehow managed to pour water down my shirt. I'd done it! That hadn't been nearly as humiliating as I'd expected.

In fact, reading my old writing, I was proud of my former me. Where had that spirit gone?

Miranda took the stage and slipped something into my hand. As I stepped down from the raised platform, I held it up over my head to better see it in the spotlight. It was a shiny golden star that read, "*Good for one glass of beer or wine.*"

I wound through the tables toward the bar to the applause generated when Miranda asked the audience to give me another round. "Remember that Sierra was contestant number thirteen. You are voting for contestant number thirteen."

I caught Alfie's eye, hoping for some signs of approval from my new ally, but he had a pinched expression, like the nurse just before she explained I had a UTI—concerned, slightly horrified. *My God.* I'd never checked to make sure my fly was zipped. My hand flew to my crotch before I thought to take a more surreptitious examination or remembered I had on a skirt. The wheels of my imagination began to turn.

Had my mascara run down my face under the flop sweat? Did I have pit stains? I pushed my way back to my barstool as the contest continued on behind me.

Before I could ask Alfie why he looked like my nipple had popped out of my T-shirt, Miranda announced contestant number fourteen.

"Everyone please welcome Tristan Spencer."

Chapter 5

According to war movies, when a bomb detonates, the world goes into slow motion and the sound narrows to the pulsing of helicopter blades, chopping the air, *whomp-whomp-whomp,* before everything rushes back. For a moment or an infinity, my senses cut out entirely. And then, all I heard was laughter.

Everyone was laughing at me.

There wasn't a hole big enough to throw myself into. I grabbed my bag, slung it over my shoulder, and took one full stride before a hand wrapped around my elbow and defied my valiant attempt to disappear.

"Where do you think you're going?" Aida's eyebrow rose as if daring me to take one more step.

"Home."

A voice came over the loudspeaker. "Well, that was a nice compliment."

I couldn't help my curiosity. I turned around to see him. Ten years might have blunted his beauty, but life wasn't fair and, under the glow of the spotlight, Tristan looked like a god in human form, bursting at the seams to become a source of light. He no longer sported the shoulder-length blond hair I'd always wanted to drag my fingers through, but the cut proved he'd grown up. Maybe we all had.

"Whoa." His eyes grew wide, like the shock had just registered, like his whole face was saying *whoa.* "That's going to be an impossible act to follow."

My heart slowed as it became clear he didn't intend to make fun of me.

"Maybe next week I should dig out my journal from that class. If I'm here next week, of course."

He had the audience laughing, and he hadn't even started his performance. At least they were no longer laughing at me. I climbed back on the barstool and listened as Tristan shared what he considered an embarrassing anecdote, though it seemed more flattering than humiliating to me, especially since the whole story hinged on him being confused for Sam Claflin.

"They kept calling me Finnick from *The Hunger Games,*" Tristan informed us. With his shorter hair, I could definitely see it.

Alfie touched my wrist and asked quietly, "How about that drink now?"

"Definitely. But instead of the free drink, can you get me a Tanqueray and tonic?"

"Yup."

Watching him skillfully spin my drink glass, scoop ice cubes in, splash the Tanqueray, then spray the tonic mesmerized me and calmed me down even further.

He sliced up a lime and garnished the drink before setting it before me. "This is still on the house." I raised a hand to protest, but he shrugged. "You've earned a small reward."

I suddenly remembered the star I'd been given and held it out to him.

"Keep it. Let it remind you of what you did today."

"A literal gold star for achievement." I opened my notebook and laid the star across the page I'd read. "Thanks."

I went back to listen to the rest of Tristan's story, but he'd wrapped it up to applause Miranda hadn't needed to coax. At least if I didn't make it to the next round, Aida would let me off the hook. I was about to tell her so when a blur of blond passed behind me and Tristan took up residence on the stool beside me.

He laid his elbow across the bar so that he faced me, and I mean, he truly faced me. "Hey, Sara!"

I might've misheard him, though it was a common mistake, made by baristas my whole life. I couldn't pretend I didn't know his name, so I said, "Hey, Tristan." Like I was cool. I took a casual sip of my Tanqueray but somehow missed my lower lip, pouring the cold liquid onto my thigh.

"Oh, shit." I reached for the cocktail napkins, and my hand nicked the edge of Aida's glass, tipping it precariously. I grabbed for it, but another hand stopped it from falling. "Alfie, I'm so sorry."

He blotted up the spill and then leaned in like nothing had happened. "Hey there, Tristan." His hand reached over. "Alfie Jordan. Long time no see."

Tristan took his hand. "Hey man! How's it going?" Damn he had perfect teeth, glossy white, pearly even. And his lips . . . Kissing those lips had once been my dream, but I was older now, and I shouldn't be flustered, but when he flashed that smile at me, the fluster-o-meter broke. My heart rate doubled.

"Oh, yeah." He reached into his pocket, arching his back to lift his fine ass off the stool enough to produce the gold star Miranda had handed him. He slapped it down on the bar. "Newcastle, please. Thanks."

When he broke eye contact with me, my brain fuzz cleared up enough to act. I'd already made a fool of myself in front of him twice now. If I stuck around any longer, I'd probably knock out a tooth or set the bar on fire.

I grabbed my backpack again. "I'm just gonna head out."

"You can't leave." Tristan's forehead creased with his confusion. He'd probably never run for cover in his life. "You won't be able to come back next week if you don't stick around to the end."

"Oh, no. I'm not doing this next week." Not now. Not with my most embarrassing confession straddling a barstool beside me. "This was strictly a onetime deal."

"But why? You're a shoo-in to make it to the next round." He tilted his head. "And I'd love to hear more of your"—his mouth twisted as he thought of the right euphemism—"thoughts."

The heat rushed like a fireball from my chest straight up my neck, engulfing my ears. "I am so, so sorry about that. I had no idea—"

"That I'd be here. Oh, I'm sure, but why are you sorry? That was truly flattering." He chuckled. "Glory days, right?"

I held up the journal. "This is only going to get worse for me."

He eyed it like he'd find more schoolgirl gushing in there. He would have. "So what? It was a long time ago, right?"

"Ten years, yeah." I dropped the notebook back into my backpack.

"Crazy."

"Seriously."

"What have you been up to in all that time?" With his elbow back on the bar, he leaned his head against his fist, looking at me like I was the most interesting thing in the world.

"I've been developing video games mostly."

"Oh, yeah? For what company?" We were nearly eye to eye, so when he bent toward me, I could feel his breath on my lips.

"Extinction Level Event Game Designs."

"No way. You work there?"

"Yeah." I blushed. "You've heard of it?"

"Hell, yeah. I submitted my art there . . . what was it?" He twisted his pretty, pretty lips. "Maybe three years ago. Do you draw for them?"

I shook my head. "Like I said, I'm a developer. I write code. You're an artist?"

"Yeah, graphic designer."

I pointed my thumb at Aida. "Aida here works with me, too. Her husband, Marco, is the lead artist at ELE."

Aida gave him a polite but chilly smile and kept sipping her Sprite.

"Hey." Tristan lifted a hand in a quick wave, then looked at the guy sitting on the other side of Aida. "Is Marco here?"

"Nope. Just us." I grimaced as I took the first real sip of my strong drink.

"You're lucky you found a job there. I've heard amazing things about them. Is it as chill as they say?"

"Yeah. It's great."

"Man, I'd love to work on video game art."

My interest redoubled. "Do you play?"

"Oh, yeah. I'm over level one thousand in *Candy Crush*."

"Is that good?" I'd honestly never played it.

"Pretty good."

"What's the goal of the game? Like, why do you like it?"

"It's completely addictive. There's always some new thing you need, always *just*"—he lifted his hand like he was picking an apple off a high limb—"out of reach."

I understood that phenomenon. "We build those kinds of incentives into our games as well."

"Always keep them wanting more, right?"

My eyes fell on his mouth, something I'd always wanted, just out of reach. I could think of any number of things I might do to make it to level one thousand with him. "Mmm-hmm."

"Hey, if you ever need any input about gaming, I'd be happy to talk about it."

"I uh—" I bit my tongue. That probably would never be necessary, but I wasn't about to shut down any avenue of conversation that might lead to something more with him. I batted my eyes and flashed my best imitation of a flirtatious smile. "Yeah, sure."

"Hey, do you have a card?"

Bingo.

I rustled through my backpack to find my wallet and dug out a business card that had seen better days. People didn't usually ask me for something so impersonal, but I was more than happy to share it. It had my phone number on it. And my actual name.

He scanned it and then slipped it into his wallet. "Thanks. Could I call you sometime?"

Was he hitting on me? Tristan Spencer? Hitting on me. I couldn't stop blinking while my brain tried to make sense of this insanity. I grabbed the gin and tonic on the bar and finished it in one swallow, then held up a finger to get Alfie's attention and said, "Another, please?" I faced Tristan again with a coy smile. Maybe humiliating myself had paid off for once. Maybe for once I'd catch the hot guy's eye.

Alfie set my drink before me. "I worried you might leave. We're about to announce the results." His eyebrows rose. "Good luck, both of you!"

Tristan leaned over. "So what are you going to do with the grand-prize money?"

Whatever I might have responded was cut short by Miranda's voice over the speaker. "May I have your attention, please. We've tallied your votes and are prepared to announce the contestants who will be invited to move on to next week. We want to thank everyone profusely for coming out tonight. Let's have a round of applause for all our participants."

I golf clapped, feeling awkward applauding for my own self. My fingers had begun to tingle from nerves, and I honestly didn't know if I wanted to hear my name called or not. On the one hand, it would be a relief to get cut tonight and have my decision taken from me. On the other, it would be a kick to the ego to fail to make even the top twelve.

"When I call your name, please come stand beside me. I ask that the audience hold your applause until the list is complete."

She called out Bryce, and the crowd ignored the rules, cheering as he stepped forward. Miranda continued to read off Dana, Gary, Heather, and Hillary. I counted on my fingers, knowing it wasn't necessarily a bad sign that nearly half the people had been called before she'd even made it to the M's. My heart began to pound, and Aida laid a hand on my shoulder, like she knew the writing was on the wall. There was no way I'd been good enough to amuse a room filled with strangers.

Mike was called up, and I somehow recalled he'd been the sixth contestant. So far, nobody had been cut. I squeezed my fists, realizing I was rooting to hear my own name, but preparing to be disappointed.

Porter, Quinn, and Shannon were called up, *boom-boom-boom*. Only three more spots were left. My mouth tasted like ash.

"Sierra."

My eyes sprang open in surprise. "What?"

Aida punched the sky. "That's you! Get up there!"

Tristan whooped. "All right, Sara!"

As I took my spot next to Shannon, I fought back a stupid grin. I'd been picked. I wouldn't think about next week. I'd make my decision later. For now, I savored the feeling of not being rejected.

Miranda said, "Tristan," and that feeling of victory was doused by visions of confessing a decade-old crush to the same boy week in and week out. Maybe there was something else in that notebook. Maybe he wouldn't assume my infatuation continued on today.

But when he slid in beside me, he leaned over and whispered, "Looks like you've got competition," and a fire ignited in my belly. Suddenly, I wanted nothing more than to hold my own in this contest. Maybe even win it.

When Zane was called as the final contestant, everyone cheered and snapped photos.

Miranda said, "Each night, the contestant with the most votes will be awarded a Get Out of Jail Free card." She held an actual *Monopoly* card up. "Remember those twists Alfie mentioned? Here's the first. This is good for one save, meaning if you get eliminated, you can play this to be reinstated in the game. However, nobody can win more than one of these during the competition. We don't want *someone*"—she glanced at Tristan significantly—"hoarding them up and then skating to the win."

The crowd murmured.

Miranda let the dramatic pause build and announced, "Tonight's winner is . . . Tristan Spencer!"

He gaped as we all applauded his victory.

I knew I'd never win one of those cards, so it meant someone else would have better odds than me. Tristan had just made himself even harder to beat. Why was I even trying?

Immediately after the contest ended, without much fanfare, the other contestants dispersed, and the bar began to clear out. I pitied the three people who had felt the cruel sting of rejection, especially considering I'd likely forfeit my spot.

When I went to grab my backpack and finally flee the scene of the crime, I waved good night to Alfie and thanked him for his encouragement and the free drink. Aida fell in with me, but as soon as we exited onto the sidewalk outside, Tristan chased us down.

He held up my business card. "Mind if I call or text tomorrow? We could hang out."

I hitched the strap on my backpack further up my shoulder. "Yeah. That would be cool." My giddy smile advertised my own lack of cool. I forced my face back to nonchalant neutral. "Whatever."

"Cool! See you around, then."

I breathed in and held it while Aida and I turned right, the opposite direction from Tristan, and headed toward our town house. Once the coast was clear, I blew it out.

"Oh. My. God." I stopped dead. "Did he just ask me out?"

"I thought we were mad at Tristan."

Was she serious?

"Yeah, ten years ago, Aida. I think I can let it go."

Did she not see the boy?

"I dunno. This is an eerily similar situation."

"I guess. I mean, it's another contest." The school-sponsored event sophomore year had not gone so well for me, thanks to Tristan. "But this is for fun."

"And one thousand dollars." She grimaced. "That's not nothing. He once sabotaged you for a lot less."

"Noted. But he has more competition than me." I reflected on how funny some of the others were. "How the hell did I make it through? What just happened?"

Aida laughed. "You killed it is what just happened. Let's go home and celebrate."

Oh, yeah. I planned to celebrate. I'd slain a dragon tonight and caught the eye of a prince. Game on.

Chapter 6

Aida's idea of celebrating was a mug of hot tea and a foot massage, so I couldn't blame her for my Saturday morning exhaustion. No, my late-night partying came courtesy of insomnia. I slept fitfully, woken by a series of stress dreams. I'd try counting sheep, but then visions of my diary reading would play like a silent movie across my eyelids. Only less documentary and more alternate-reality horror show, as I picked apart my performance, sprinkling in unedited bonus material of all the things that could have gone wrong.

To make matters worse, when I checked the time on my phone I discovered I'd been tagged in an unflattering group photo on Instagram with the other surviving contestants. The camera had immortalized me glancing at Tristan, my eyes glowing like a trash-can-diving raccoon caught in motion-activated security lights.

My stomach cramped up at the residual embarrassment. Why had I put myself out there like that?

The physical pain drove me upstairs to grab a glass of apple juice and some ibuprofen. I sat at the kitchen table, scrolling the Vibes Taproom Instagram account for other candid shots of me. Relieved to find none, I returned to the group photo and clicked on Tristan's profile.

I hadn't thought about him much in the past decade. It had

certainly never occurred to me to hunt him down on social media, but there he was, living a life like the rest of us, as if time hadn't frozen him forever in my memory.

He'd posted a picture of himself last night, flashing a backward peace sign in front the Vibes marquee. He took a ton of selfies, but he looked amazing in every picture, like a model, so who could blame him? His smile was made for advertising. I ran a finger along his photographed jaw and accidentally clicked on the Like heart. *Shit.* I hadn't meant to alert him to my stalking. The picture was weeks old. If I unliked it now, would he still get a notification? Would I look like a bigger freak for unliking it?

Since he was going to figure out I'd been spying on his account, I went ahead and hit Follow, hoping it wasn't sending any kind of message. For good measure and plausible deniability, I followed each of the other contestants, the bar's account, then also Alfie's and Miranda's personal accounts.

Since I was up, I flipped on *Mario Kart* and discovered my after-hours antagonist already racing. I challenged him until my eyes were closing, and then I dragged a blanket over me and fell asleep on the sofa.

The next morning, only a huge mug of coffee kept me alive as I rolled into the yoga studio.

"Hello, everyone." I stowed my backpack in the corner and started gathering my mat and blocks.

A variety of greetings met me.

The regulars had already rolled out their mats, and I walked around patting each person on the shoulder before settling in position at the front of the class. Thankfully nobody new had dropped in. Visitors made me nervous. I always wondered if they would know yoga better than me and judge me on my lack of expertise.

I'd been taking yoga classes for years, ever since a nasty ankle injury had forced me to put away my running shoes. Running had centered me, relaxed me, but I couldn't tolerate the jolt of feet hitting the pavement anymore. I'd rediscovered my Zen with yoga. I still got plenty of low-impact cardio from riding my bike, but yoga helped me with strength, stamina, and balance. It helped me with confidence as well, but not in the ways I needed at the moment.

When I first moved to VaHi, I started riding my bike over to the Y on Saturdays to take the yoga class as a student. One day, the former instructor asked me to temporarily fill in. I only agreed when the other attendees begged me to keep the class going. When her absence became permanent, the Y said they'd have to cancel the class if they couldn't find a replacement. I made the decision then to get my yoga certification.

It was a slow and natural transition from student to teacher, much like yoga itself.

Still I battled impostor syndrome nerves every time I entered the small room, though the familiar friendly faces encouraged me to give them my best.

I sat back on my heels, hands on my thighs, and began walking everyone through a breathing and stretching exercise.

We moved from position to position. As I demonstrated Marichi's pose, Mr. Baxter complained, "Sierra, I can't seem to turn my hips far enough. Would you help me?"

Mr. Baxter always sat front and center. Despite being old enough to be my granddad, he was never shy about checking me out, so I tried to avoid any positions that might give him a view down my shirt. He was harmless, even when he claimed he needed help adjusting his limbs.

I didn't move. "Mrs. Garrett, could you demonstrate to Mr. Baxter how to do the pose?"

He scowled but managed the pose just like he'd done a hundred times before. The man was surprisingly flexible for his age.

Almost all of my students were older, and I loved helping them. The occasional young person wandered in, but the class wasn't a regular routine for them. They usually had kids or classes or hangovers.

The sound of my ring tone—Mario yelling *Woohoo!*—broke the serenity. Again. And again. I apologized and got up to turn the volume down. The phone vibrated once more, and I stole a glance, surprised to find I had texts from Tristan. I blinked my eyes hard, convinced I was seeing things, but the messages continued to exist when I'd cleared my vision. I knew I should drop my phone back in my bag, but I set it down next to my mat, curiosity already beginning to fester.

I let everyone finish out the current pose, then moved them into Downward Dog, skipping over Mountain pose. Nobody questioned the change, and it allowed me to slide the phone under me so I could quickly read the texts.

Hey, it's Tristan Spencer.

It was cool to see you.

I was wondering if you're free tonight.

Can you meet me for dinner in Little Five Points around six?

I nearly fell out of my pose. I nudged my phone to the side and glanced up at the class to catch Mr. Baxter watching me. My shirt hung open, and he had a clear view of my cleavage. I told everyone to stand back up for that missed Mountain pose and glimpsed the wee tent pitched in Mr. Baxter's shorts. Good for him, I guessed?

We made it through Triangle pose and then settled into the final relaxation, the *Savasana.* As we all lay on our backs, quietly breathing in and out, my brain was running a mile a minute. What should I write back to Tristan? Obviously, I'd tell him yes. But was he asking me out on a date?

With a quiet gentle tone, I said, "Inhale deeply. Raise your legs as you tense your muscles. Clench your fists."

He'd asked me to meet him. Why wouldn't he offer to pick me up if it were a date?

"And lower your legs, releasing all your tension. Let go of your anxiety."

How should I get down to Little Five Points? And what would I wear? What if I dressed for a date and he didn't?

My stomach cramped, and I took my own advice to breathe in, then out.

Oh, my God.

I was going on a date with Tristan Spencer.

I sat up and calmly said, "Namaste." The class repeated it back and began to rise.

I stood and gathered my things, anxious to get home and talk to Aida.

Mr. Baxter approached as I was rolling my mat. "Great class, Sierra."

"Thanks, Mr. Baxter."

"Call me Leon."

"That's nice, but—"

Mrs. Garrett sidled beside him. "Leave the poor girl be."

"How about we go for a cup of coffee?"

I smiled, attempting a demeanor of serenity that belied my inner tumult. "That's sweet, Mr. Baxter, but I have to get ready for a date."

"You have a date?" Mrs. Shih had joined the trio.

I carried my mat to the far wall, aware they all awaited my response. "Seems so."

"With who?" Mrs. Martinez was always asking me how I was still single. "Do we know him?"

"No. He—"

Mrs. Shih interrupted me. "Is he handsome? I bet he is."

"He is. Very."

"Of course he is," said Mrs. Garrett. "But is he nice? What's he like?"

Honestly, I didn't know the answer to those questions. "I'll let you know."

"He has to be better than the last guy," said Mrs. Martinez, and the women all nodded.

By "the last guy," I assumed they meant Howard, but that had been a year and a Wyatt ago. I never told the yoga women about my sex life. I barely told them about my love life. "He's someone I knew in college. We're just going out for dinner."

And it might not even be a date.

"Oh, a boy she used to know. I bet there's a story there." Mrs. Gupta must have been eavesdropping.

I grabbed my backpack and made sure everything was squared away before throwing it over my shoulder. "I'll give you all a full report next time, okay?"

We filed out in the same direction, but they headed toward their cars while I unlocked my bike from the rack. I hopped on and began pedaling up the sidewalk. Normally, I took side streets to the town house. I loved the beautiful homes, the lush magnolias and dogwoods, and all the colorful azaleas. I did not love the sun beating down on me in the early summer Atlanta heat, however.

Today, I decided to take a detour through the stretch of restaurants and shops surrounding Alfie's bar. The bar hadn't opened yet, but I slowed my bike and took a good look at the place in daylight. I'd barely registered it prior to the night before. Glossy black paint covered at least twenty more uneven layers before it hit brick. The second floor had a New Orleans–style balcony and gorgeous tall windows.

For a heartbeat, I thought about knocking to see if Alfie might be around, but the place seemed devoid of human activity. What time did bars usually open? I circled back and checked the hours out of curiosity:

5:00 PM-2:00 AM MONDAY-SATURDAY

What I wouldn't give to work those hours instead of fighting my natural sleep cycle. I pedaled away, at first laughing at the idea of suggesting to Aida we change our office hours. But as I turned off into the residential neighborhoods, the idea stopped being so funny. If I could work instead of battling insomnia, maybe I wouldn't be so tired all the time. Maybe we could consider flex hours at the least. Why not?

I turned the final corner and locked the bike against the side of the house. As I climbed the steps of the front porch, I scrolled through my text messages, trying to think of a cool response.

I knew I was supposed to play some kind of game, pushing back to make it seem like I wasn't too available, that I couldn't be expected to be free on such late notice, that I should act hard to get. But none of those things were true.

Sure. Just tell me where.

Inside, Aida and Marco sat on the sofa playing *Call of Duty*, and I headed to the kitchen to make coffee, but finding a pot already brewing, I poured a mug and carried it to the living room to watch their murderous rampage.

My phone buzzed and I checked it to find another text.

Mexican?

I'd go to Taco Bell if it meant hanging with Tristan. *Sure.*

His next text had the name of the restaurant and the time.

Tickled by this new development, I wanted to share with someone who'd be equally excited. Aida was not that person, but she was all I had.

"So." I left that hanging there.

Aida pounded on her controller, shooting at a group of enemy fighters. "So?" She didn't even glance at me.

"I have a dinner date tonight."

Her avatar crept through a dark postapocalyptic hellscape. "With?"

"Tristan."

"Son of a bitch." A hail of bullets caught her from the left, and she spun to return fire. "What the hell, Marco?"

"Sorry. Sorry." Marco swept the room and moved out in front. The game gave me a headache even playing alone, but watching them together made my nausea return with a vengeance. I ought to switch to a nice herbal tea before my insides ate themselves.

"I was wondering if you might be heading out tonight. I could use a ride to Little Five Points. I'll get an Uber home."

"Mmm-hmm . . ." Aida had a way of sounding skeptical whenever she said this, like it was a question, not an agreement.

"What?"

"Like you'll be coming back home tonight." She opened her inventory and scrolled through her guns.

"I will be."

Marco asked, "Why doesn't your date come get you?"

"Great question." Aida paused the game and faced me. "Why doesn't he?"

"I don't know. Maybe he can't for some reason."

"He made it here last night."

She was right, but maybe he'd taken an Uber. Maybe he'd walked.

"Can you take me over or not? I don't want to have to fight for parking. If you can't, I'll ride my bike. It's not that far."

Marco looked up. "Don't do that. It's not safe at night."

Aida set her controller on the coffee table. "No. We can take you." She stretched. "I wanted to go check out this restaurant over in Decatur anyway."

Marco added, "Promise you'll call us or take an Uber to get home. Please don't try to walk."

Aida laughed. "In the morning. When you're ready to come home."

I flung a coaster at her. "I will be home tonight."

I couldn't imagine any scenario where Tristan would invite me back to his place. In fact, this would be the perfect opportunity to take Aida's advice to kiss good night and walk away. If he didn't call, I'd be seeing him on Friday night regardless.

But just in case, I'd be sure to shave and wear my date underwear. One could never be too prepared for spontaneous romance.

Chapter 7

What to wear? What to wear? Did I want to go with normal or look like myself? Tristan had seen me in ordinary-person camouflage, so I figured I should do a repeat, twisting my hair up to hide the multicolored ends and accentuating my eyes and lips.

Wyatt was wrong about me. My boobs alone started me at a solid six. Seven for some guys. With makeup, nobody could call me a butterface. With makeup, I could turn myself into a ten if I really wanted to. Tonight, I really wanted to.

I was tempted to wear the vintage dress I'd recently ordered. The cut was pretty simple with a fitted bodice and flared skirt, but the soft light-blue fabric was covered with various planets that had smiling faces. It was fun and funky, but probably too offbeat for Tristan. Still, I wanted to look pretty, flirtatious, and feminine, so I dug in my closet until I found a snug black V-neck blouse I knew flattered my shape. I allowed for a little whimsy, slipping into a stretchy purple skirt silk-screened with tiny video game controllers. And although it was possibly a real date, I opted for my Converse. I did own dress shoes, but they hurt my feet, and I reserved them for emergencies only.

As we drove up Moreland, Marco said to Aida, "So let me get this straight: Sierra had a crush on this guy in college."

"Right."

"And you say he's the same guy who—"

"Yup," Aida answered before he finished whatever he'd been about to say.

"And now he's—"

"Yup."

He scratched the side of his neck with one hand, the other on the steering wheel. "And she's going out with him?"

"Seems like it."

I called up, "I can hear you. I'm in the backseat, not on Mars."

Marco ignored me. "Can you explain to me why? I thought—"

"She thinks he's cute. Remember?" Her sarcasm pissed me off. She did *not* have a right to be madder at Tristan than I was.

We came to a stop at a red light a couple of blocks north of our destination, and they both turned around and looked at me. Marco shrugged. "I guess she can make her own decisions."

I opened the car door. "I can walk from here."

I jumped out and made it to the sidewalk when Aida rolled down her window and yelled, "Don't forget to use a condom!"

Ha-ha.

The light turned green, and I shook a fist as Marco turned left and drove out of sight. And that was the moment I noticed my backpack wasn't slung over my shoulder.

God dammit.

I had no money, no driver's license, no keys. Shit. No phone.

To stop myself from freaking out, I mentally listed all the problems I might encounter.

Money. I wouldn't need if this was a date.

Driver's license. I only needed for alcohol. I wouldn't order any.

Keys. I wouldn't need until I got home.

Phone. I needed. I had no way to call for a ride. Fuck.

Okay, so I could walk home and wait on the porch for Aida. Or sit at Alfie's bar for an hour.

Or go home with Tristan.

Freak-out averted. I could survive.

However, the stress hadn't left me unscathed, and I discovered

I had an urgent need to pee. Most businesses in Little Five Points had strict policies against using their facilities without ordering anything, and I didn't have money for that. There was a comic book store on Euclid near the Mexican place, and I knew the owner. I could swing in, borrow his restroom, and be on my merry way. Though this side venture wasn't without its own perils.

The comic store's sign came into view as I rounded a pack of teens clogging the sidewalk.

I swung open the glass door and did a quick sweep of the interior for any signs of my ex-boyfriend.

"Hey, Sierra."

I'd overlooked Howard hunched behind the cash register.

I didn't want to make this into a whole reunion, so I powered on through the store. "Hey, Howard. Mind if I use your bathroom? Thanks."

"Sure." He said this to nobody since I didn't stop walking until I had the door locked behind me.

And then, blessed relief. I tugged out a wad of toilet paper, which was so stiff and rough it could have been made from gum wrappers. That didn't bother me until I noticed the reddish stain on my underwear.

Fuck my life. No wonder my stomach had been so crampy for the past couple of days.

Could stress bring on a period a week early?

I reached over to grab a pad from my backpack before I remembered my inventory was at zero. Ugh. Time to live like the cavewomen did. I took a long strand of toilet paper and Mac-Grubered it around my underwear as a makeshift sanitary napkin. This barely qualified as paper; an actual napkin would have been of more use.

I looked around for a tampon machine, doubting I'd have such luck.

Hallelujah! Howard had one installed.

But curses! It required a dime. A dime! I laughed at how the loss of a simple bag had stymied me. Granted, I doubted I'd have such an archaic form of payment in my backpack.

Who had a dime?

Howard probably did. But how could I ask for change without him knowing why? *Argh*.

If I'd been inside a video game, I'd just mow down some bushes or decapitate a gorgon, and I'd be flush with coinage.

In the real world, one had to beg.

I squeezed my fists to fight back a scream and muster the courage to do something I really did not want to do, then peeked out the bathroom. There was a straight view to the cash register. I slipped against the wall and actually said, "Psssst." I never knew people did that outside of the movies, but it got Howard's attention. I waved him over.

"Can I borrow a dime?" I whispered.

"A dime?" He spoke in a normal voice so I shushed him, and his eyes grew into massive all-seeing saucers as he took in my plight. This would have been a good time for an earthquake.

Why was this still such an embarrassment in this day and age? Why was I protecting Howard's genteel sensibilities from a predicament that afflicted half the population? I straightened my back and looked him in the eye.

"Please? I'm in a bind. I can pay you back."

"Oh, of course. No." He turned back toward the register. "I mean, no, you don't have to pay me back. One second."

Thank God.

Time stood still as I waited and watched him work the cash register.

He'd gained weight. He'd finally gotten a decent haircut. And he was no longer wearing bowling shirts as everyday fashion. Score a point for his wife, Dahlia. It figured some other woman would reap the benefits of another one of my failed relationships.

Howard and I had broken up over a year ago. Things were still a bit awkward between us, although our split had been inevitable and neither of us harbored ill will. We were possibly too compatible, like chocolate icing on chocolate cake. I might have been content to remain in a comfortable loveless relationship indefinitely since I no longer expected much more than companionship anymore anyway.

My mom had told me there were three kinds of love: *Eros*, *Philia*, and *Agape*. Sex, friendship, and some other third kind of love. I think that was her way of explaining her sterile marriage with my dad wasn't altogether normal, and I should aim higher, but without a decent role model I didn't know how to.

I'd loved Howard with the most ardent *Philia*, but we lacked any sparks, any real sexual chemistry.

I knew the difference. It wasn't too hard to hook up with someone like Wyatt for a night to satisfy *Eros,* but those relationships were short-lived without the basic friendship.

And *Agape*? I was unclear on that. I'd always pictured it as this mysterious all-consuming love. Whatever it was, I'd never experienced it that I knew of.

I'd be content to find a man who could give me two of the three at the same time.

Howard wasn't that man.

After I found the courage to end things with him, he moved on and met Dahlia. I still couldn't believe he'd gotten married. Meanwhile, I was a pinball, bouncing from one guy to the next without any stability or *Agape* in sight. Whatever that was.

Howard returned with the dime aloft, like he'd retrieved a treasure of real value. I guessed it was worth gold to me in that moment.

Once I had the dime, I shot back to the machine and plunked it in. There was only one choice for a pad, and I turned the dial and waited.

Nothing happened.

Maybe the machine had been hanging there neglected since the dawn of time, and Howard had never refilled it.

Frustrated, I smashed the box with my palm, and my violence rewarded me with a loud clunk as pink plastic dropped down into the well. I stared at the foreign object. It was perfectly square, three inches high and three inches wide. When I un-wrapped it and opened it, I discovered why. The pad itself was thick and solid, like the cotton dentists use to keep teeth dry. It must've been manufactured before women's liberation. I was surprised it didn't come with a harness.

Whatever. It was a step up from the budget toilet paper. It would have to do.

One thing I knew for sure. I wasn't going to be needing a con-dom tonight.

When at last I emerged from the precipice of disaster, a new one awaited me. Tristan leaned on the counter, chatting with Howard. My stomach clenched at the prospect of them talking about me, of Howard telling Tristan where I'd gone and what had befallen me. It was far-fetched, but within the realm of pos-sibility.

"Hey, Tristan. Funny to run into you here."

He looked up. "Sara! Hey!" I sighed. We were now outside the borders of when it would be acceptable to correct him on my name. He gestured to Howard. "This is my friend Howard."

I nodded. "Hey, Howard."

Howard said, "Yeah, Si-err-a and I go way back."

I loved him for articulating my name in a singsong voice, but this was a battle I'd lost with teachers and investors and gamers. Tristan had my card. If he were going to notice my name wasn't Sara, that should have happened already. Some people were oblivious.

I promised myself I'd correct him if we ever got beyond pleas-antries, if he ever kissed me. It was an honest mistake, and I wasn't going to get hung up on it.

Howard gave me his attention, as though we hadn't just shared an intimate sanitary moment. "Will you be going to Gamescon this year? I understand Marco and Aida will be a bit occupied, eh?"

"That's the plan," I said, wishing the logistics had worked out so I could tag along with them and enjoy the event without all the anxiety. "I'm hoping to get a chance to demo the new game."

"Oh, yeah? What's it called again?"

"*Castle Capture*. It's an MMORPG. A little *Final Fantasy*, but totally medieval."

"Sounds badass. Can't wait to try it."

"Well, I'd let you test it out right now, but I'm working out the kinks."

"Is it another martial arts fighting game?"

The first game I'd developed for our company, *Roundhouse*, was full-on hand-to-hand combat.

"Nuh-uh. It has loads of weapons—broadswords, maces, cannons, even a trebuchet."

"Shit, no way."

"The artwork is luscious." I reached for my nonexistent phone to show him some of Marco's drawings before I remembered my predicament.

Tristan said, "I'd love to see it."

I'd gotten so absorbed in the conversation with Howard, I'd kind of forgotten about Tristan, and it was great to know that at least for a moment I could appear confident and knowledge-able without my lizard brain tripping me up.

"Maybe you'll show me sometime?" He looked into my eyes, and my derpiness returned full force.

The words *Come back to my place and I'll show you right now* formed in my mind, but I stuttered out, "W-well, yeah. Sure."

Tristan seemed unfazed. "You ready to go grab dinner?"

Time to test the waters. "Yeah. It's just that I left my back-pack in my roommates' car, and I don't have any way to pay, so—"

"Dude. I've totally got this."

Even Howard glanced up from his comic at the choice of ep-ithet.

Tristan turned toward the door waving me to follow. "Come on. I have something I want to show you."

I was more confused about the status of this so-called date, but he'd left me intrigued. Plus, I was starving. Aida and Marco would be gone for a couple of hours, so I was stranded until further notice anyway. "Okay. That would be nice."

As Tristan exited, I turned to Howard and whispered, "Please lend me some more change."

He smiled. "Sure thing, *dude.*"

"You're a saint, Howard."

He dropped a fistful of dimes and quarters into my hand, and I felt like a real-life Mario collecting coins out in the wild.

Chapter 8

I chased after Tristan and slammed into the glass door that didn't open. He pushed it inward, toward me. "You okay, there?"

Tristan had a way of turning me into a personification of Murphy's Law. Maybe the universe was interceding on Aida's behalf.

We headed to the nearby Mexican restaurant, and Tristan grabbed a table outside. I didn't think I could handle spicy food, so I ordered a quesadilla and then excused myself to go to the bathroom in the hopes of upgrading to a pad that had been manufactured this century. Of course they didn't have a feminine products machine. Thankfully, I was still mostly high and dry, but that could change at any minute. I could probably make it through dinner, but after that, I'd have to call it a night and head straight home. No way was I pushing my luck on this museum artifact of feminine hygiene.

I just needed to get through one date without making a fool of myself, and I felt like I was already walking on a tightrope.

If this even was a date. Would Tristan have offered to pay if I'd had money?

I peered around the corner before I went back to our table. Tristan sat in the fading evening light, reading his phone, smirking a little bit, like he'd read a funny meme. I still couldn't believe it was really him.

Back in college he'd been over-the-top attractive, with his shoulder-length thick blond hair and a near constant bronze coloring. His sparkling blue eyes had dazzled me. And his devastating smile could make me lose my wits every time.

Now, he'd matured, but it suited him. He'd softened up and filled out a bit. His tan had faded, and his hair was trimmed. It was kind of a relief his beauty had descended to the realm of mere mortals. It gave me a boost of relative confidence, like I could talk to this version of him. In video game terms, my heart container lost a quarter of its size, but my power meter increased. I could almost hear the sound effects.

"Behind you." A waitress passed around me, carrying a tray, and headed toward our table. I followed her and sat across from Tristan as she distributed our plates. Tristan held up a finger, and I thought he was going to insist on a prayer, which seemed peculiar at a restaurant, but he did the next best thing by taking out his phone and snapping a picture of both our plates. Food worship.

Or as he said, "Foodstagram."

I regretted the lack of my own phone. Not for the food, but for the Tristagram I wanted to take. This moment felt so surreal.

We both dug in. Eating was a social activity I could get behind, even if I didn't feel the urge to document it.

When his burrito was demolished and I was pushing around the last of my refried beans, he said, "So I wanted to show you something."

He reached into his messenger bag and pulled out a comic book protected by a thick plastic cover. His lips pinched together in a giddy smile, like he had a secret I was going to be delighted to learn.

If he hoped to impress me with some first edition *Superman*, he was going to be disappointed. It was true a lot of Howard's comic book customers were my video game customers and vice versa. I, however, fell outside that neat Venn diagram. I did not give two shits about comics.

But when he held the comic up with a hopeful and beautiful smile, I willed my eyes to feign genuine interest.

The cover read *Skate Punk* and featured what appeared to be an actual skate punk, wearing a hoodie and low-rise jeans fashioned into a casual superhero costume. I was confused until I noticed the byline. *Tristan Spencer.*

Then my smile truly lit up my face.

"You drew this?"

"Wrote. Designed. Drew." He handed me the comic, and I gently thumbed through it. "Howard helped me get this copy printed, but I'm looking to produce a whole series."

I wasn't a connoisseur of comic art, but he had a bold style. "Wow, Tristan. This is amazing. I love how rich the colors are."

"Thanks. I had a hunch you'd understand how important that is to me. Why I entered the contest last night."

"To cover the costs of production?"

"Defray the costs." He took the comic back and slipped it back into a plastic case.

"Oh." Had he asked me here to convince me to drop out of the Chagrin Challenge? That could be a win-win situation. He'd lose a competitor, and I'd have an excuse to quit. "I mean, I wasn't all that serious about the contest anyway."

His eyebrows shot up. "No! I didn't mean to ask you to forfeit." He rubbed the back of his neck, and pink dotted his smooth, perfect cheek. "I was hoping I might impress you, to be honest."

"Really?" That was an unexpected twist. Tristan Spencer trying to impress me? "I'm duly impressed. I swear."

The waitress dropped off the bill, and Tristan glanced at it before turning back to face me with a curious grin.

"So."

The word hung there, as if he expected me to be the kind of person who could fill voids in conversation. Like I was the loquacious person I always wanted to be. Could I be that?

I tilted my head. "So?"

Maybe my chatty side needed some work. Did he want me to make the next move? Had Tristan the charmer grown shy over time?

"So what now?"

To be honest, I wasn't sure what I wanted to happen next, but it didn't involve *Eros*. Not tonight with the ticking time bomb in my uterus. I wasn't sure the brick I'd taped to my underwear was going to be there for me when I most needed it. If only I had my backpack, I'd make a quick plunge into the nearest drugstore and rid myself of the sword of Damocles hanging between my legs. As it was, I was attuned to any sudden signs the flood waters were rising.

"I should head home."

Tristan got up. "I could take you if it's not too far."

I suddenly knew what I wanted to happen next: A kiss good night, then wait for a phone call. "Yeah? That would be nice."

He pulled out his wallet and counted out the bills. "Come with me."

I followed him off the patio, and he turned up the sidewalk, saying, "The reason I didn't come pick you up is that my car's in the shop."

"Oh." That was a decent excuse, though he could have explained it earlier. "So how are you getting around?"

"I've got a set of wheels, but I didn't know how comfortable you'd be on the back of a motorcycle."

My heart sped up. A motorcycle sounded super sexy, but it would have definitely traumatized me. We turned a corner, and I began thinking up excuses. I wasn't sure how best to extricate myself without coming across like a coward. Which I was. I loved the speed and freedom of my bike, but motorcycles were out of my league. Just like Tristan Spencer, apparently.

"It's right up here."

He approached the only vehicle on the side street with two wheels—and I stifled a laugh. *Motorcycle* was an exaggeration. It was just a powder blue Vespa.

"It's cute."

He patted the seat. "Are you up for some adventure?"

Two miles on the back of a Vespa? I could do that.

"Will you promise to take the back streets the whole way?" I touched the handlebar. "And drive super slow?"

He handed me a helmet. "Hop on."

I boarded the Vespa, acutely aware of that damn cinder block from Howard's historical hygiene machine. I couldn't wait to get home and return to the sanity of modern sanitary napkins. Tristan put his helmet on and took his place in front of me.

We drove up Highland Avenue, pressed together. The dogwood trees had bloomed earlier, but some still held on to their flowers. The weather was perfect, and I had my legs straddled around the thighs of one of the hottest guys I'd ever seen, once upon a time. It was a scene out of my wildest fantasies circa sophomore year in college. I wondered if at some point "past me" felt a disturbance in the Force.

With my arms coiled around his torso, it occurred to me that the out-of-reach Tristan Spencer I'd crushed on in college wasn't a real person. The real Tristan was more like this Vespa: less sexy, less scary, and maybe more my speed.

All my uneasiness transformed into excitement, and I felt a voltage spark, a growing hope that Tristan had set this whole situation up in order to get my hands on him, to make a move on me. I couldn't help letting my schoolgirl imagination play out, wondering how his mouth would feel against mine.

By the time we arrived at my place, my hair had fallen loose. I tried to twist it back up as I hopped off the Vespa, but it wasn't obeying. Tristan swung a leg over the seat of his motorbike. The effect was less than heroic, like a beautiful real-life elf dismounting a small pony. A powder blue pony. I stifled a snicker.

He looked up at the town house, then scanned up the street. "This is where you live? It's so nice."

"Yeah. I share it with Aida and Marco."

I glanced up at the second-story windows to check for light, hoping they could let me in.

His eyes followed mine. "Are they home?"

I suddenly fast-forwarded through his possible intent. Would he walk me to the door for that kiss good night, or did he want to be invited inside? Really get to know me.

No. That couldn't happen. Not tonight. Not with the weather forecast in my southern hemisphere.

I backed toward the porch. "So, thank you for dinner."

He strode toward me, his clear blue eyes shimmering with the last of the evening light, and I retreated. My foot snagged on the lowest step, and I lost my balance and fell on my ass. *Oof.*

He laughed, then held his hand out to help me back up. Standing on that lower step put me eye-to-eye, inches from him. He reached up and touched my hair. "Hey, cool colors. I hadn't noticed it. That's rad."

I pulled at the strands. "Thanks?" He didn't move away, and I gathered my courage to mirror him, touch his hair. "I like what you've done with yours."

"Yeah? I was planning to grow it back out. What do you think?"

"I think it would look good either way." It was still long enough that I could grip it, and my fingers threaded through his locks and tightened. I told myself I should let him make the first move, but I was lying if I said I didn't want to at least find out what Tristan Spencer tasted like. I tugged him closer, and as his lips met mine, a sense of déjà vu washed over me.

Had we kissed before?

I drew back to give him a chance to decide what to do next, and he licked his lips, then leaned in again for another kiss. And yeah, it felt weirdly familiar for a moment, but I relaxed and let it be. Kissing was a luxury, and I could easily lose myself in the swift currents of desire.

A car slowed in the road, and Aida called out her window: "We're home."

They continued on by, heading to our garage behind the building.

At first, I was pissed at the buzzkill, but then grateful. I shook my head, clearing the fog of desire, and broke away from Tristan. A kiss good night. Then wait for the call.

Tristan half smiled, dreamily, and I took that as a good sign.

I stepped away. "Good night, Tristan."

He didn't pursue me. "So I'll see you on Friday?"

Would he? Even if I dropped out of the contest, I guessed I could go and support him. "Possibly."

He climbed on his Vespa, put on his helmet, and kick-started the motor, which purred like a tiny kitten. "See ya later, Sara!"

Mother fuck. I yelled, "It's Sierra!"

But he made no indication he'd heard as he waved and sped down the road.

The front door opened. "Sierra? Everything okay?"

I brushed dirt off the back of my skirt, spinning to fix her with a death glare.

She came out and let gravity pull her down to one of the rockers on the porch. "I'm sorry for earlier tonight. I need to learn to bite my tongue."

"Yes."

"I thought you would have lost your impossible glorification of the golden boy by now."

Trust Aida to never bite her tongue.

"Maybe I have. I don't think he's perfect. Who is?" I climbed the steps and sat beside her. The first stars glittered against a periwinkle sky, and already the cicadas were overtaking all other sounds. "So maybe my fascination with him outlived a ten-year-old grudge. That's a long time to be mad, Aida."

She grunted noncommittally.

"Did you know he's an artist? He's developing a comic book. Isn't that cool?"

I thought that might soften her up since she'd married an artist herself, but she just gave me that same worn-out skeptical look. "So you're romanticizing him, now? He's still the guy who broke your confidence. Have you forgotten that?"

I hated when she called me out. "No. Of course not. But isn't it possible that he's no longer the same guy he was when he pulled that prank?"

"It's possible," she conceded. "He still pings my douche detector."

I sighed. Aida was opinionated and stubbornly protective, but it was my choice to date who I wanted, and a little support would have been nice. "It's weird, but seeing how hard he's working to develop his comic made me appreciate how easy things have been for me."

"*Easy?*" She scoffed. "You've worked damn hard. Nothing was handed to you. Not to mention all the obstacles you had to overcome people like Tristan will never encounter." She held up a hand, like she was belting out a gospel song. "Don't talk to me about easy."

I stretched. It suddenly seemed incredibly late. "We don't have to hold this rally today. You're right. Of course you are, but look at where we are, how far we've come. We're incredibly fortunate."

"Fine. But don't ever try to tell me you haven't earned it." She rocked forward and used the momentum to hoist herself out of the chair. "Come on inside. I've got a hankering for hot chocolate."

"You go on in. It's been a weird weekend. I'm gonna sit here a while longer."

Before the door closed, I yelled over, "Oh, and my backpack's in your car."

"On the kitchen table." The door clicked shut, and I was alone with my thoughts.

I stayed on the porch for another hour, rocking and processing the past twenty-four hours. I hadn't given myself time to decompress and overanalyze what had happened the night before and then this evening. The diary reading had been far less traumatizing than I'd expected, but like Aida had said, knowing everyone would be embarrassed had helped my competitive side edge out over my fears. Still, the thought of doing it again brought new anxieties. I was more likely to get knocked out now that there were fewer contestants, and that would be a different kind of awful.

And then there was Tristan, who could use the money.

Tristan. That was a whole other nut to crack. I'd obsessed over him, but I never truly knew him. I probably never would if I stopped going to the contest. If he really did plan to bring his journal from our class, I might get some insight into who he was, who he'd been. At the same time, I'd be revealing a lot of my innermost secrets from a period in my life when I'd idolized him.

It might be worth the discomfort. Or it might be like rushing into battle without a plan while shouting *"Leeroy Jenkins!"* I'd probably get annihilated.

With no further decision made, I yawned and dragged myself back into the town house. I snagged my backpack and checked my phone before descending to my personal cave where I fell face-first onto my futon and drifted off to sleep, completely forgetting to change that prehistoric pad.

Chapter 9

I awoke in total darkness. Things were happening belowdecks, and I raced for the bathroom to correct my nighttime negligence. Once I'd fixed my napkin needs, I crawled back in bed, hoping to fall back to sleep, wondering what time it was. I flung my arm over the edge of my bed to hunt for my phone, squinting through the glare of the light as it woke up. Shit, it was still only two a.m.

Why did I always wake up at two a.m.?

I flopped over onto my side, trying to turn my brain off. After a few minutes, I flipped onto my back and counted backward from one hundred. When I got to ten, I sat up and stretched. Insomnia and I were old friends, and I'd learned it was better to lean into it than waste the whole night tossing and turning unproductively.

Upstairs, I heated a mug of milk then stirred in the cocoa powder Aida had left out. I dropped onto the sofa and powered up my Switch. When the main menu appeared, I chose my user, Asuna, and got comfortable, holding the controller in the well made by my crossed legs. I loaded up *Mario Kart* and clicked through the options, choosing to play with friends, scrolling the list of user names. These weren't actual friends, but people I'd collected over time by sending or accepting requests after a particularly brutal race. I smiled when I saw the checkered flag beside Parzival's name, indicating he was online. All I knew about him—assuming it was a guy based on the avatar he'd built—was that he lived somewhere in Atlanta, according to the geo listing by his user name. Often I picked up friends of friends, so we might have had fewer than six degrees of separation.

I loved his user name, which came from the virtual reality fantasy *Ready Player One*. It wasn't even the character's name, but his avatar's user name. It paralleled my own user name from another VR fantasy, *Sword Art Online*. I loved the idea of meeting someone in a VR, like *Second Life,* and getting to know them through facsimiles we chose to represent our physical selves. I did meet people online sometimes, mostly in the middle of battle campaigns, but it's hard to flirt with a Goblin Death Knight when he's trying to kill you.

Parzival only seemed to play in the wee hours of the morning. We were two night owls who raced each other from time to time. He was super hard to beat, but that made things more challenging, which was why I searched him out. Coming in first over and over got boring fast.

I relaxed my hands and then squeezed them into a fist, preparing to face my rival for an epic battle nobody in the history of the world would be talking about for generations.

After I picked my driver and wheels, the game dropped me into the lobby, and I hung out there until his current race finished and other avatars dropped in with me. Cartoon bubbles popped up around them, but all the chat phrases were preset. It was frustrating, but there was no way to actually trash talk the other players. Probably for the best. For all I knew, Parzival was actually eight years old. It would explain his avatar. He'd intentionally chosen the ugliest features from the Mii options. His nose was nothing more than two holes in his face. His eyes were a pair of dots, but his eyebrows took up most of his forehead in a Nike swoosh. He'd given himself a receding hairline. The mouth was the most disturbing feature, stretched out and revealing overly defined teeth, like a jail cell. His stupid face always made me laugh. What kind of lunatic would go to so much trouble to trash their Mii?

Mine, in contrast, was fairly nondescript. Only the blue pig-tails made it stand out.

Parzival's arm raised in a wave, as his avatar said, "*Go easy on me.*" I laughed and selected from the options available. My avatar waved and said, "*I'm a little nervous.*" I was given an option to vote on the game I wanted to play, and then all the other choices appeared above our heads. The dial scrolled over our picks, roulette style, highlighting each as it passed. At last, it slowed and landed on someone's choice. And then we found ourselves in our cars at the start of Rainbow Road.

Fuck. I sucked at Rainbow Road.

I pressed the button to make my engine rev as I waited for the traffic light to go from red to green.

Parzival and I each took off like a shot, side by side, and swapped places several times, but he nudged me out in the end.

Back into the lobby, I chose the preset dialog "*So unfair!*"

Parzival said, "*What a shame!*"

We played Bowser's Castle, Moo Moo Meadows, and Toad's Turnpike, which was usually my best race, but I was off my game, and Parzival won every time.

Consistent losing wasn't much fun, so I figured it was time to throw in the towel. I chose "*This is my last game*" from the prompts before choosing the track. Parzival waved, and his avatar said, "*I'll get you next time.*"

Somehow Parzival and I had managed to become stranger-buddies. Maybe he was just a kid, but I liked to picture him as someone like me: a shy twenty-something who found it easier to flirt over a gaming system than an actual dating app. And yet, these limitations were a virtual cock block preventing me from ever having a real conversation with anyone I raced. Maybe that was how I played it safe.

Maybe life would be easier if it came with prewritten dialog.

The town house was quiet as a tomb as I made my way downstairs. Aida and Marco would be up in a few hours, with the sun, but they slept like the dead all night. Someone had to be alert for any vampire invasions.

I stretched and checked my phone one last time, mainly to swipe off any notifications to stop the green light from blinking. There were only a few, and the text message icon stood out. I scratched my side and stretched, wondering who might have gone to the trouble to send me a message in the middle of the night. I started to throw my phone onto my nightstand, but the curiosity gnawed at me, and I knew I wouldn't sleep trying to puzzle it out, so I unlocked my screen.

The message was from Tristan. *It was fun hanging out.*

At least it hadn't said, *You up?*

I stared at the message, trying to formulate a proper response. I wished I could choose from a preset and write back *Go easy on me* or *I'm a little nervous.* I had nothing, and besides he couldn't expect me to see his message at three in the morning. I set the phone down and flopped into bed, finally drifting off for good.

Monday afternoon, I took a break from fixing defects to get some free coffee in the break room and walked in on an argument between Marco and Aida. I started to back out, but my need for caffeine prevailed.

Aida pounded her fist on the counter. "There ought to be an option to play Link in female form, is all."

Trying to avoid being pulled into the politics of games I hadn't designed, I maneuvered around them and slid a mug into the coffeemaker, changing the default setting to espresso so I could double up on the coffee packets. It was that kind of day.

While Marco deferred to Aida most of the time out of self-preservation, he never backed down from a pointless gaming argument. "Do you really think girls are out there all, *Oh, no, I'm a helpless princess,* because Link's a boy?"

I urged the coffeemaker to hurry up.

Aida said, "Yes. Yes, I do. You can't call a game *Zelda* and then make the entire game about a boy named Link who runs around saving Zelda from the destruction of the world. It's the very definition of patriarchy. And what's worse, girls have to identify with the boy, so they internalize a male-centric world-view. Would it hurt men to have to play from a female point of view every once in a while?"

I poured two creams into my mug and scurried toward the door when she said, "Right, Sierra?"

Fuck.

It was hard enough being a girl in the gaming community. I tended to tread lightly around politics. Aida was of the belief we had to burn it all to the ground and take what was ours. I respected her courage, but I had a team of developers who were for the most part men, and I'd earned their respect by being twice as good as any of them. I kind of liked to think I was changing the world one guy at a time by showing them I wasn't any different from them. In fact, I was better.

I stopped in the doorway and turned long enough to say, "It would be a nice option, but I grew up on *Zelda*, as did you, and neither of us took the helpless princess route."

Marco flashed a smile, and Aida's eyebrows rose, so I knew I should clear out before she lobbed a word bomb at me. It wasn't that I disagreed with her. It was just that confrontation made my heart race in a bad way. Forced to take a side, I'd usually find some mealy-mouthed middle ground and then hide until the argument blew over.

On my way down the hall, I was surprised to hear Aida say, "Damn straight."

Once upon a time, Aida and I had been a couple of helpless princesses, expecting life to turn out as we hoped if we just waited for it. Then my salaried job went poof along with the company I'd worked at, and nobody came to save us. People sometimes assumed Aida and I got our jobs at this company based on some kind of affirmative action, when the truth was there were no jobs like ours to be had anywhere, so we created them. Yes, I was fortunate to hold my dream job, but it hadn't landed in my lap.

I stole back to my office and swung my chair around to my desk to dig into my defect queue, but my phone began to ring, which made me jump. Nobody ever called me.

Although the area code indicated an Atlanta phone number, I suspected the call would be spam and nearly swiped the red X to dismiss it, but I figured I ought to be sure, so I answered but didn't say hello, waiting to see if a robot voice would kick in.

Silence.

And then a man said, "Hello? Sierra?"

"Yes?"

"Hey, it's Alfie. From the bar?"

I froze, fearing he was calling about the contest. I tapped my fingers on the side of the phone, nervous. "Of course! Hi. What's up?"

My voice had gone up an octave.

"Well, I just wanted to check in with you and see how you were feeling about the next round. I know you had some qualms."

Yup. My anxiety cranked up a notch.

I ran a hand through my hair and pulled forward a long strand, staring at the juxtaposition of purple and green. "Yeah. I don't know. I don't think I'm cut out for the pressure. And I'm just going to get eliminated anyway."

"I see. Well, you know, one hundred percent of people who don't compete lose." He laughed. "Wow, that sounded better in my head."

But it made me laugh, too, and I relaxed a little. "My cross-country coach used to say, 'Success is for the people who show up.' And I knew what he meant, but what happens when lots of people show up? It can't be true for everyone."

"Oh, my God. You're right." He was laughing again, and I settled into my chair, anxiety back down near zero. His voice had such a comforting quality to it—not too low, not too high, a little raspy when he chuckled. I wanted to keep him talking just to hear it.

"We should come up with honest aphorisms. Like: You'll probably suck, but you might not."

He snorted. "How about: Giving up is for losers."

That one made me cackle. "Exactly. Or, Why quit when you can humiliate yourself publicly and still lose?"

"Ouch."

I may have gone too far. "I've given this a lot of thought."

"But you did so great on Friday."

"Do you think so?" I nearly whispered it.

"You were incredible." He cleared his throat. "Listen. I don't mean to sound like a self-improvement guru, but you have as much right as anyone else to win."

"Oh, I never expected to win."

"And yet you had almost as many votes as Tristan."

"I did?" My heart rate picked up. "I was just trying to make it through one night."

"And you did." His quiet encouragement eased my residual embarrassment, but upping the expectations only intensified my stress for next time. Chances are I'd only disappoint him.

"I don't think I could do that again, though. I just wanted to survive."

"Tough love right here: Don't be a loser, Sierra." There was gentleness in his voice, and it made me smile since I knew his harsh words were an extension of our earlier joke. "Challenge yourself," he said more earnestly.

I swallowed hard. He was reminding me exactly why I'd started the contest. "Let me think about it, okay?"

"Sure. Just let me know soon so I can contact our alternate." Back to business.

I don't know why I'd been reading flirtation into the whole conversation. If he was with Miranda, I wouldn't want to think of him as a cheater anyway. I matched my tone to his. "Will do."

After we hung up, I dove into analyzing a defect in level two of *Castle Capture*, but his words were echoing in my mind.

Testing became more difficult as I progressed in the game because the challenges became more difficult. The monsters were deadlier. The bosses took more skill to defeat. Level one gave a player a chance to explore the world and figure out the rules, how the controllers worked, how to swing the garbage piece of wood players got as a beginner sword. In order to move up to level two, a player would have to gain mastery over these basics, and as a reward, they could collect better inventory and learn more advanced moves. So while the game got harder, they in turn got better at it.

I thought about Alfie's sports advice as it related to gaming. A player who hung around level one without taking risks could never advance. The game wouldn't allow them to proceed without conquering the level, but more importantly, they'd never learn enough to help them in their next quest.

In the same way, I'd been a total newbie the week before at the diary slam, but I'd leveled up, just a little bit. I'd gotten the lay of the land. I knew the rules. I knew how the game worked. I knew my competition. I hadn't won outright, but I'd defeated the first challenge, and I'd earned my spot in the next round.

Wasn't this entire exercise about taking risks and confronting my fears? If this was a video game, my final battle would be to face Reynold, the big boss, and convince him I could present at Gamescon, and the only way I was going to do that was to better myself, one step at a time.

I sent a text to Alfie: *Count me in.*

Chapter 10

Friday night, Aida wasn't feeling well, so Marco accompanied me over to Vibes to check out the scene. I'd let myself believe there'd be fewer people there since the number of contestants had been cut to twelve.

I was in for a disappointing surprise: A throng crowded the entrance.

We squeezed through and pressed against the bar. I waved at Alfie as he whizzed past like a blur and began filling a tall glass with beer. He glanced over once with a quick smile that made me feel self-conscious, and I dipped my head, hoping I hadn't been too bold with my appearance.

My makeup was still precise. I hadn't reached a point where I'd show off my freckles, scars, and nondramatic eyes. But encouraged by Tristan's passing approval, I left my hair down, flaunting all the colors of my rainbow.

Speaking of Tristan, I didn't spot him near the front, but he may have been farther in the bar near the makeshift stage. I didn't want to abandon Marco to go find him.

Miranda and Alfie danced a choreography behind the bar, communicating sometimes with nothing more than a gesture. Whenever they'd pause and whisper to each other, I felt a twinge of envy, like I often did when I encountered people who'd found their mates. Miranda was lucky to have nabbed one of the good ones. I shouldn't have been surprised. She was beautiful, blond, statuesque.

I knew I shouldn't stare, but I really loved watching Alfie's eyebrows furrow in concentration as he poured drinks, then how his face lit up whenever he interacted with a patron. Same as how he often looked at me.

As if he'd noticed me tracking him, Alfie slowed down enough to materialize in solid form. "Hey, Sierra. Hey, Marco. What can I get you? Club soda?" He narrowed an eye at Marco. "And if I'm not wrong, Dos Equis?"

Marco said, "Hey, that's pretty good. How's it going?"

I swung my head from one to the other. "You know each other?"

Marco shrugged. "This bar has been here for a year. I've stopped in a few times."

Alfie didn't challenge Marco's claims in any way. I wondered if there was such a thing as bartender-customer privilege, and Alfie was sworn to conceal how often Marco actually turned up on one of these stools.

"Does Aida know?"

He shot me a look like I'd lost my mind. "Do you honestly think I'd do anything without her knowledge? Sometimes she needs space. Sometimes I need the company of others."

Alfie set our drinks on the bar, then disappeared to handle the increased demand. It had to be good for him the place was hopping. Not so great for me. I was starting to feel like it was a bad idea to come out, wishing I'd stayed home in my pajamas curled on the sofa, testing out the new *Black Desert Online*.

Before I could act on my desire to translocate, I heard a voice in my ear: "Hey. Sierra, right?"

I spun around to find a vaguely familiar face. I combed my brain to recall how I knew this cute red-haired guy. He shifted a wallet from his right hand to his left and reached out to shake. "Zane. I'm in the contest. You might have missed me since I followed your act. Once I was done last week, I wouldn't have been able to pay attention to anyone else. Terrifying, right?"

He lifted a folded twenty out to get the attention of either of the harried bartenders.

What a relief to hear it wasn't just me. "That's an understatement."

"I'm so nervous about tonight, I decided to hit the bar a bit early. I might live to regret my decision." He spoke fast, charged with energy.

"I considered that last week but worried it would only lower my inhibitions and make me do something I'd regret. Onstage. In front of an audience."

His face dropped. "Oh, my God. I hadn't even thought of that."

His reaction made me snort. Despite his profession of terror, his eyes twinkled kindly. Before I'd left for the night, Aida had commanded me to check out the other guys at the bar, so I gave Zane a once-over. He was smartly dressed in a high-quality, light-blue button-up shirt that contrasted well with his ginger hair. His lips passed kissable muster, aided by the slight smirk he wore, like he was seconds away from a sarcastic observation. He seemed easy to talk to. It wouldn't hurt to show some interest.

I leaned forward and confessed, "Honestly, I almost didn't come back tonight."

"What? You?" He straightened up, his whole face registering cartoonish shock. "Girl, my boyfriend says you're the one to beat."

Oh. Never mind the flirtation, then. I relaxed, weirdly relieved I didn't need to keep performing for Zane. Maybe I could make a friend instead.

Zane waved his twenty a foot higher, and Miranda appeared. Damn, she was really pretty. "What can I get you?"

He placed his order, and I asked for another club soda and lime, never knowing when I'd see another server.

When we each had our drinks, Zane said, "Come sit with us!"

I glanced at Marco, prepared to turn Zane down, but Marco lifted his half-empty bottle and said, "Go on. I'm probably going to head back home anyway. Call me when you need an escort."

The walk home was only a few blocks, but Aida was convinced there were shady bad guys hiding behind every plastic trash can and azalea bush, waiting to cart me off to some sex dungeon. She'd read too many terrifying Facebook stories. But like Marco, I was more afraid of Aida than kidnappers, so I agreed to text when the contest was over.

I followed Zane through the crowd to his table and recognized the guy sitting there from the week before. His face lit up. "Hey! If it isn't the girl with the secret weapon!"

Zane politely introduced us, saying, "Bryce dragged me here last week, and I swore I would murder him if one of us doesn't win the money after all this."

Bryce dismissed him with a wave of his hand. "Promises, promises."

I took the extra seat, wondering what he'd meant. "What secret weapon?"

Bryce leaned way forward so he wouldn't have to shout. "You brought your crush with you! Did you plan that?" I shook my head, but he didn't even pause to catch a breath. "Oh, my God. Everyone cringed so hard for you last week. You should have gotten first for that performance alone, but then that boy was here?" He giggled. "Priceless."

Zane slipped his hand into Bryce's as he turned to me, head shaking. "Seriously. I hope you don't bring that kind of secondary mortification every night, or we'll never beat you."

"I think you can relax," I said. "I didn't even win last week."

"That's only because while you were reading nobody knew a bomb was about to go off." Zane lifted his beer, but just before it hit his lips, he said, "He stole the glory that was rightfully yours."

I sat up a little taller. Glory? Because of my embarrassment? Aida was right. I was in my element, like a level-forty Paladin fighting a swarm of crypt fiends in the Ghostlands. I grinned, enjoying their praise.

"Look at this." Bryce flaunted a sparkly silver journal with a bright rainbow arcing across the cover. "You made me pull out the big guns."

"What is that?" I'd fallen into the spell of these two. If they could go onstage as a duo, they'd bring the house down.

"Junior high. Puberty. I'm going for broke, thanks to you."

They were making me rethink what I'd planned to read. There were entries in my journal that had nothing to do with Tristan, and I'd found one that was only slightly embarrassing, but it was sure to disappoint my two newest fans.

I took out my notebook and turned to a page I'd originally ruled out, but now they'd left me aiming to impress. Thankfully, I'd documented a horrifically shameful moment from that semester. Not the *most* shameful, but good enough for tonight. And bonus, it referenced Tristan. Maybe I could coast on my newfound brand—she whose past had come back to haunt her.

Someone thumped my back, and a second later, Tristan was gliding around the table, spinning a chair around to straddle it. "Sara! You made it."

My heart hammered from the shock of his boisterous arrival. "Hey, Tristan. Do you know Zane and Bryce?"

Tristan reached out a hand to each of them. "Most excellent to know you! You're both in this tonight?"

Zane pursed his lips into a prune of a frown, then condescended to utter, "Indeed."

He and Bryce shared a knowing look before they each picked up their drinks and began sipping at the same time, simultaneously turning to face the stage, where Miranda sorted through some cards.

Bryce said, "God, I hope we don't go alphabetically every week."

Zane said, "Amen."

Tristan leaned closer to me. "Guess what I found?"

With Zane and Bryce demonstrably shutting us out now, I had a private audience with Tristan. "What?"

His left hand appeared from where it had been hiding below the table, and he slapped a Mead notebook almost identical to my own on the table. The cover had been turned into a work of art, with profiles of what I assumed had been the other kids in our class. In the center, in block letters, were the words *Comm 1000*.

"Oh, wow." It would be fun to hear what he'd been thinking that semester, and I wouldn't feel so alone with my own journal. "Solidarity, huh?"

"Exactly." He half-smiled in an endearing way and added, "I found something in here I think may have been about you."

I stammered, "Wh-what?"

My stomach went into free fall. Confessions about someone in the audience had been *my* secret weapon, according to Bryce. If I was the target of Tristan's reading, that might dilute the impact of my own journal. Even worse, if his diary centered on me, he was going to expose *me* somehow. My heart clenched at the possibilities.

"No worries." He lifted up so he could sling his leg around the chair and face forward. As he did so, he said, "It's all flattering." That smile again. "For you, anyway."

I locked eyes with Zane, who'd been listening despite his pretense otherwise. "Don't let the competition get to you. You've got this."

As Miranda stepped up to the microphone, I felt a light tap on my shoulder and looked over to find Alfie crouched beside me. Somehow seeing him calmed my nerves, probably because he'd given me such empowering advice twice now. "Everything okay? You ready?"

I winced. "I think so."

The top of his hair glowed red from the stage light, and I resisted the urge to muss it up. His eyes were nearly black in the dim room, like pools of ink, but they turned down slightly at the corners, and he had the longest eyelashes. He came across so friendly, I wanted to pat his head and scratch behind his ear.

As if he'd read my mind, he rubbed his neck. "I decided to dig up my journal from Ms. Maxwell's class. Would you believe I still had it?"

"Looks like there's three of us."

He glanced back at Tristan, then returned his attention to me. "Well, I just wanted to wish you good luck and warn you I'm probably about to out-humiliate everyone here."

"You'll be great."

Without thinking or asking for permission, I reached over and touched his shoulder in a gesture of encouragement. He inhaled sharply, like I'd shocked or offended him. Mortified, I withdrew my hand, aiming to tuck it under my thigh to hide the criminal appendage, but his hand lurched out and wrapped around mine. I nearly jerked back in surprise, but then I relaxed at his touch. It was as if he had a reservoir of peace and he'd passed it to me via some superpower or magic. His grasp tightened briefly before Miranda announced, "Welcome back to the second round of our first annual Chagrin Challenge."

The crowd applauded, and Alfie squeezed my hand for a beat longer before heading up to the stage, leaving me confused as to his intent. He touched Miranda's arm and leaned in to say something before taking the microphone from her. She lay a hand on his shoulder, whispered in his ear, laughed, and then jogged off the stage to tend the bar. They made a very cute couple, and I hoped I hadn't inadvertently done anything to make his eyes wander. I shook my head at my own hubris. Why would he ever stray from gorgeous Miranda?

Alfie blinked in the spotlight. "Thank you all so much for returning. Last week was a lot of fun, and I'm counting on you all to bring the chagrin-g." Yes, he managed to rhyme *bring* and *chagrin*. He wrinkled his nose, evidence he heard how wrong that sounded. "I'd been planning to continue my recitation of horrific poetry, but I was reminded that I, too, kept a journal for one semester, so I dug it out." He held up the nondescript note-book. "I should probably burn this thing, but alas, I am one with you all in over-sharing."

He shook his head. "This one's gonna cost me."

Who knew those notebooks could conceal such subversive commentary?

Chapter 11

Alfie flipped the journal open and paused to breathe in, then out. I willed some confidence his way. As if my imaginary strength had found its mark, he began.

"People always told me I'd make friends easily in college. I hadn't in high school, so I didn't understand why things would be any different. My mom met my dad in college, and she promised it would be a small city comprised of people whose ages and interests would align with mine. She was right about the concentration of potential friends. I've never been more immersed, and yet somehow, once again I've become invisible."

He took a drink of water before continuing.

"I wonder if Ms. Maxwell reads these journals. I ought to pay her for the free therapy." Laughter stirred through the audience. "I don't usually speak this many words. Why speak when people don't hear me?

"I've grown used to the solitude, and honestly, I prefer my own company to bad company. I never disappoint myself."

More soft laughs. It was weird to me, because he wasn't saying anything really funny or even embarrassing, but I could sense the audience rooting for him. Rooting for that boy he used to be. Wanting to go back in time to be the good Samaritan who would reach out a hand of friendship.

Oh, to have a time machine.

A smile crossed Alfie's face. "But today, I saw a girl, and I thought she saw me. She has a certain style, like she moves in another dimension, and I thought, maybe she's different enough she might see the world I inhabit. I walked toward her, though walking isn't exactly the right verb. It was like being drawn by a magnet. I was mesmerized by her spirit. I approached her to introduce myself, but she stumbled. I bent to help her up, and she glanced at me. Her eyes held infinite depths of perception, and I thought she saw into my soul. I thought we'd formed a connection. I opened my mouth to say hi, but then she looked away. I picked up her notebook and handed it to her, catching her attention for another fleeting moment as she stood and hesitated. In that moment, I could have said anything. I wish I'd just said hi.

"But she turned to take a seat, and she didn't see me, so I didn't speak, and she didn't hear me. I resolved to try another day."

He closed the notebook and stepped away from the microphone, and then the silence broke. I started to applaud with everyone, but I was stunned.

That girl was me.

I knew that because I'd journaled that same incident and had bookmarked it as an option for tonight. I hadn't mentioned Alfie, though. Or had I?

Wouldn't it have been crazy if Alfie had crushed on me the way I'd crushed on Tristan? What a blind love triangle we would have made. And it might explain how affectionate Alfie had been toward me. Those decade-old crushes lingered. I ought to know.

Zane elbowed me. "You okay?" He pointed to his cheek, like he was miming.

I reached up, surprised to find wet cheeks. I scrubbed them with a napkin. "What? That was moving."

Bryce said, "Well, now I'm going to feel like a jackass following that."

Zane said, "That's kind of the point."

Miranda called for more applause for Alfie, who'd tucked tail and fled to tend the bar. As Bryce expected, she called his name next.

Bryce flashed his silver rainbow journal at me and Zane with a cheeky wince before trotting up to the mic. I took a sip of my drink to wash away the nerves I felt for him. It had been easier to watch the carnage when I didn't know these people.

Bryce opened to a bookmarked page, cast his gaze out into the audience, and without further introduction said, "My mom caught me masturbating today."

My drink sprayed from my lips, and I frantically snatched up a napkin to blot up the liquid dribbling down my chin onto my dress. Tristan turned his head and shot me a look that could only mean he also knew we were now competing for second place.

Bryce went on. "It was my fault. I hadn't locked the door and she walked in. The look on her face will haunt me until I'm in my grave. When I'm older, this will be a day I will tell my therapist about."

He paused to look up from the journal to say, "And I did." He shook his head. "I told all of them."

I thought for sure he'd end there, but he started back in.

"I threw on some pants and tiptoed down the hall, thinking up some excuse I might have had for sitting half naked in my swivel chair with my hand wrapped around an impressively large erection. I'd just invented a story about homework for health class when I heard her talking to someone. I peered around the corner and caught her on the phone, shrieking to whoever about my penis. I had to know who was now privy to a private moment between me and imaginary Zac Efron."

Everyone in the audience was howling.

Bryce closed the book, leaving us all in that moment, silently urging him to keep reading, for his teenage self to have finished writing.

"Who was it?" someone yelled.

Bryce leaned toward the microphone. "That, ladies and gentlemen, was the day I went to live with my dad."

And with that bomb blast still detonating, he turned and walked off the stage to deafening silence. Nobody seemed to know if they should laugh, applaud, or surround Bryce in a mob hug. As he sat down, Zane reached over and rubbed his back. I wanted to stretch a hand over to him, but we'd just met and I didn't want to be weird, so I caught his eye and smiled awkwardly. Miranda called out for everyone to applaud, and we all did, but it wasn't the raucous reaction he might have gotten if he'd chosen a safer route, if he'd finished on a comedic note. But I was awed by the raw honesty, and it made me feel a bit ashamed of my frivolous diary.

But then Bryce winked and grabbed his bottle of beer, and the world moved on.

Poor Dana had to follow that. I zoned out on her and her ill-fated audition for a school play. I watched Zane and Bryce whispering with each other and felt a stab of envy for their relationship, their obvious friendship. I longed for that kind of ease with someone I cared for.

When Gary was called up, I headed toward the bathroom to calm my nerves. I emerged as Heather was telling a story about a swimsuit malfunction. I went back to the bar to look for Alfie. The crowds from earlier had thinned almost completely as everyone had taken a seat or leaned against a wall.

Alfie stood behind the counter, listening as Heather swam in the deep end, searching for her missing bikini bottom. His smile widened as I approached.

"Club soda?"

I nodded.

He set the glass down, and we both applauded as Heather left the stage, and Hillary took her place.

"I loved what you read," I said in a stage whisper.

"Thank you!"

I made a show of glancing around the bar. "Looks like you've found a way to keep yourself surrounded with friends."

He laughed. "Very observant of you."

"I was wondering." I bit my lip. This felt intrusive. "Do you know who that girl was?"

"Why do you ask?" He pulled a towel off his shoulder and began to wipe down the completely polished bar.

I noticed that wasn't an answer. "It's strange, is all. I had planned to read something about a day when I happened to drop my notebook in the same class."

He shrugged. "Happens, right?"

I narrowed my eyes at him. "You sure you don't remember?"

"That was a long time ago." He sighed. "If you're asking if it might have been you, it might have been you."

I'd have to live with that answer. "Well, it was a very sweet journal entry." I said, "And if it had been me—" at the same moment he said, "Actually . . ."

We both stopped, and I prodded him. "What were you going to say?"

He held out his hand, palm up, like he was offering me a chair. "You first."

"Just . . . if it had been me, then I should have paid more attention. I should have noticed you. And I should have thanked you."

He twisted his lips into a half frown. "If that was you, you were embarrassed and I understood."

"Yes. I was embarrassed." And smitten and entirely focused on another guy. "I'm still sorry, and I wish I would have said hello."

His smile returned. "Hello."

"Hi."

Our eyes locked for a beat, his dark and mysterious, mine no doubt wide-eyed and curious. I wondered why I hadn't noticed him when he'd clearly noticed me. I started to say as much when Miranda's voice broke in, like a reminder of missed opportunity.

She thanked Hillary and introduced Mike, and the awkward silence that had grown between me and Alfie was shattered when Mike said, "I shit my pants in fourth period."

I raised my eyebrows at Alfie, who was blinking in overexaggerated shock. We turned our attention back to the stage for the horror that would follow.

Mike's disgusting story met with more groans than laughs

and kept me preoccupied. I nearly forgot the buffer before my turn was running out. But when I heard Porter's name called, my body became an alien creature to me, and I had no more control over how the nerves in my fingers or the gasses in my stomach or the cells in my brain would behave.

How could my hands be cold and numb, while my ears were so hot and my heart pounded so painfully in my chest? How could I need to pee again so soon? What was that taste in my mouth? Copper?

Porter was replaced by Quinn. I threw a trapped-animal glance at Alfie, calculating how disappointed he was going to be if I left. How disappointed he would be if I stayed. I couldn't compete with any of these people. My diary entry wasn't funny. It wasn't sad. It was boring. Like me.

My bag was still hanging on the chair next to Zane, so I'd have to retrieve it, and then I could sneak out. They'd call my name before they realized I was gone. Then they'd carry on without me. I wound my way back around, and as I picked at the strap of my bag, Tristan reached over and grabbed my wrist. "Oh, good. I thought you might have left."

"I'm considering it."

"You can't. I told you, you're gonna like what I have to read." His eyes were puppy-dog saucers of gentle begging.

I dropped into my seat. "Fine."

When Shannon was called up, my hearing ceased to work because my pulse had gravitated to my ears, and everything was *blood! blood! blood!* But I smiled when everyone else did. And I applauded.

Then Miranda called my name.

I was going to shit my pants in front of the whole room. That would beat Mike's story.

Zane leaned over. "It's just reading, right?"

Bryce nodded. "And that"—he pointed at my journal—"is no longer you. It's a fiction. Okay?"

God, that was great advice, though even presenting a dry and impersonal demo in front of friends was murder. But knowing I had a few allies in the room now, a few people who were urging me on, who were behind me, and most importantly had *all* bared some scary secret from the past, gave me the courage to take one step, then two. I reached the small platform and turned to scan the audience before moving into the spotlight. And along the wall, for the first time, I noticed Reynold, leaning back, drinking a beer.

Mother fuck.

Maybe it was a good thing. I'd started this entire farce to win his approval. Maybe I could convince him I could do this.

God, I hoped I could do this.

Chapter 12

The microphone sat in the stand, ignorant of its menacing significance. I hated it, but I reminded myself it was just a tool to project sound. Since I didn't want to endure the additional embarrassment of being told to speak up again, I approached. As soon as I stepped into the spotlight, I was practically alone. Other than the muffled chatter and the occasional cough, I could have been in an empty room.

I closed my eyes and imagined myself in a void. When I opened them, the bar no longer existed. Only me and this cursed microphone.

With the journal opened to the page I'd marked, I began to read.

"I tried a thing today.

"I nearly talked myself out of taking the chance, but I remembered what Mr. Shepherd always said: Success comes to those who show up. I could at least show up.

"All last week, I noticed he always sat in the same seat. It's kind of a first-come, first-served situation.

"My plan was simple: I'd arrive early and take the seat next to his. Then when he got to class, he'd sit next to me.

"But this morning, it was raining, hard, so everyone was riding the bus. I waited, pelted with rain, for at least ten minutes. By the time I arrived in the class, I was soaked, and he was already settling into his seat. I could see that girl Marilyn Crusoe eyeing the empty chair next to him as if invisible dashes floated in the air to advertise her precise trajectory. I had to hurry. The steps down the amphitheater aren't steep, but they also aren't carpeted. When I drew near, my left sneaker skidded. My arms windmilled as I tried to prevent the inevitable, but I misjudged the steps and my right foot overshot the landing.

"I dropped everything trying to break my fall, but fall I did. On my butt. I managed to keep from sprawling by forcing myself straight down to a sitting position, but then I heard a terrible sound as my jeggings ripped.

"A few people laughed, but someone had the good grace to pick up my notebook while I gathered my phone and backpack. I yanked my shirt over my literal ass hole before I stood, head held high with a pride I did not feel.

"I should have bailed right then, but as Mr. Shepherd would say: Destiny favors the bold. I knew that if I aborted my mission, it would be one hundred times harder to execute this plan tomorrow.

"Now or never.

"He stood and bent toward me to ask if I was okay. My knees buckled. Those eyes. Blue seems like an inadequate name for the color of those gorgeous spheres, like a vision of Earth from outer space. I was lost in the cornflower when he stood to help me. His hand touched mine, and static electricity passed between us.

"We laughed at the unexpected shock, and I interpreted that spark as a sign.

"I asked, 'Is this seat taken?'

"He gestured toward the empty chair as he returned to his. Then my phone, which had become precariously perched after my stumble, slipped right off my notebook. I reached after it, trying to catch it in midair before I saw where it was headed. Straight for his crotch. Oof.

"That would have been the right time to turn my tail and flee. But as he handed me my phone, somewhere I found the gumption to plop right down and introduce myself.

" 'Sierra Reid,' I said. 'S-I-E-R-R-A. Sierra.' "

Okay, I'd added that line in an attempt to get the message across to current-day Tristan.

"And as if I hadn't known it, he smiled and said, 'I'm Tristan Spencer.'

"And just like that, Tristan Spencer was talking to me. Mission accomplished."

I took a huge breath and stepped back from the mic. I hadn't noticed if anyone had laughed. The audience could have picked up and left for all I knew. But the spell broke as soon as people started clapping, and I staggered off the platform, focused on not tripping down the stairs yet again, unaware of the star in my hand until I sat back down.

Tristan leaned back. "Dude. That was awesome." He beamed, and I thought if all I managed was to build up the ego of a guy who didn't need it, then at least someone would feel better at the end of the night.

I would have loved to be anywhere else at that moment. Sitting beside him after baring more confessions of a ridiculous crush made my skin burn from the shame of it.

"Sierra, huh?" His face scrunched up, and he said, "Sorry?"

"Thanks." At least that awkwardness was managed.

I stuffed my notebook back into my backpack, hoping I'd never have to look at it again. Reynold caught my eye and gave me a thumbs-up. I didn't know why he'd shown up, but gaining his approval calmed me considerably. Maybe I could humiliate my way to Germany.

"Next up, Tristan."

Before he stood, he said, "Such a coincidence, by the way. Seems I documented that same day." It surprised me he'd even taken the class seriously enough to write anything worth reading, but maybe I had a lot to learn about him.

Zane lifted his beer bottle like a toast. "That was hilarious, Sierra. You'd get my vote, if I wasn't partial." He winked. Contestants weren't even eligible to vote, anyway, but it was sweet.

Tristan grabbed the mic, and we all focused our attention back to the stage.

"If Ms. Maxwell collects these notebooks, my humble apologies for what is to follow because I had a raging boner in your class today. Your lesson today was on *Show, don't tell*. And dude, I totally was. Showing that is."

A burst of loud laughter erupted.

"It started before class when this hot chick came up the aisle wearing a see-through T-shirt, thanks to a bountiful rain this morning. The outline of her bra lit up like a candle in a window, and my imagination took off."

My blood turned to ice as I imagined myself practically naked in public, as I was sure everyone in the bar would now as well. *What is he doing?* That had been *my* mortification. He couldn't turn it into *his* moment.

"Then she slipped and fell, and I shit you not, I caught a view of her panties through a rip in her pants. That was it for me. I got a chubby right away.

"To make the situation more dire, when she decided to sit by me, she dropped her phone directly on my erection. Ouch. She started to reach for it, and I'm more than a little certain she noticed the camping tent pitched in my crotch."

The audience rewarded him with snickers and cackles. Everyone present knew it was me who'd done all this. I'd revealed it myself, but any laughter I'd solicited at my own confession felt conspiratorial. They'd been laughing *with* me. The hilarity of Tristan's reading was at my expense. This felt mean.

"Then she introduced herself, and for the first time I got a look at her straight on. The girl's a righteous knockout. Eyes like an angel. Lips like sin. I stared a little too long and told her my name. Before I could pull it together to ask her for her phone number, Ms. Maxwell called the class to order."

And just like that, I wasn't mad anymore.

"And so, Ms. Maxwell, I'm so sorry, but I had a hard-on in your class today."

He grinned and looked out in my direction. Though I knew he couldn't see me, I could tell he thought I'd be pleased. And to be honest, I was flattered by the last bit. I never knew that he thought I was cute. He'd never shown any interest in me. I certainly hadn't noticed this mythical erection. Maybe it had been someone else who showed up on a rainy day and flashed the class after a nasty spill. Maybe.

He took his star and jogged back to our table, eyebrows raised. "Well? What did you think?"

I punched him. "That's for stealing my thunder."

"No way! Your story was way better than mine."

"Yours turned out to be"—my cheeks warmed—"very sweet."

Miranda welcomed Zane to the stage, and I gave him a thumbs-up.

The corner of Tristan's mouth lifted. "I wish we could get out of here."

My stomach lurched. "Yeah?"

"You wanna go outside and talk?"

Did I? "We should pay attention to Zane."

"Yeah."

Easier said than done. When Tristan turned to face the stage, I stared at him. Did I miss a million signals in college? Had he really meant to ask me for my phone number? He had it now, and he'd used it already. I'd never even responded to his late-night text the other night. Was something happening here, and I was too scared to realize it?

My thoughts were broken by an eruption of laughter.

Zane said, "And that is why you should never take your phone into a changing room."

Full-on applause. Zane took a deep bow and bounded off the stage, flashing his yellow star.

I grabbed mine and stood as Miranda invited us to take a short break while she collected the votes. "I need a drink."

"I'll come with you."

Tristan followed me to the bar, and I laid my star out next to his on the counter, a pair of yellow pasties. I blushed, remembering not much more than that had prevented Tristan from getting an eyeful of my bare bosom that day.

"I can't believe you wrote that all down." That's not what I wanted to say. I wanted to ask him if he'd meant it.

"It obviously made quite an impression on me." He leaned his arm along the bar so he was facing me.

Alfie arrived, looking a bit harried. Everyone had taken this moment to refresh their beverages. "Great job, both of you. What can I get you? Gin and tonic, again, Sierra?"

He was a good bartender to remember my order like that. I nodded.

"And for you?"

Tristan said, "Newcastle, same as before."

Alfie reached below the bar, retrieved the bottle, and uncapped it in about ten seconds. Then he began mixing my drink. I kept my gaze on him because I was too aware of Tristan beside me, and I couldn't meet his eyes or I might say something that would embarrass us both.

Alfie scooped ice into my glass. His sleeves rode up, revealing toned forearms with a hint of corded muscle.

Tristan took a swig of his beer. "What are you doing after this tonight?"

Did people go out after they'd already gone out? "Probably go home. Play video games."

Alfie poured a stream of gin into the glass. Tanqueray. He remembered. He reached for the tonic spray gun with a wink, his dark eyelashes framing those mystical eyes. A little smile played at his lips, like he knew I was staring and enjoyed the attention.

Tristan set his bottle on the bar. "Do you need an escort back home?"

The tonic spritzed from the hose, and Alfie's hand slipped just enough that a jet arced across the counter and caught Tristan right in the shoulder.

"Oh, God." Alfie grabbed his towel. "I'm so sorry. I thought I had a better handle on that."

Tristan blotted at the spot. "It's no problem, man. Just a little soda." But his voice belied his calm words.

Alfie finished up my drink and garnished it all with a wedge of lime. Tristan took it and said, "Let's get back to our table. Looks like they're about to announce the results."

I winced at Alfie. I knew he hadn't meant to spray us, but he didn't smile back at me. In fact, somehow he looked as annoyed as Tristan sounded. Maybe I should have paid for the drink. He probably hadn't meant for my star to cover non-sanctioned drinks forever. I made a mental note to settle my tab after the announcements.

"Here we go, everyone." Miranda held a list before her. I quickly took my seat and swapped hopeful grins with Bryce and Zane. I glanced over to the wall, but Reynold was gone. I took a deep breath, hoping for some reason that I might have won the night and gotten one of those Get Out of Jail Free cards. I chalked this sudden wish up to my video game addiction. A free life could always come in handy.

"If I call your name, you'll be advancing to the next round. For everyone who doesn't make it in tonight, thank you again for coming out. Tonight's top vote-getters are: Bryce, Gary, Heather, Porter, Quinn, Shannon, Sierra, Tristan, and Zane. We hope to see you all again next week for round three."

My whole body crumpled. I hadn't known how worried I'd been I wouldn't get picked until the stress evaporated. I searched for Mike, who'd told his pant-shitting story to an unreceptive audience. He was busy laughing with Shannon, so I figured he wasn't too put out.

"And our big winner tonight is"—Miranda paused for dramatic effect—"Zane!"

I patted his back as he stood and chucked Bryce in the shoulder. He jogged up and took the card from Miranda, holding it up like a trophy.

After the applause died, Tristan stood. "You ready to rumble?"

"Sure." I picked up my half-finished drink and swallowed it in one face-melting gulp. "Let's get out of here."

Chapter 13

Outside, the voices and laughter from the bar sounded muted and far away. The only light came from streetlamps and a pale, shrouded moon. Tristan left me alone on the sidewalk while he retrieved his Vespa from around the corner, then he walked it beside me as we headed toward my place.

I finally said what I'd wanted to before. "I was really surprised by your journal entry. I had no idea you were even aware of me that day. Did you really write all that?"

That was as close to fishing for a compliment as I could get short of asking, "*Hey, did you really think I was cute?*"

He looked up toward the sky for a few steps, then exhaled. "Well, you know, I embellished it a little."

Gut punch. "What do you mean?"

"For the contest. I tweaked it to make it funnier. Didn't you?"

Was I supposed to? Had I been sharing my truest secrets while everyone else was making a game of reading fictional accounts? "So . . . what exactly did you change?"

"Like the part about the boner. As if I'd write that in a journal."

"Then what *did* you write?" He'd obviously added the funny parts to compete with Bryce's masturbation story. What about the flattering parts? "Did you make the whole thing up to copy me and win the crowd over?"

He stopped dead. "You think I just came up with that on the fly at the last minute?"

"I have no idea. Did you even mean what you said about me?" I hated how childish I sounded, but it was important.

"About how pretty you were?"

This was so humiliating, but I needed to know he wasn't just riffing for the sake of the contest. "Yeah."

His eyebrows drew together. "Of course I did. You were pretty then. You're even prettier now."

I stared at my hands. The polish had chipped on my thumbnail, and I futzed with it. "It's just that you never struck me as shy, so I'm surprised you never told me before, is all."

"Sort of like how surprised I was last week to hear you say you liked me? To hear it again this week?" He took a step toward me and lifted my chin with a knuckle. "I promise—I only embellished that entry to make it funnier. It's entertainment, not the nightly news."

When he looked at me like that, I got butterflies. I thought he might kiss me again.

But I heard Mrs. Shih asking, *"What's he like? Is he nice?"* My yoga moms would ask me again tomorrow, and he was a complete mystery to me.

I drew back and continued up the sidewalk. "You told me about your comic book, but where do you work?"

"In Edgewood."

"Doing what?" I hoped he didn't mind the third degree. I glanced over to check his expression, but we'd left the streetlights behind, and the moon did nothing more than set his hair to glowing.

"Oh. Like I said. I'm a graphic designer."

The only places I could picture in Edgewood were a Target and a Lowe's. "At what company?"

"It's a small company. You wouldn't have heard of them."

He was probably right. If it had been a gaming company, I would have. Marco had all the art connections. "Are you happy there?"

Tristan frowned as if considering the question. "Actually, I'm always keeping my eye open for a better job. Do you know if your company needs anyone?"

"Oh, I'm not really involved with the hiring of artists."

We were a small company, and Reynold or Aida handled the day-to-day operations. Marco oversaw the artists. I managed the developers and testers. Our employees could pile into an airport shuttle. We'd done just that the year we flew to Las Vegas to celebrate the launch of *Roundhouse*.

"Of course not, but maybe if you hear of any openings?"

"You ought to talk to Marco."

"That would be great."

We only had about a block to go, and I wanted to find out more about him. "How did you get started with comics?"

His whole body seemed to unspool, and he grinned. "I've been reading comics since I was a kid. God, I used to be so into *Green Lantern*. At first, I copied the drawings, and then when I got better, I tried making my own. And then . . . I don't know if you remember, but I always used to hang out at that skate park in Auburn."

I didn't know that at all. "There was a skate park?"

He chuckled. "Yeah. It was a great place to blow off steam."

It made sense. He'd always had that skater vibe. "So you decided to make a skater superhero."

"That was the idea. I dunno. Maybe it's dumb."

I knew only the basics about comics, but I remembered worrying my first video game might be too stupid to bother with. I searched for some advice that might have helped me then. "Tristan, you created something, and you should be really proud of that."

"I guess. Howard thinks he could help me self-publish. But that's an expensive investment, and so far, nobody's been willing to front me that kind of cash. I've tried to raise the money via Kickstarter, but that's stalled out."

"Hence, the contest."

"Right. A grand would cover the printing expense. I'd still need to figure out how to market it to get kids to buy it, but if I could get that one issue into the hands of readers, it might be enough to launch the entire series. I've got more stories ready to go."

"Wow. That's ambitious."

I kept walking, trying to think of other intrusive questions. "Where did you grow up?"

"Roswell."

"No way! I grew up in Norcross. We were practically neighbors."

"Oh, yeah? I had a summer job over at Peachtree Corners."

"Me, too! I wonder if we ever ran into each other."

He nudged me. "I think I would have remembered."

When we got to my porch, I expected to say good night and angle for another kiss, but he said, "So you were going to play video games?"

I shrugged. "It's how I unwind."

"What games?"

"*Sonic the Hedgehog, Crash Bandicoot, Mario Kart.*"

"*Crash Bandicoot?*"

"Yeah. It's stupid, but fun."

"Mind if I play it with you?"

"Oh." I glanced up at the apartment. The lights indicated Aida and Marco were up, though probably only waiting on me to get home. I could invite him up to play a game, and then once we were alone, we could talk more, get to know each other better. And maybe he'd show me some sign he was truly interested in me. I pictured myself straddling him, kissing him, slipping his shirt off. All the lost fantasies that rattled around the attic of my memories could finally be acted out, like fulfilling a sexy bucket list.

"You want to come in?"

He moved closer. "If you want me to."

Oh, yes.

I dug out my keys and led him up the steps to the front door. As soon as I entered the town house, Aida hollered from the kitchen, "You were supposed to wait for Marco!"

"I got an escort," I called back.

She poked her head out. "Oh, hey Tristan."

I led him back to the kitchen where we found Marco at the table, nursing a beer. "Marco, this is Tristan. Tristan, Marco."

Tristan held out his hand, and as soon as they clasped, Tristan said, "You're Marco Vargas."

"That I am."

"I remember you from when I submitted my application to your art department."

Marco frowned. "When was this?"

"A couple of years back. But you were looking for someone more experienced in Unity Pro."

"Ah. Yeah, we're pretty deeply embedded in that drawing tool right now."

"I've actually been working a lot with that program lately. I would love to show you my work sometime."

"Hey, Tristan. Would you like a beer?" Aida gave me the wide-eyed *what the fuck* look.

I shook my head at her. I didn't know. "We're just gonna go play some *Crash Bandicoot*."

She raised an eyebrow. "Can't. The PlayStation's at work."

"What? Ugh." New plan. "Come on, Tristan. Do you like *Mario Kart*?"

"Yeah. I'm pretty good at it."

Turns out that wasn't true, and I had to decide whether to play for real or soothe his ego by half-assing it so he could win some. After a few races, where I won despite refraining from hitting any power-ups or taking advantage of speed boosts, mainly because he kept falling off the track, I said, "Would you like to play something more collaborative? I've got *Mario Party*. Or maybe we could just talk?"

He put the controller on the coffee table. "Nah. I should be heading out."

"Sure." Disappointed, I got up and walked him out to the porch, wondering again if I'd completely misread his intentions.

He paused at the edge of the steps. "What are you doing tomorrow?"

"I've got yoga until around noon."

"Yoga, huh?" His nose scrunched up like I'd mentioned some offensive vegetable. "Are you free tomorrow night?"

"Yeah. Why?"

"Do you think you could swing out to Decatur?"

"Um. Sure. When?"

"Around six? Or I could come get you, but it's kind of a long way on the Vespa. Believe me."

"Car still in the shop?"

He laughed. "Oh, yeah. They haven't found the problem. Do you mind driving?"

"No, it's not a problem."

"Cool. I'll text you my address."

I waited for him to clarify why he wanted me to come to his house. Was he planning to take me out to dinner in Decatur? Was he planning on making me dinner? Did he just need a ride to the grocery store?

I tried another tack. "What should I wear?"

He gave me a once-over. "Might want to wear something more casual."

"More casual than a T-shirt?"

He glanced at my skirt. "Maybe yoga pants or sweats?"

The hell? "Are we going to be doing yoga?"

He laughed. "Maybe."

"You're awfully mysterious." There was no way the guy who grimaced at yoga a minute ago had a sudden change of heart. This was no doubt nothing more than a booty call. Not that I was entirely opposed, but advance notice would set up my prior expectations.

"It'll be fun. I promise." He winked, and I was ninety-nine percent certain I'd need to shave closely and find my sexiest panties.

Wasn't this exactly what I wanted? I was getting closer to Tristan, but I didn't know if he saw me as a friend, a date, or a potential fuck buddy.

He leaned in for a kiss, and I closed my eyes, imagining where tomorrow night might lead. But he didn't linger, so I was left wondering if this was a prelude to anything more.

He bounded down the steps, and I shut the door to find Aida hovering behind me, waiting.

"What the hell was that?"

I leaned back against the door. "I don't know. I think . . ." I sighed. "I think it was a job interview."

"I don't know why you keep doing the same fool things, expecting different results." She turned and disappeared into the kitchen.

I grabbed my backpack and peeked in to say good night and apologize to Marco. "I had no idea he was going to do that. I guess he saw an opportunity and couldn't let it pass."

"More like made an opportunity," Aida muttered.

I put my hand on my hip. "Are you saying he planned this? He knew he'd find Marco sitting at the kitchen table so he flirted with me to walk me home?"

"It worked, didn't it?"

Marco held up a hand. "Would you please take it down a notch? I can't blame him for trying. But there's probably nothing we can do for him right now. So you should know which of you is right soon enough."

"Which one of us is right?" I asked.

"Yeah. Is the guy interested in you? Or is he interested in what you can do for him? If it's the latter, he'll stop pursuing you when you can't help him."

Marco could be so brutally honest at times.

"I suppose so."

Aida grunted. "Don't get your hopes up."

"You should have heard what he read tonight, though." I tried to recall the words he'd used. "He'd written about me in his journal, and he called me a knockout. It sounded like he noticed me more than I thought back in college." Although most of that was physical, and a lot of it borderline voyeurism, but hadn't my interest in him been equally shallow? Still, he'd revealed some vulnerabilities when he walked me home. "Maybe he hasn't changed that much, but maybe he has. Or what if we were always wrong about him?"

She snorted. "Whatever, Sierra. You make your own decisions."

She turned back to the sink and began washing dishes, and Marco muttered something about digging up Tristan's old job application to take a look.

Halfway down the stairs to my lair, a text message sent my phone vibrating. *Sorry for tonight. I sometimes forget how to relax. Maybe tomorrow night could be a do-over.*

And with that, I scored a point against Aida to move to the top of the leaderboard. Aida was wrong.

Aida was the queen of the grudge holders, which was why Marco worked so hard to stay on her good side. She still threw shade at me for the time I saved over her *Super Smash Bros.* game. And that was years ago.

I didn't see the point in wasting energy on negative emotions. Focusing on unjustified fears and long-forgiven slights couldn't be healthy. However, I wasn't a patsy. If I trusted a guy and he betrayed me, he'd be done.

Yeah, I had reasons to mistrust Tristan, but I loved a good redemption story, so I hit the reset button. We were playing a whole new game now.

Chapter 14

In the deep recesses of my dreams, a voice niggled at me until I floated back toward consciousness. The drink. The bar. Alfie.

The free drink.

I sat bolt upright. I'd never paid Alfie for the gin and tonic.

I checked the clock. Half past one. The bar would close in thirty minutes. I rolled over, thinking I should forget about it until tomorrow, but my legs were already bouncing and I knew I'd never fall back asleep anyway.

The kitchen was dark and quiet as I crept out to my car. Opening the garage door would probably wake Aida, but she wasn't my mom. Besides, they wouldn't want me walking or biking across town in the wee hours of the morning. In my pajamas. Well, sweatpants and a T-shirt, anyway. I'd taken half a minute to put on a bra, brush my teeth, and don my tennis shoes.

Parking was easy to find. I had ten minutes to spare as I jumped out and raced to the bar doors, worried that maybe they'd closed early. But a couple of people staggered onto the sidewalk as I approached, and the muffled *mmmph-mmmph-mmmph* of the bass blossomed into a song I recognized from the radio.

Entering a bar at night always gave me the sense of going on a camping trip and finding myself in a cave as I transitioned from the cool open air into an encapsulated universe of stale cigarettes and the promise of sin. Maybe because I'd always arrived before sunset, Alfie's place had never given me that vibe. Maybe because Alfie always welcomed me when I came in, the place felt safe and friendly. The few customers remaining at this hour were gathering belongings and heading toward the exit.

I climbed onto a barstool, scanning for Alfie's smiling face, but Miranda looked up from the register. "Hey, Sierra. Sorry, you just missed last call."

"Oh, I wasn't here to order a drink. I'm looking for Alfie."

"Ah." She paused, holding a stack of bills in her hand. "Alfie's gone home. Can I help you with something?"

"Gone home?" I pictured them in their apartment, waking in the morning together. He was so thoughtful, he probably made her breakfast while she slept in. She'd landed a good one. I should have been happy for her, but suddenly I wanted that drink I'd missed out on.

She finished counting a stack of bills. "What did you need? Should I call him?"

I slid the ten out of my pocket. "No. I forgot to clear my tab before I left earlier. He gave me a gin and tonic instead of the free drink. I wanted to square up."

She dipped an eyebrow at me. "There aren't any outstanding tabs here. He probably meant for it to be a comp. You'd have to talk to him about it."

"Would you mention it when you see him?"

"Sure, but I won't see him again until Monday. I'm off tomorrow."

My head jerked over to her. "Aren't you going home to him?"

She laughed. "To Alfie?"

"I figured—"

"Ha. No. I love Alfie to death. He's a good boss and a great friend. But no. We just work together."

I couldn't explain the relief I felt, and it wasn't really fair to poor Alfie that I'd been rooting for him to be single, like me. Like I wanted some solidarity with my loneliness. "I see. Well, I'll try to drop in tomorrow night and figure it out."

"Sure. No problem."

I slid off the stool, somewhat disappointed that nothing had been resolved. Still, I would have been at home tossing and turning if I hadn't at least tried. I waved to Miranda as I exited the bar and headed down the sidewalk to my car.

"Sierra?"

I spun around as Alfie turned the corner, pulled along by a beautiful speckled dog, with brown, white, and gray fur. My heart melted, and I dropped to my knees. "Hello, sweetie."

The dog dragged Alfie forward, tail wagging, tongue hanging out one side of its mouth. I held my hand out so it could sniff me. It put its paws on my lap and licked my face. I laughed and pulled back to scratch under its chin and ruffle its fur, like I'd wanted to ruffle Alfie's hair. "What a good dog. Look at those beautiful blue eyes."

I looked up at Alfie. "Girl or boy?"

"Boy."

"What's his name?"

"Jasper."

"Hello, Jasper. Aren't you a good boy?"

"Don't encourage him. He's full of energy and wants to go for a run."

"Poor baby." I patted his head.

"He thinks he's a puppy, but he's got arthritis." Alfie squatted down and scratched behind Jasper's ears. "Good old boy."

I could have sworn Jasper smiled at the attention, eyes closed in total bliss. Was it possible to envy a dog?

I lavished more attention on Jasper and met Alfie at eye level. "How long have you had him?"

"He was my sister's dog. She was obsessed with Twilight, hence the name."

"And where's your sister now?"

"Paris."

"Oh. I see."

"And my mom can't take care of him."

"Right."

We'd run out of dog small talk, and the weirdness started to creep in.

Alfie stood. "What brings you out so late?"

I noticed he'd changed into sweatpants and a faded Auburn T-shirt.

"Oh. Right." I rose and reached in my pocket for the money. "I forgot to pay you for my drink earlier."

He laughed. "You came out in the middle of the night to close a bar tab?"

"Well, I thought you were mad at me earlier."

"You thought I was mad?"

"Yeah. And I couldn't stand making you mad because—"

"Because?" He tilted his head, looking both amused and confused.

"Well. Because I think you might be the nicest person I've ever met."

"Oh." He side-eyed me. "The nicest, eh. Not the prettiest?"

I snorted at his reference to my journal from the week before. "You want to be the prettiest?"

"Just kidding." He smiled, but now that the question was out there, I decided it deserved further analysis.

In the streetlight, I gave him a thorough examination. I'd initially thought he was cute with that rumply hair, but I was wrong. "There's nothing pretty about you, Alfie."

He double blinked. "Okay. That was honest."

"Well, maybe your eyes." I couldn't make out the color, but those long lashes framed dark eyes that sparkled, like a starlit canopy of night.

"My eyes? I guess I'll take it."

"Nope. Alfie, you're not pretty at all." I bit my lip, worried I might be too forward, but now that I'd stopped and considered him, I'd seen something I hadn't before. He had beautiful features under that slight beard he wore. High cheekbones, a long pronounced dimple in one cheek, and soft lips covering a smile that warmed my heart. "You're not pretty. You're gorgeous."

"What?" He shook his head. "You're crazy."

I should have felt embarrassed, but what are friends for if not to offer free praise? "You're welcome."

"I wasn't fishing."

"Sure." I would have challenged him to repay the compliment, but I'd rolled out of bed without a speck of makeup on, and I didn't want him to examine me too closely. "I should head home."

Alfie wrapped the leash around his wrist to regain control of Jasper, who was urging him forward. "You want me to walk you home?"

I pointed at the Ford Escort parked behind me. "I drove over."

"All right." He hesitated a beat before stepping away. "See you Friday?"

This late-night rendezvous had been more relaxing and entertaining than a video game alone on my sofa. There was something comfortable about Alfie, and I would have liked to be friends with him, but I hadn't asked someone for a playdate since I was a kid. Maybe I could offer to come walk his dog some nights.

I opened my driver-side door. "See ya around, Alfie."

Saturday morning, my yoga class greeted me like a pack of fleas in an abandoned apartment, like they were waiting for blood.

Mrs. Martinez was first to ask the question. "So? Details?"

"Y'all." I gave them all the stink eye. "It's way too early for details."

"But you had a date, right?" Mrs. Shih had the look of a woman who wanted to live vicariously through her idealized vision of my love life.

"We went to dinner last weekend." I smiled. "And he walked me home last night."

"So he's nice?"

I started to tell them he was, but my mind drifted back to my midnight stroll for some reason. If they wanted nice, they'd love Alfie. "Yeah. I guess."

It wasn't really fair to compare them. Alfie was just . . . Alfie.

"You don't know?" Mrs. Garrett's concern touched me, but what did they expect after a week?

"We'll see how it goes." I unrolled my mat to indicate the end of the conversation by plopping down and directing them to relax their bodies and ground themselves. They took the cue and settled down to focus on their own meditation.

As I talked them through the *Sukhasana*, I let my mind skip over the moments I'd experienced in the past week, trying to release anxiety. Yoga had been great for my body, bringing me a flexibility I'd never achieved while running. I used to think I stretched enough, but it had taken me years to be able to bend at the waist and touch my toes while keeping my knees straight. Running had helped relieve stress, but there was nothing compared to a sustained pose for gaining focus, clarity, and peace while also strengthening my core.

Moving into another position, I made sure the class followed suit, but this was my yoga class, too, and I sank deep into that place where I could better understand myself.

I thought about the presentation the night before. I'd probably blown my wad on that performance, and I still hadn't won the night. But putting things in perspective, it didn't matter if I'd won or lost. I'd made it through two separate readings, and this time I'd done it with Reynold in the audience.

My heart rate increased as I pondered the implications of his presence.

"Let's move into Warrior One." I pushed my front foot out.

Mr. Baxter said, "I can never do this. Can you help me get my balance?"

I rolled my eyes. He was persistent at least. "Mr. Baxter, yoga is about uncovering your own pose. Follow your nature."

He grunted and settled into a perfect stance, lifting his arms up over him. Other than the gentle sounds of the calming music playing from a boombox in the corner, the room quieted again.

I let myself think about Tristan, about the way he'd looked at me the night before, about the way he'd kissed me a week ago. Was he seriously interested in me?

My shoulders tightened with the stress I was dredging up. I took a deep breath, intent on focusing on something pleasant. I replayed that kiss again, remembering how his lips had felt against mine, but when I drew my face back from his, in my imagination, I saw Alfie.

Chapter 15

GPS led me to a bungalow with a fenced-in yard. I pulled into the driveway about ten minutes too early, and not wanting to look too eager, I sat in my car, scrolling through Instagram posts from the contest the night before. Alfie had shared a picture of Jasper, and I got lost in his feed. He didn't post often, and the few times he appeared, he was usually surrounded by other people who looked an awful lot like him. I assumed they must be his family, and I wondered where they were, where he came from, where he'd grown up, what it was like to have such a large family. I knew so little about him, and I wanted to know more.

A buzzing sound like a lawn mower engine intensified. I looked out and saw Tristan tooling up the road on his Vespa. He waved and slowed to a stop. I rolled my window down.

"Hey!"

"Hey, Sierra." Thank the Lord he had my name straight finally. "Sorry I'm a bit late. I just got off work." At a normal hour. When regular people work.

"No problem. It's not that late."

"You ready to go?"

I climbed out of my Escort. "Where to?"

"Hop on. It's just around the corner."

My stomach grumbled, and I hoped we were going to a

restaurant. Decatur had a yummy Indian place that sounded divine right about then. He wore slacks and a button-up shirt, making me feel extremely underdressed in the clothes he'd told me to wear.

I settled in behind him on the Vespa, wrapping one arm around his firm torso. He smelled like sunshine, tanning lotion, and fun. I was tempted to lay my head between his shoulder blades and breathe him in, but before I had a moment to act on that crazy impulse, he hit a curb to jump onto a sidewalk and entered a park. Literally right around the corner.

He rode past a swing set and a jungle gym, until we reached what appeared to be a skate park.

I slung my leg over the bike, and Tristan jumped off, kicking the stand as he did so.

"One sec." He unbuttoned his work shirt and pulled it off, revealing a T-shirt below. "Much better."

I wondered if he'd strip his pants off, too, but alas they remained. He grabbed a skateboard off the back of the scooter and said, "Follow me."

In an area made of concrete with a few different kinds of ramps, kids of various ages swooped to and fro. I tensed, expecting to witness a horrible spinal injury. Tristan set his board down, stepped on it, and pushed off. Then he gave me a heart attack by jumping up and kicking the board somehow so it flipped completely over before he got his footing again, landing perfectly and gliding to a stop. He turned and grinned.

"Wow." I was legitimately impressed. "What's that called?"

"That? A kick flip."

"Oh." I shaded my eyes from the sun. "I was expecting something more colorful. Like a Zombie Tornado."

"No tornado, but I can show you a Back Slide Hurricane."

And he was off toward a ramp in the far corner. When he got to the top edge, he slid across it for a foot or so before riding back down. Unsure of proper etiquette, I applauded. Another one of the skaters tried the same trick, but he wobbled at the top of the ramp and ended up jumping off the board and running back down.

Tristan skated back over to me. When he stepped off, the board continued toward me until I stopped it with my foot. "Hop on," he said.

"Oh, no."

"Come on. It's fun."

"Nope. I always end up on my ass around you. This is just too on the nose."

"What?" His eyebrows knitted together, then he seemed to remember. "Oh, you mean like you wrote in that journal."

"Exactly. And also later." The more embarrassing example. "During that contest."

He frowned. "Which contest?"

"You know. The one for comm class. The big one. Where students from all the sections competed?" When he shook his head, indicating no recognition, I wanted to punch him. "How do you not remember that? You and I made it to the finals. It was a big deal."

"Sounds kind of familiar."

"We competed against each other on a stage?" I was starting to get angrier.

"Wait." He laughed. "You don't mean the slideshow sabotage?"

"Yes!" I was on the verge of tears now, and I really hated that. I clenched my fists to try to get better control. I'd long ago stopped being mad about it, but his reaction was dredging up all the bad feelings.

"That was you?"

"I was humiliated."

He shook his head. "But you weren't the one humiliated. I was."

"Oh, please. You made an ass out of me that day."

"What?"

"We went over this years ago. You totally planned it." He'd tried to deny it then, too, but he had motive and opportunity. Plus, he'd manipulated me to step right into his trap. "I'd rather you didn't lie about it on top of everything."

"Why would I lie about that?"

"Because you like to win, Tristan."

"Well, damn. I don't know what to say."

"You could start by apologizing."

He led me to a bench that had been a skater's prop a minute before. We sat down, and he took my hand. "I'm sorry, Sierra. I really mean it."

I relaxed. "That's all I wanted to hear."

"That's it? You're not mad anymore?"

"Tristan, it was years ago, right? I'd already let it go." I focused on our hands entwined, feeling the rough callous of his thumb against my palm. "I know it wasn't that big a prank in the grand scheme of things. Some funny pictures to make the audience laugh at me. Ha-ha." A tear slipped onto my cheek, and I wanted to die from the humiliation of it. I wasn't that upset, but my body always betrayed me. "It's just that it was a huge deal to me at the time. It was that much worse because I always idolized you, so when you pulled that stunt to embarrass me, it hurt in ways you couldn't have known. Plus, I broke my ankle that day."

"No shit." He squeezed my hand. "You idolized me?"

That made me choke-laugh. "My journal wasn't a giveaway?"

"I can't believe I didn't notice then."

The sun had reached the point in the sky where it drenched everything in golden hues. Tristan's eyelashes were tiny flames around eyes so blue, they reminded me of dyed Easter eggs.

He fished his phone out of his pocket. "You look so pretty. Let's take a picture together."

He held the phone high, and the light hurt my eyes, but I smiled. Then just before he snapped the picture, he turned and kissed my cheek. When he showed me the picture, I thought, that's what we'd look like as a couple. We'd be stinking adorable, and people would envy us.

He reached over and ran a finger across my cheek, dragging loose hair to the back of my neck and making me shiver with his touch. I watched the scene unfold from the vantage point of my past self, wanting this moment so bad I could taste it. I couldn't help but give in to the temptation of touching his soft cheek. The setting sun brushing his cheeks dusted him in gold. His skin felt rougher than I'd expected. Manlier. I'm not sure why I thought he'd feel like silk.

He licked his lips and leaned a little closer. I willed him to kiss me, and when his lips grazed mine, it tasted like victory.

My stomach growled again, and I broke the kiss.

I looked around the skate park, watching a dozen Tristan clones showing off for one another. "Why did you bring me here?"

"Because you told me you'd never seen me skate."

"What?"

"Last night, I asked if you'd ever been to the skate park in Auburn, and you said no. I wanted to impress you with my mad skills."

"Impress *me*?" First the comic book, now this. "You're impressive, Tristan."

"As are you." He leaned back against the bench. "You must be to end up working at Extinction Level Event." Before I could preen from the praise, he went on. "Or was it a diversity thing?"

"How do you mean?" I blinked my eyes rapidly, waiting for him to extrapolate on this topic.

"Well, I mean it's obviously tough to get hired there. It's a small company, I guess. I applied and never heard back. Your girlfriend who works there, she's what? Middle Eastern?"

"Uh, American. Her parents are French-Algerian."

"You see what I'm saying? I'm sure you're both talented enough, but maybe they aren't looking for plain vanilla dudes like me."

I took a deep breath as I tried to figure out where to begin, but then I exhaled. This wasn't an argument I was prepared to have. Aida would have eaten him alive, but I didn't want to be disagreeable, and it really wasn't worth trying to make him understand. I could have explained that Aida and I had started the company, but what would that have accomplished?

"I think maybe I'm just gonna go home." I stood.

Tristan reached over and touched my wrist. "I'm sorry. That

was unfair. It's just that I don't know why they wouldn't hire me. You've seen that I have the talent, right?"

He seemed sincere, but I couldn't let it go if I didn't at least set him straight. "Tristan, I've worked really hard to get where I am. The tech market is actually harder for women. Okay? It's hard for everyone."

"You're right." He sighed, looking more stressed out than he had before.

"Are you that unhappy at your current job?"

He shook his head and smiled. "No. I'm good. I'd just like a change."

"I wish I could help you. Maybe I could talk to Marco." But if Marco had seen any hint of that attitude, Tristan wouldn't have made it past the first interview.

Tristan stood and held out a hand. "You want to head back to my place?"

I was well prepared for that question. I'd showered and shaved and spritzed myself with pleasant scents. I'd even packed a condom at Aida's rude prompting, but now I wasn't so sure. His comments about my job rankled.

Tristan retrieved his bike, and I got on, but already I was making excuses in my mind, so that by the time we got to his house I was ready to say, "You know, I'm gonna head home."

"What? Why?"

"I'm not feeling well." This wasn't even a lie. My head felt woozy, which I attributed to lack of food. My mind wasn't clear enough to make a decision, and maybe Tristan wasn't going to ask me to sleep with him, but stepping into his house felt like a promise that would be harder to break on the other side of the threshold.

Part of me still wanted to follow through, but I wanted it for the wrong reasons. For Instagram reasons. For reasons that made sense to me once upon a time, when I didn't need to like a guy to sleep with him.

When I didn't need to know a guy to fall in love with him.

Tristan followed me to my car. "You seemed to be feeling well enough a little while ago. What changed?"

How do you explain a total eclipse of your long-held world-view?

"Nothing changed, Tristan. Nothing at all." I'd just come to recognize reality, a truth Aida had already discerned.

I could have spoken up and told him how he'd offended me, but it was easier to pack up and leave. I pulled my keys from my backpack, already wondering if I was overreacting. "I'll see you Friday?"

"Friday? I'm free tomorrow. I could come over. We could hang out." Is this what happened when hot guys got turned down? I'd never had anyone beg to spend time with me. I'd never been chased after, and I kind of liked the feeling of power he'd given me. It almost made me want to bestow my charity upon him and tell him yes. I could live out a decade-old fantasy this very night. We could have one night of meaningless sex and satisfy the great unresolved yearning of my life.

But I didn't want to.

"Sorry. I can't."

He sighed. "Okay."

Before I opened my door, my butt hit the side of the car as his hands pressed against my shoulders. "One for the road."

His lips hit mine, and I froze from the surprise of it. The front of his pants met my hip bone, and I no longer had any doubt about Tristan's intentions.

Eros, *Philia*, and *Agape*.

Now that I'd spent time with him, I knew Tristan could only ever satisfy my physical desire. I longed to find a man who'd be both lover and companion, and Tristan obviously wasn't that man. Sure, I could imagine being friends with him, but I didn't think our tentative friendship would survive a night of sex. Beyond some basic attraction, we weren't in any way compatible.

Quite simply, despite my body's traitorous desires, my heart was no longer Tristan's.

When I pushed him off me, he broke the kiss and made some

space between us. At least he was a gentleman enough to take no for an answer.

At least he'd made me sure of my decision.

"I need to go."

And with the weight of every possible alternate reality on my shoulders, I got in my car and drove away into the one concrete future I'd just created. One with Tristan in my rearview mirror.

Chapter 16

I was navigating the shadowy catacombs under the abbey in the level-three dungeon.

The reported defect claimed that casting Morgana's Charm of Making a second time would raise a duplicate army of the dead. Fascinating. The charm was only supposed to work once and then extinguish itself. Defeating the entire army would open the tomb of Gilead that contained another nastier monster who protected an unbreakable longbow. I loved weird defects and wanted to find out what would happen if I had two armies to defeat, and also what would happen if I summoned a second army after the tomb had opened. Either way, the defect needed fixing, but I was curious if repeating the same steps would make my situation much better by allowing me to obtain double the longbows. Or much worse by giving me twice the trouble for no extra gain.

Occasionally, if a defect yielded interesting results, I'd argue to leave it unfixed as Easter eggs for users to discover. This didn't feel like that kind of defect, but I loved playing with un-intended consequences—when the code didn't do what I thought it would do.

A tap on the door distracted me from the game long enough for the swarm to extinguish the last of my life, and I exited out with a grumble.

Reynold came in and took the extra chair. This didn't bode well. I hadn't spoken to him since I'd flubbed the demo over a week ago. He was busy with his other investments, including a locally sourced designer jean manufacturer, a wholesale vape distributor, and a sunglass vendor. From what I could tell, the sunglasses were his most profitable. We were his least, but he believed we had the most potential. Otherwise, he would have dumped us or sold us ages ago. Still, I knew we were on borrowed time.

When he visited our offices, he didn't waste time on pleasantries.

"How's the game coming? Will it be ready for Gamescon?"

"Most definitely. Most of the bugs we have left are edge case."

Unlike the rest of us, he dressed the part of a professional, wearing a nicely tailored suit and tie. He unbuttoned his jacket and leaned his elbows on his knees. "How edge?"

Reynold didn't know code, so there was no point giving him a technical answer. I'd learned how to speak to him at his level.

I tilted my head side to side. "Like you'd have to be trying to break the game to find them."

"Our users are always trying to break the game."

"You know what I mean. We owe the testers a bonus." I raised a brow at him in response to his darkening expression. "And not pizza this time. Actual money."

Reynold hated to shell out for perks before the cash flow offset his investment. His role here was different from everyone else's. When Aida pitched the company to him, he'd agreed to become a hands-on investor because he believed we had potential, but he didn't think we had the experience to bring our products to market in a way that would pay dividends for him. His condition was to stay involved, in charge of the money and the business strategy, but his end goal was to sell us to a bigger development company eventually. Unless we could begin to turn a sizable profit on our own. Until then, he made sure we all earned a fixed salary while he took on the risk of failure. Hence, his reluctance to reach into his own pocket to fund extras.

Although he owned us, he was a beneficent despot, letting us run wild with our imaginations when it came to the actual work.

He considered himself a rudder steering the boat, but the artists and developers were the waters below.

True to form, he groused, "We wouldn't need testers if the developers coded right in the first place."

Ouch. I laughed. "You know developers test for the happy path. We need the testers and their devious minds to look for the holes."

That shut him up for a moment. He stood and moved over to my credenza, where my family of Funkos and other assorted kitsch gathered like a coven of sorcerers plotting a devilish uprising. He picked up my Mishiko figurine, the only toy I'd collected from the *Roundhouse* line. "This looks like something out of the Matrix."

"Actually, Mishiko was based off Kirito from *Sword Art Online*."

"I have no idea what you just said." He turned the statue around in his hands, either admiring the sleek design of the long black coat and elegant longswords, or stalling for time.

He put Mishiko down. "About last Friday."

Stalling, then.

I took an elastic band off my wrist and pulled my hair into a ponytail just to be doing something with my hands. I waited for him to finish.

"That was an interesting thing you did."

"Interesting?" I wouldn't know where Reynold was going until Reynold arrived there. It was pointless to answer his non-questions until he asked questions.

"Interesting. Unusual." He bit his lower lip. He had a soul patch that morphed from triangular to trapezoid whenever one side of his mouth defied the other. Combined with his eyebrow-like mustache, his facial hair looked like a third eye. "When Aida told me what you were doing, I had to come see for myself."

"Ah. Aida's who I have to thank for your presence there." I set my hands on my lap and looked at him straight on. "And?"

"And I think it's good. Not a traditional approach, but you seemed to manage with the material you'd chosen to present."

This was where I was supposed to plead my case to him, but he had that scheming look. There was more to this visit than my overcoming the obstacles of my painful anxiety.

"What do you want me to do?"

He laughed. "You were always a step ahead of me. What gives me away? Or am I just that predictable?"

"You're never predictable, Reynold."

He scratched at the part of his chin that remained clean-shaven. "I want you to find a way to promote one of our products next week."

"You want me to pitch our game between guys telling stories about sharting?"

"Think of it as practice. Show me you're ready."

"You realize I've been reading from my diary, right? None of these products existed then."

"So make it about some other game. I just want to see you sell something."

Reynold was a pain in the ass, but he was my path to Gamescon and I needed to impress him.

"Fine. I'll squeeze in some product placement next week. Okay? Will I get to go to Germany if I do that?"

He closed his eyes and sighed. His mustache-beard continued to stare at me. When he fixed me with an actual steely gaze, I stiffened.

"Aida may not have told you how much is riding on the demo. Our last game has been losing market share to our chief competitor, and sales are flat. We need to build excitement with this next title, and a lot of game reviewers will be at the presentation. We need to blow them away."

Oh.

The implied *or else* was that he'd start to find a bigger company to absorb us so he could cash out, or, worst-case scenario, we'd fold. If he sold the company, there'd be no guarantee any of us would still have jobs under a new regime. It was the gamble we'd agreed to.

My desire to travel to Germany suddenly felt selfish and immature. Surely, Reynold would rather send a powerhouse.

"So why aren't you hiring some big salesperson to go to the convention?"

"Believe me, I'm thinking about it. But Aida has convinced me it would be better to send someone who knows the game rather than an outsider. I want you to show me you have the chops. Otherwise, I'm sorry, but I'll have no choice but to look elsewhere."

"So if I can show you I can pitch one of our products, will that be enough?"

He shrugged. "I think we've got a little ways to go. But think of this as a part of your redemption journey."

"Level three. A quest." I almost got goose bumps at the visual.

"And that reminds me. Please don't leave any Easter eggs behind in the game this time."

"Sure," I lied. He might know business, but he didn't know gamers. Easter eggs turned serious gamers into fanatics.

When he left, I considered how I could satisfy Reynold, and the same option presented itself again and again: I'd need to fabricate a diary entry.

Tristan had planted the idea in my head with his confession the week before. I'd balked at the prospect of outright lying, but there were several reasons a fictional entry appealed to me. First, I could incorporate the product placement easier. Second, I could share something less humiliating. And third, I could finally read something that wasn't a love letter to Tristan. It wouldn't have to be totally invented, either. I knew just the anecdote to share.

Chapter 17

I got to the bar a little early to chat with Alfie, but Miranda greeted me, and I worried for a heartbeat he'd taken a night off. It was strange how quickly I'd grown accustomed to seeing him each week.

Miranda reached into a plastic bin to retrieve a steaming wineglass, wiped it down, and hung it above the bar. She didn't stop moving, and it was a little mesmerizing and soothing to watch her polish each glass methodically.

"Did you get things settled with Alfie?"

"Oh. Yeah." My cheeks warmed as I pictured myself out on the sidewalk in my sweatpants, telling him he was gorgeous. He probably thought I was a freak. Somehow I didn't think he did, though.

"Can I get you a drink?"

I'd been spoiled by Alfie knowing what I wanted before I ordered it. I shook my head and watched the other patrons taking up residence on stools around me.

When Alfie returned from the kitchen, I picked him out of the crowd immediately, like a celebrity had appeared in the faceless mob. He glanced over and saw me and, without asking, slid me a glass of club soda with a wedge of lime. What a sweetheart. I held it up like a toast.

I dropped a five on the counter and sat back to mentally prepare myself for the contest, still unsure about my plan. Some of the contestants had told anecdotes, and Tristan had convinced me that improving on the truth in this situation wasn't the same as lying. I knew I wasn't constrained to my diary, but I still needed the crutch of reading. People like Tristan had the talent to wing it, but not me. Would it be too deceptive to pass off my story as a journal entry?

The first moment Alfie stopped moving, I flagged his attention. "Hey, Alfie. I've got a question for you."

He threw his towel over his shoulder and sat back against the counter behind him. "Shoot."

"Is there a rule against making things up for the contest?"

He rubbed his chin. I liked how he kept a neat dusting of facial hair. It wasn't enough to count as a full beard, but more than a shadow. It suited him. "Well, there's no rule. I mean, how could we possibly verify?" His lips pressed together as he continued to weigh the question. "But it does take away from the spirit of the fun somehow. I'd like to think people are sharing authentic stories."

Guilty. I shifted on my seat. "Have you embellished anything you've shared?"

"Me? What would I have had to gain from that?"

True. He wasn't even competing.

"But if someone was obviously lying, they wouldn't be disqualified."

"Why? Is someone inventing false narratives?"

I laughed like a defensive robot. "Ha-ha. How would I know?" His quizzical expression made it obvious he suspected me. I didn't want him to think I was confessing to anything overtly shady, but I also didn't want to betray Tristan, so I said, "My boss wants me to introduce something specific into my reading this week, but I'd have to revise history in order to jam it in."

His forehead wrinkled. "What does your boss have to do with it?"

"Have I not told you why I'm even here?"

Someone flashed a twenty at him, and he excused himself for

a few minutes to mix a drink, but then he whispered in Miranda's ear before stepping out from behind the bar. He waved me to follow him. "Come talk."

We took a seat at an empty table. As he stretched out his long legs, I ran my eyes all the way up his body. A pair of chocolate brown boots peeked out the ends of his dark blue jeans. He'd left his heather gray Henley untucked and unbuttoned just enough to reveal his collarbone. That little glimpse made me imagine his chest underneath, and my eyes followed the buttons one by one down to where they stopped above his sternum. I remembered that brief peek at his forearms a week earlier, and I swallowed, picturing his pecs, his abs, his . . .

I dragged my wayward eyes up to his curious stare, sure he'd read my mind. I flushed.

"So tell me. Why are you here, doing this contest?"

"Well, first, I have a crippling fear of public speaking."

He tilted his head with a wry smile. "I hadn't noticed."

"Shut up." I rolled my eyes at his deadpan joke. "You coached me into staying that first night, and I thank you. I needed to get over that initial hurdle. And then your pep talk on the phone got me here again last week."

"You're welcome." He leaned back and crossed his ankle over his knee. Damn, he was sexy sitting like that. "I'm still waiting to hear your story."

"So there's this gamer convention in Germany in a couple of months, and someone needs to go there to present a demo of our next video game title. Normally Aida would go. You remember Aida? She's—"

"Your friend that came with you the first week."

"Right. And she's—"

"About to have her hands full with a newborn."

"Exactly. So there's an opening, and I want it. Badly."

"Why exactly?"

How to explain my reasons? "I mean, why do people go to Comic Con? To geek out with other fans over shared interests. I love video games, and I want to hear pitches for games that are yet to be developed and meet the people who design the games I play, or who play the games I've designed. Not to mention, I've never been out of the country, and that would be a kick-ass trip."

"Okay, but why do you need to go for a demo? Can't you just go?"

"That's a good question. But, well, it's pretty expensive. And yeah, I could swing it, but . . ." I didn't want to go into my entire financial situation with him. The games we'd developed had done well enough to allow Reynold to reinvest in the company, which meant hiring more developers and artists and building customer service, not to mention paying Reynold his cut. We needed one breakout title to ward off the existential threats. Meanwhile, my salary covered rent and essentials but didn't stretch far. I'd been putting money in savings, of course, but I'd have to borrow from myself or someone else to afford a flight to Germany. It seemed like a frivolous way to spend my money when I could go on Reynold's dime. Instead of telling Alfie all that, I said, "But then I wouldn't be able to eat for a month."

He laughed. "So I take it the demo involves public speaking."

"Exactly. And Reynold—that's my boss—doesn't think I can do it. He thinks I'll choke."

Alfie tapped his thumb against his lip, listening, thinking, hearing me. "So this is your way of proving it to him? And now he's throwing in additional challenges."

"Bingo."

"So what's the endgame? How do you prove yourself worthy of this great reward? Do you have to win the contest?"

"No. This was never meant to be my proving ground. Aida initially suggested using the weekly readings to gain confidence in myself—the confidence I lost a while back." I took a breath because my voice cracked and I didn't want to start crying over this.

Alfie scooted his chair forward, then reached out and took my hand. "Hey, we've all got things to work through, but I'm willing to bet you haven't lost all your confidence. You seem to be doing pretty great with your life."

I loved that he saw that. Sure, I was a mess in certain social situations, although somehow Alfie hadn't once made me feel weird or panicked. My fear of public speaking had intensified over the years, but I'd gotten way better at what I did best—developing games. I had no problem talking through initial designs with the team or making sure our plans got executed. "You're right. I guess I've been focusing on my failures."

"No failures. For the record, you killed it the last two weeks on that stage."

"Thanks." That left me with my initial question. "So you're not going to kick me out if I shove in some talk about video games?"

He smiled. "I'm not the one doing the voting. And I love video games."

Zane and Bryce appeared out of nowhere. "Hey, Sierra! Hey, Alfie!" They pulled out chairs and sat with us.

Alfie stood. "Guess I need to get to work. Thanks for talking."

As he headed back to the bar, I followed him with my eyes, realizing I'd talked to him all of three or four times, and we'd always ended up talking about me. I needed to change that pattern if I truly wanted to befriend him.

More people arrived. I saw some of the people I'd been competing against and had never spoken to. I waved at Heather, and she smiled back. I scanned the rest of the arriving crowd. There was no sign of Tristan yet, but I glimpsed Reynold squeezing in to order a drink at the bar.

"You want to get in on some soft pretzels?" Bryce was reading the short bar menu.

"Me?" I might barf if I ate anything before the show. "Thanks, but no."

"Suit yourself." He flagged a passing server and placed an order.

Zane said, "What's in your magic journal, tonight?"

"Something a little different," I confessed.

Tristan pulled out a chair. "Different how?"

I smiled at him. "Well, for one thing, you'll be glad to know it's not about you."

"Oh?" He slumped. "I like hearing about me."

Zane and Bryce exchanged an eye roll.

"I think my shtick was getting old," I said.

"Never." Tristan waggled his eyebrows, and I shook my head, laughing.

The room suddenly seemed full, and the chatter had risen to a level that drowned out our casual conversation. I scanned the crowd. "Looks like word has gotten out we're all making fools of ourselves in public."

Zane nodded. "There's not much else going on right now. Alfie picked a good time to host this."

Miranda headed to the stage, and a moment later, Alfie patted my shoulder as he passed by. That little tap made me sit up straighter. Bryce and Zane had quickly moved from strangers to friends, and I loved that they were so supportive, but Alfie in the audience rooting for me fed me an extra shot of confidence. Even though I barely knew him, he'd slowly wormed his way into my heart, like we'd been friends much longer than a couple of weeks.

Maybe we'd spent time together in college. Maybe we'd been paramours in a former life.

The thought gave me a chill.

Once Miranda welcomed everyone, Alfie took his spot at the mic to do his promised solidarity reading.

"Hey, everyone." He lifted the comm journal and cleared his throat, then just as he seemed about to read, he added, "I hope the nonparticipating audience members appreciate how mortifying this really is."

After a brief pause, he held the page out beyond the mic and began.

"Alfred Alfie Alf.

"My parents hated me. There's no other explanation. There's not one good variant of my name.

"I'm either a butler, a Jude Law movie title, or a Muppet alien. At least nobody remembers the movie.

"I've been considering . . ."

He paused for a moment but didn't look up from the journal before continuing.

"I can't believe what just happened. I'm sitting on the brick wall outside Haley Center, trying to get a little sun, writing in this journal before class starts, and that totally cute girl sits down next to me. She sees my notebook, which I flip shut immediately, and says, 'Rushing to finish your morning pages?' I nod, unable to remember what words are.

"She leans a little closer. She smells like autumn. 'I really like the journal, but could you imagine if Ms. Maxwell ever read them to the class? I would die of embarrassment.'

"The idea had never occurred to me, and I swallow hard.

"Then she asks, 'So what are you writing about?'

"And for some reason, I tell her. I say, 'I don't like my name.'

"She shrugs. 'So why don't you change it?'

" 'Change it?' I say. I don't get what she means. It's not like I can just march down to city hall and pick a new name.

"She goes, 'When you get an account online, you get to pick a new name, right? Nobody thinks twice if you call yourself Nymeria or Star-Lord. It's just who you are. Like a pseudonym. Why can't you have a pseudonym in real life?'

"I say, 'What? I just go up to people and introduce myself with a fake name?'

"She laughs, and that makes me laugh. 'Try it maybe. Who cares?'

"Who cares? I love her attitude. I consider for a minute what name I would choose. I picture that guy in *Ready Player One*. I always thought that his avatar had a pretty epic name, but I imagine the looks on people's faces if I said, 'Hi, my name's Parzival.' Maybe I could go by his real name, Wade Watts.

"Then again, maybe not. Wade isn't much of an upgrade from Alfie.

"The girl gets up and slings her backpack over her shoulder. I want so badly to touch her cocoa hair. 'So what's your real name, anyway?'

"I could say anything, but I don't want to be a fiction to her. 'Alfie,' I say, and I wait for her to cringe. But she tilts her head, considering, and her smile grows ever so slowly, like she's testing out a new flavor and has decided she likes it.

" 'I like Alfie. You should keep it.'

" 'Why?' I ask.

" 'It's sweet, like you. It makes me feel like I could trust you.'

"Then she turns and walks away, and I realize in that instant, I forgot to ask her her name."

He stopped talking, and everybody applauded. Everybody but me. I sat there stunned, once again, wondering: Was that girl me? Had I crossed his path again and again, missing him every time?

It seemed crazy, but as he described that conversation, it had sounded familiar. I'd sat on that brick wall outside Haley Center a million times, and I could swear I once talked to a guy there about his name. Maybe I'd created a false memory out of thin air, wanting to remember it. Besides the boy I pictured hadn't looked like Alfie. Or maybe he had, and Alfie had grown up and filled out. That boy had been . . . well, a nerd. Granted, I liked nerds, but Alfie was no nerd.

Then again, what if he was? What did I really know about him other than he gave inspired advice. And wrote about a nameless version of me in a journal ten years ago.

Had that been me?

And a second realization hit me: Was it possible that he was *my* Parzival?

Chapter 18

Bryce was called up, and I went in search of Alfie. Instead, I found Reynold sipping some kind of brown liquid. Scotch, I guessed. He indicated a free stool. "You ready?"

"I think so."

"What did you decide to do?"

"You'll see." I acted cocky. I was anything but. I couldn't let Reynold see me sweat, although if he stuck around he might see me puke.

Bryce left the stage to thunderous applause. Gary was called up.

When I got to the table, I caught Tristan flipping through my journal. I snatched it back. "Mind your business," I whispered, with a soft smack to his hand.

"Scoping out the competition." He didn't even look abashed. He reached over and turned it around, pointing at the cover. "Did I draw this?"

"Did you?" It looked a lot like the ones on his own notebook. I searched my brain for any occasion when Tristan might have doodled my image on my journal. Maybe we'd sat next to each other in class more than once. Or had we hung out on that same brick wall between classes? I would have remembered if we'd ever gone out on anything resembling a date. Even if he'd just asked me to drive over to his place for mysterious purposes. I shook my head. "I can't remember."

"It looks like you." He turned back to face the stage, and I stared at the drawing again, but my traitorous memory had left me with more questions than answers. I'd have to dig through the journal later to see if it held a clue. I'd intended to read the entire thing, but every time I sought out a single entry for the contest, I broke out in hives. It was worse than watching videos of myself or hearing myself speak. My own prior private thoughts gave me the willies.

Gary was followed by Heather. I spotted Alfie carrying a massive bag of ice over his shoulder to the bar and watched as he set it down with a gravity-intense thud. His Henley did a poor job of camouflaging his back muscles, and I had to drag my eyes back to the stage.

Porter spoke, and I couldn't resist another glance at the bar, where Alfie mixed drinks while chatting amiably.

Quinn was called up. Alfie headed back to the kitchen, carrying a bin I assumed held dirty dishes. It wasn't my fault if his shirt rode up and allowed me to ogle his ass, which was far more entertaining.

Shannon read about the day at camp in middle school when she'd been talked into streaking. The counselors had called her parents, and then she'd been sent to vacation bible school with the elementary school kids. It sounded like the worst summer on record, and I knew my story wasn't remotely close to that level of cringeworthy. But it didn't involve Tristan, and it did relate to my video games. And that was the only requirement I had tonight.

Miranda called my name, and I stood for the third time in as many weeks at a microphone in front of an audience of mostly strangers. The story had the virtue of being mostly true. However, I'd recreated it for the contest, copying techniques from the others. For instance, I tried to start out with a bang.

"I got my ass kicked today.

"My new best friend Aida thought it would be fun to take a self-defense class, and since I don't have that many friends, I thought, sure, whatever. I've always loved watching martial arts, so I imagined us emerging from the class with ninja skills. I thought we'd spend an hour with a hot guy teaching us how to ax-chop bad guys. Maybe I'd learn how to break a board.

"Sadly, we spent a good twenty minutes telling each other to stop and stand back because we didn't want to fight. Which was bullshit because I kind of did want to fight, and also because I could have done that without any training. My opinion would soon evolve on this topic.

"Our instructor, a tiny little Keebler elf named Cindy, overheard me griping to Aida that the class was totally lame. She said, 'Imagine you find yourself alone in a dark alley with me coming at you.' I giggled at the image. Seriously. Cindy came up to my shoulder, and she probably weighed as much as a falling leaf.

"Cindy marched toward me with the expression of a miniature warrior, and I held out my hands like she'd told us and, without much conviction, said, 'Stop. Stand back. I don't want to fight you.' She nodded and stood still. I looked over at Aida. 'Scary, huh?'

"Next thing I knew, I was on the ground with my arm behind my back. Before I'd finished speaking to Aida, Cindy had grabbed my wrist and swept my leg. Holy shit that hurt.

"Then it was a massacre. She pulled my arm straight up behind me, and I couldn't move without agony. Cindy told the class, 'This is called an arm bar. It's an effective way to disable an attacker, even if they're bigger than you.'

"Such a kick to the ego. She had all the other women in class take turns using me like a rag doll to practice on until my shoulder grew sore. Finally she let me up and said, 'Strength isn't always a function of size.'

"I wanted to go hang my head in shame, but she added, 'You should avoid fighting if you can, but what I'm here to teach you is how to survive if you can't.'

"Humbled as I was, I paid attention and learned how to carry out that cool wrist twist.

"At the end of the class, Cindy filled me in on her secret. 'I'm a second-degree black belt.'

"I gasped and said, 'I apologize for underestimating you.'

"She said, 'When you're kicked down, you have to stand up and try again. You did that today. You got back up. Good job.'

"I took a deep breath, and for the first time since she'd kicked me to the curb, I no longer felt embarrassed, until she added, 'By the way, you might need a new pair of pants. Yours are ripped down the back.'

"Mother fuck, again?

"I yanked my T-shirt down to hide the hole. Why was I always showing my ass everywhere?

"As we left, Aida said, 'Next time, we'll try yoga, okay?' "

I wasn't eliciting any of the laughter I'd hoped for, and I had to transition awkwardly into the plug. I trusted Reynold was still at the bar.

"I later developed *Roundhouse* for Extinction Level Event. It's a martial arts hand-to-hand combat-style video game with hundreds of kicks and punches programmed in. It's available online. If you get a chance to play it, you'll fight a simulated Cindy at the end of the first level. And you can take her down in an arm bar."

I paused again, then muttered, "God, I hope Cindy doesn't appear in the audience tonight."

That last line earned me the laughter that had been missing through the rest of my story. As I took my yellow star and headed through the crowd, people stood and reached over to pat my back. Someone said, "I got my ass handed to me at karate and never went back." Someone else said, "That brought back nightmares."

I reached our table, grabbed my backpack, and said, "Good luck, Tristan," before heading back to the bar to find Reynold, grateful he hadn't left.

"Not bad, Sierra. You did the bare minimum, but you met the challenge." His soul patch didn't change shape as he pressed his lips together.

"I'll probably be eliminated tonight. Are you going to hold it against me if I can't finish this contest?"

"What did your self-defense lady say? 'When you get kicked down, you stand up and try again'? Sometimes in life you face challenges you can't overcome, and yet you have to step up and try. That's the kind of confidence I want out of you."

"So what are you saying?"

"Let's talk on Monday." He laid a twenty on the bar. "Whatever you're drinking, I'm buying."

I slapped my yellow star on the counter. "It's on the house."

Alfie arrived at that very second and slid me a Tanqueray and tonic, as though he'd mixed it before I'd even left the stage. I loved how that played out like a choreographed dance, as though I had the world at my command. I lifted the glass to Reynold in a silent toast, like a badass.

Tristan was onstage already. He'd started into a monologue about something unrelated to college entirely.

"Beware of technology and those who don't know how to use it."

He got a laugh right away as he launched into an anecdote about agreeing to ride share with someone down to Florida. He wasn't reading from the comm notebook tonight, but like a true storyteller, he held the audience in thrall.

"How was I supposed to know Craig was a psycho recently let loose into society?"

The story didn't seem to be terribly mortifying until the GPS entered the picture, and Tristan and Craig ended up driving on the University of Florida campus.

"When we were confronted by a set of steps leading down, I said, 'Yup, we're totally driving on the sidewalk.'

"That's where Craig jumped out and left me in a running vehicle, with students passing by, pointing and laughing at me.

"It took supernatural reserves of patience not to back up and abandon Craig on the spot."

Reynold leaned over. "Now that boy has a good sense of delivery."

"Yeah?" I tried not to react sarcastically.

"Nice looking. Good strong voice. Confident. You could maybe learn a thing or two from him."

I wanted to say, "*So why don't you hire him?*" But I stopped myself. I'd come here with a purpose, and I didn't need to be giving myself competition. Instead, I said, "I'm getting there, Reynold."

He finished his scotch and patted my shoulder. "I'll see you in the office next week."

As he slipped off the stool and disappeared out the door, a different voice startled me.

"So should I be afraid of you, ninja?" Alfie had snuck up behind me.

"What?"

"Your story. I'm thinking you could take me down with that trick."

"I thought you did karate."

"Oh, right. No, I only took it for a few months until my brother got bored. My parents weren't going to drive just one of us to town for a sport."

"Well, no worries here. I can only do video game karate."

"Ah, yes, I noticed you managed the transition. Did your boss like it?"

"Maybe. I'll find out more next week." Now that I had him here, I wanted to talk about what he'd read. "So that girl you talked about, on the wall?"

"Mmm-hmm." Had he moved closer?

"You should have told her." My voice had become a hoarse whisper, but he was near enough to hear me.

"Told her what?"

"That you liked her."

"Yeah?"

I leaned in. "I still like your name, by the way. It suits you."

A smile broke out across his face. I was working up to asking him if the Parzival connection was pure coincidence, but Tristan had finished his performance and grabbed a stool beside me, dropping the drink coupon on the counter.

"Hey, Alfie. Newcastle?"

While Alfie rounded the bar to obey his command, Tristan said, "Well, that went better than expected."

I pretended I'd paid attention. "Good job."

I watched Alfie crouch down to fetch the beer from the fridge.

Tristan said, "I'll walk you home when this is over."

"Oh." I bit my lip, considering his offer, but I really wanted to finish that other conversation, so I hatched another plan. "I'm sorry. I already asked Alfie to."

Alfie's head popped up above the bar, his eyes wide with surprise. "Right. We were . . ." He scratched his neck, then stood and set the bottle on the counter.

"It's just that there's something I wanted to show him." I produced an apologetic smile. "Thanks anyway, Tristan."

His eyes narrowed for a beat. "What are you doing tomorrow?"

"Why?"

"There's a comic con in Atlanta this weekend."

"Seriously?"

"Yeah. I thought I'd check it out, maybe get my artwork seen." He tilted his head to give me that pleading look he'd mastered.

"Sorry. I've got yoga until noon."

He grimaced again. "It's okay. I'll give Howard a call and see if he'll give me a lift."

Had he just been looking for a ride?

"Seriously? Still no car?"

"Oh, yeah. Beyond repair. I'll have to buy a new one." He shrugged. "I just haven't gotten around to it."

I was starting to wonder if there ever was a car. "Have fun tomorrow."

He nodded, then took his bottle and disappeared into the throng.

I winced at Alfie. "Hey, sorry for the ambush."

"No problem. I'd be more than happy to walk you home if you don't mind hanging around here a bit. I need to do a little work after the contest before I can leave."

"Of course."

He lifted a plastic bin filled with empty glasses. "Don't go anywhere."

I felt an unexpected thrill of anticipation. It would be nice to talk to him for longer than a few stolen minutes.

Zane finished whatever performance he'd prepared, but the response wasn't very vocal until Miranda reminded everyone to applaud. We all seemed to be having an off night tonight. It made me feel better about my chances.

I sat nursing my drink until the results were announced. Bryce, Heather, Quinn, Shannon, Tristan, and I were all declared safe for the next round, which meant Zane had been eliminated. Tristan was declared the victor once more, but he couldn't get a second *Monopoly* card, so he won a twenty-dollar gift card, and the knowledge he'd just blocked everyone else from winning a free life.

As Bryce and Zane passed me on their way out, I reached over and said, "Sorry, Zane. That sucks."

He laughed. "I'm not done. I've got a Get Out of Jail Free card from last week!"

People left in pairs and trios, and I watched the crowd thin.

Once only a few people remained, chatting and finishing their drinks, Alfie returned and asked Miranda to hold down the fort until he got back.

I slid off my stool, feeling a little excited and nervous at the same time.

Alfie opened the door for me as we stepped outside onto the same sidewalk where we'd shared a clandestine meeting the week before.

Chapter 19

As Alfie joined me in the dark, the silver moonlight caressed his face, revealing the beauty I'd only begun to truly appreciate.

He followed me across the street to the sidewalk, then fell in beside me. "So that guy at the bar earlier, was he your boss?"

"He's not exactly my boss. It was easier to call him that, but he's the guy deciding my fate."

"And so if you get his approval, you get to go to . . . what's the conference called?"

I laughed. Like anyone else would have heard of it. "Gamescon."

"And what exactly would you do there?"

That was a big question. "We have a slot reserved to demo our newest game to an assortment of people—bloggers, You-Tubers, Twitch streamers."

"Twitch?"

I'd gone too far. "It's just a bunch of influencers who can help to make our game a success. There's so much competition, but if we can hype the game and get these people on board, then we'll inspire word of mouth promotion that can't be bought."

"Got it. So you need to prove you've got what it takes to win the bloggers over."

"In a nutshell, yeah."

He whistled. "That's a pretty big incentive to get out of your shell."

Once again, I wasn't learning anything about him. "Can I ask you something?"

"Shoot."

"Why did you decide to host this event?"

He slowed down to a snail's pace, like he wanted to extend the conversation. "Nothing so romantic as your reason."

"Romantic?"

"Heroic, then?"

"It's not heroic." My anxiety wasn't some monster I could slay with the right arsenal of weapons.

"I think it is. It's brave. And you have a pure and noble goal."

"You're not answering my question."

"I'm not overcoming a personal demon to prove myself worthy of my ultimate dream or anything like that." He shrugged. "I just wanted bodies in the door."

"Money?"

"No. I won't make much money off this. The prize will eat most of my extra profit."

"But it's advertising. People will be back once the contest ends. I know I will."

"I hope so. There's nothing lonelier than an empty bar."

Trying to offer unsolicited advice, I thought about what might lure customers. "What about bringing in musicians?"

"Tried that. There's too much competition in the area, and musicians need to be paid." He drifted closer to me, and his shoulder briefly brushed mine. "We do karaoke on Saturday nights with a cover charge. That's usually pretty popular. I thought I'd try something different and see how it goes."

"Well, it seems to be a huge success."

"And that's in large part because of the excellent entertainment. Thank you." He tipped an invisible hat.

We approached my town house, and I said, "This is my place."

"So soon." He shoved his hands in his pockets and rocked back on his heels, like he was going to plant himself in that spot until he saw me safely through the front door.

"Do you have a minute to come in, or do you have to get right back to help Miranda?"

He grinned. "She can manage."

I unlocked the door. The inside of the house was dark and quiet. Aida must have assumed Tristan would walk me home.

"Come here." I led him into our living room where the TV dominated.

"Your screen is huge!"

"Yeah, well, it's useful for split-screen games. Marco and Aida are *Call of Duty* freaks." I led him toward the sofa. "Do you ever play *Mario Kart*?"

He laughed. "Actually, I do, almost every night. After I walk Jasper, I'm usually still wired. Most people get off work at five and run errands, then make dinner and watch TV to unwind. It's hard to finish work and go straight to sleep."

While he was talking, I set up the game, with the volume turned down low.

"So." I bit my lip, hoping this wasn't going to be a bust. "Earlier when you mentioned you'd considered taking the name Parzival . . ."

"Yeah." Now he looked a touch wary. "Funny you should mention that."

"Why? Is it because that's your user name when you play *Mario Kart*?"

His eyes widened. "Have you seen me online?"

I gestured to the screen that showed my profile.

"I'm Asuna."

As soon as I said it, I realized that I may have read way too much into our childlock-restrained interactions. Maybe he hadn't even paid attention to who he was playing. Maybe he'd coincidentally chosen the preset dialog that sounded like flirting. Maybe—

He leaned in close, a breath away, and said, "I'm using tilt control."

I burst out laughing. It was the stupidest of all the possible phrases available, and one I'd never had a reason to use. And so I said, "Go easy on me."

He smiled. "I'm a little nervous."

I couldn't think of any other presets all of a sudden. "Don't be. You wanna play?"

"Hell, yeah." He shook his head, laughing. "Asuna. Wow. My racing rival in the flesh."

I held out a controller set into a steering wheel. "You can take it out if you don't like the wheel."

"And give you an edge? No thanks. I need all the help I can get to beat you." His expressions kept registering the surprise I'd felt when I'd heard him say the name. "This is so crazy."

The game screen loaded, and we set up our race cars. Alfie went with a motorbike as always. I took a wide four-wheeler to handle turns. "You wanna play Grand Prix?" Grand Prix mode consisted of four races against each other and ten computer-generated avatars to win the ultimate trophy.

"Sure. What's your favorite?"

"You choose."

He thought for a minute, making a clicking sound with his tongue, before arriving at an answer. "Let's do Lightning Cup. I want to race you on Rainbow Road in real time."

"Oh, no." I made the selection, then crossed my legs and laid my wrists on my knees, ready to take him on.

And we were off.

It was funny to see him in action. When he turned the wheel, he leaned into it as if he could steer with his body. I elbowed him once to make him fly off the course, and he bumped me in retaliation. We switched the lead any number of times and ended up both losing the first race to computer-simulated Donkey Kong.

"I think he cheated," Alfie said.

"Let's take him down."

In the next race, instead of battling each other, we both started lobbing our weapons at the CGI players until we'd established a lead.

I asked, "What's the deal with the face on your Mii?"

"My avatar's ugly face? My sister created that."

"The one in Paris?"

"Nope. A different one."

"How many siblings do you have?"

"Five. Two sisters and three brothers."

"Holy shit."

"I know. You?"

"Only child."

"Whoa. I can't imagine."

We flew across the finish line, one, two. I set my controller down and looked at him. "This is so weird."

"So weird. You've kept me company more nights than anyone I've ever known."

"Same. I have terrible insomnia. You have no idea how often I've hoped you were online. Next time, we'll have to FaceTime each other so we can talk while we race."

He put his controller on the coffee table beside mine. The next game started, and ten cars shot out of the gate, while ours idled, ignored. "I never would have predicted I'd end up sitting here playing against you of all people."

I searched his eyes, wishing I could read his mind. "We were less than a mile apart. We could have been real-life friends all this time."

Alfie took my hand in his. "You know when you told me—"

The stairway hall light flipped on, and a floorboard creaked. I jerked my hand back as Aida peered over the rail. "Sierra, is that you?"

"Yup."

"We were wondering if we should send the police."

"Oh. Sorry. Alfie here walked me home."

"Is that so?" Her tone became decidedly friendlier. "Hello, Alfie."

I blushed. She'd never spoken to Tristan like that.

"It's Aida, right?" He blinked in the sudden light. "Nice seeing you again."

"You, too. Good night, Sierra." She flipped off the light and crept back upstairs.

Alfie stood. "I should probably be getting back."

Disappointed to cut our conversation short, I followed him out onto the porch.

He said, " 'Night, Sierra," as he took the first porch step.

"Wait," I called.

He stopped.

"What were you going to say before Aida came down?"

"Oh." He stepped back toward me, rubbing the back of his neck. He looked at his feet, then raised his eyes. In the light of the porch, they revealed flecks of gold. "I was thinking about what you said earlier tonight."

"When?"

"When you said I should have told that girl I liked her."

"And?" It came out as a whisper on an exhale.

"And I do." A blush crept up the side of his cheek, and he turned to go.

I blurted out, "What are you doing tomorrow?"

He spun back. "Nothing until the bar opens at five. Why?"

I hadn't thought it through at all. I just knew I wanted to hang out with him again, but what could we possibly do together? I could only come up with one thing. "Do you want to go to yoga with me in the morning?"

His brow lifted, and I braced for the rejection. "Yoga? Sure. But I've never done it."

"That's okay." I sighed with relief that I hadn't weirded him out. "Can you meet me here at nine thirty? We can walk over."

"Absolutely."

I'd be up all night replaying this sequence of events, but I told myself it wasn't a big deal. We were just a couple of friends, spending more time together. "See ya then."

He leaned forward and laid a quick kiss on my cheek. "Can't wait. 'Night."

As he skipped down the steps and disappeared into the darkness, I held my hand over my cheek, making sure nothing else had been stolen. Other than that kiss.

And my rapidly beating heart assured me it was still there.

Chapter 20

I stared in the mirror, debating whether or not to paint my face.

On the one hand, Alfie hadn't seen me in full daylight without makeup.

On the other hand, I couldn't show up at yoga looking like I was going clubbing.

I'd easily decided on my pink T-shirt that said ROAD TRIP above *Mario Kart* characters. I thought he'd get a kick out of that.

My phone buzzed with an incoming text. *On my way.*

I'd run out of time. I texted back, *Ready, player one* and threw on some eyeliner and lip gloss. I wasn't completely insane.

In the kitchen, Aida sat at her laptop, hands planted in her hair.

"Everything okay?"

She rubbed her eyes with her knuckles. "If you'd stop waking us up in the middle of the night, maybe we'd get some sleep."

"It wasn't even midnight." I sidled up beside her. "Company problems?"

"No. Everything's fine." She turned her red eyes toward me. Were things worse than she was letting on?

"Maybe I shouldn't do the demo. We can hire someone who can actually present confidently."

She closed the laptop. "Shut up. Once you get over this block, you're going to be amazing. Nobody knows the game like you do. Nobody loves it like you do. Nobody will be able to sell it like you can. I wish you could see that."

"I wish I believed that."

"How'd it go last night? Did you make it to the next round?"

"Yup."

She gave me one of her serious soul-piercing gazes. "So . . . what's going on with Alfie?"

"Nothing's going on."

"Coulda fooled me. You two looked awfully chummy last night."

I heard a warning in her observation, like I was leading the poor boy on. How to explain it? "You know how I play *Mario Kart* sometimes?"

"Every night."

"Not quite." Was she keeping tabs on me? "Anyway, Alfie plays, too, and I wanted to race him."

"Ah." Her fangs receded.

"He's sweet, isn't he?"

"And very, very cute."

"He is. He's coming with me to yoga today."

"Nothing's going on, huh?" She shot me her bullshit-detector expression, one eyebrow raised, lips pressed together. "Mmm-hmm."

"Shut up. I need to head out. He's waiting for me." I rubbed her back, and she groaned. "You should get a nap."

"Tell him I said hi."

Alfie had just reached the steps when I opened the front door. His smile lit up his whole face, and the morning suddenly seemed brighter.

I jogged down and signaled for him to follow me. "You know where the Y is?"

He fell in beside me. "Sure. I'm over there most mornings."

"Seriously? I've never seen you there."

"You're probably at work when I go. Our hours don't exactly line up."

"Except for the literal middle of the night. At two a.m., our schedules are in perfect sync."

He chuckled. "True. Not to mention right now."

Saturday mornings and late nights.

I shot a sideways glance at him, wanting to secretly check him out in full sunshine. He had more color in his skin than I expected, considering he seemed to be a creature of the night.

As we turned onto Hudson, I asked the question I'd been wondering for weeks: "Alfie, were we friends in college?"

He pursed his lips, and I didn't know whether it would be worse if we hadn't been or if I didn't remember we had been.

Eventually, he blew out a breath. "We were never exactly friends. I'm actually kind of glad you've forgotten me, honestly. I had a lot of growing up to do still."

"I recall a guy who might have been you, but I might be imagining it. The guy I'm picturing wasn't as together as you. Not nearly as cool."

"You think I'm cool?"

"You do own a hip bar in a trendy neighborhood."

We reached Highland Avenue, and I asked, "What did you mean about needing to grow up?"

He sighed. "I didn't like myself much then, and as a result I sometimes behaved poorly. I've been working to be better."

I had no answer to that, except "You're awesome, Alfie. I'm glad we've become friends now."

"Me, too." He slowed in front of the YMCA.

"I may have failed to mention I'll be teaching this class. So, get ready to work it."

We arrived right on time, and most of the class had already begun setting up their mats. Mrs. Garrett was the first to notice I'd brought a guest. Her head tilted to one side before she leaned over to whisper to Mrs. Shih.

"Is this the guy?" she asked without the minimum of discretion.

I hoped to mitigate the disaster by simply introducing him. "Everyone, this is my friend Alfie. He'll be joining us today."

"She's never brought a boy to class before," said Mrs. Martinez.

"This is the boy you've been dating?" asked Mrs. Gupta, who examined Alfie like he were a slab of beef at the butcher. On sale. "You were right. He is very handsome."

Oh, my God.

Alfie's cheeks had flushed noticeably.

"I'm so sorry. I also failed to mention these are all my surrogate moms." I warned them all with an imperial glance. "Like I said, Alfie's a friend."

I put on some quiet music, then began the opening meditation.

When all eyes had closed, I peeked over to scope out Alfie's bare arms and legs while he wasn't watching. His muscles were toned and defined. A movement caught my eye as the other ladies turned to stare, like a pack of wild animals. Mrs. Shih gave me the thumbs-up. I shook my head.

But he was definitely attractive. While Tristan radiated energy and demanded every eye turn to him, Alfie was more like a dark star—quiet, but profound. He came to yoga with the kind of calm the rest of us sought, fundamentally at peace with himself.

When class ended, Mr. Baxter packed up and left without a word—a nice reprieve. Maybe I'd ask Alfie to come with me every week if it bought me this additional buffer.

Alfie put his mat away, unaware of my well-meaning matchmakers tracking his every move. So was I. They smiled and nodded at me like I'd brought him out for inspection.

As we left, I handed him a bottle of water from my bag. He twisted the cap off and took a few swallows, then eyed me quizzically. "You talk about having performance anxiety, but you were anything but shy leading that class."

"Well, anxious and shy are two different things. I'm not shy. It's more that I worry about things that will embarrass me. Then that becomes a self-fulfilling prophecy when my nerves make me incapable of performing without mishap. I've been dealing with this for a decade. Yoga class isn't the same. Part of it is the structure of the class. I mean, everything is controlled."

"I noticed that."

"And part of it is knowing I can't fail at yoga, but if I do, I'm only failing to improve myself." I laughed, hearing myself. "It's a cult. Plus, I know everyone. They're old friends."

"So, you're trying to break your fear of presenting in front of total strangers in an uncontrolled environment?"

I hadn't broken it down like that before. "I guess I'm trying to overcome the certainty I'm going to fall on my ass." I blushed, recalling my worst presentation ever. "It's not an idle fear."

As he turned to face me, the sunlight hit him such that I finally saw the true color of his eyes, and my breath hitched. I'd thought they were dark brown, but they were an exploding microcosm of blues and gold specks, like a cloud nebula. I would have believed entire galaxies were created and destroyed in the blink of his eye.

"What's wrong?"

I shook my head. "Nothing. Just." I took a breath. "You have beautiful eyes."

He smiled. "Yeah?"

"I always wanted blue eyes."

"I hear that a lot. But it's not something I can control, so I'm not sure why it's that big a deal. You never hear anyone gush over how cute my elbows are."

I laughed. "You have cute elbows."

"Have you noticed my neck?" He tilted his head to bare it.

It was a joke, but when I gazed at his neck something ignited inside me, like I was a latent vampire, needing to sink my teeth into him and suck his blood. I'd never fetishized anyone's neck before, but when his muscle tightened, I wanted to feast on him. "You have a very pretty neck."

"At last. She thinks I'm pretty."

I rolled my eyes. "I told you. You're better than pretty."

When we arrived at my town house, I asked, "What are you doing tomorrow?"

"Taking Jasper to Piedmont Park. Want to come along?"

"Absolutely."

He grinned. "I can pilfer some food from the bar. We'll make it a picnic."

"Sounds like fun!"

If we'd been on a date, it felt like the moment when I'd wait to see if a kiss would be forthcoming, but even if we were going out, what did one do after a morning yoga date? Kiss good afternoon?

Would this be what dating Alfie would be like? Morning dates followed by daytime sex? Afternoon delight? We were like the moon and the sun, only meeting up during the occasional eclipse.

I took one step back. "Well. See you tomorrow."

He moved toward the street, and the bonds between us began to snap. "Can't wait."

When he was far enough away that even his long shadow had disappeared, Aida yelled down from the porch, "Nothing's going on, eh?"

Late Sunday morning, as I sat on the porch with Aida, a vintage convertible Mustang pulled up. Alfie left the car running as he jogged up the walk. He'd shaved, which changed how he looked, but neither for better or worse. Just different. This was a cleaned-up Alfie, a going-on-a-date Alfie maybe. I half expected him to produce a bouquet of flowers.

Jasper barked from the backseat.

Aida whispered, "That boy's awful cute."

Alfie said hey to Aida as I descended the steps. He took my hand, and it gave me such a warm fuzzy feeling my smile threatened to stretch my face out. I waved back at Aida, and I could almost hear her thinking, "*Mmm-hmm.*"

His car was powder blue, but light-years sexier than a Vespa. As I climbed in, I patted Jasper on the head. "Who's a good boy?"

Jasper turned around once, then dropped down on the seat with his head resting on his paws. The interior was like a time machine. The vinyl seats screamed nineteen-sixty-something.

Alfie slid into the driver's seat behind the hilariously dated steering wheel.

He ran a hand over his chin. "What do you think?"

Aida was right. He was awful cute. "You're still gorgeous." I imitated his gesture. "How about me?"

I hadn't put on any foundation. Just lipstick. I'd left my hair straight, all the colors on display.

"You're always gorgeous." He revved the engine and put the car in Drive, and we headed toward Piedmont Park on a warm summer day.

"This car is something else."

He bit his lip. "It was my dad's. He collected and restored classic cars."

I'd noticed his use of the past tense and wanted to tread lightly. "Your dad? Did he . . . ?"

"He'd show them off at vintage car shows." He turned right.

The wind whipped my hair across my face, and I reached into my backpack to dig out a hair band. "So, you just tool around Atlanta in old-timey cars."

"To be honest, I usually drive a very sensible Volvo, but I wanted to impress you." He shot me a crooked half smile. "Did it work?"

Guys and their preening. I laughed, but he flipped the visor down and snatched out a pair of sunglasses. With his left elbow resting on the door and his right hand relaxed on the wheel and those aviator shades and his wild hair and this car, he went from really cute to incredibly hot in a heartbeat.

"Yeah. It worked."

I wanted to freeze this magic moment in time.

When we arrived in the parking lot, Alfie handed me the leash and popped the trunk to retrieve a couple of paper grocery bags.

We followed the path to the dog park, where Alfie let Jasper off the leash and tossed a ball. Jasper trotted after it.

"How old is he?"

Alfie squished his face up, thinking. "Eleven. I think. Yes, eleven."

He laid out a blanket. "Hope you like bar food." He'd brought some cold chicken, soft pretzels, and beer.

I watched Jasper sniffing another dog's butt and turned to find Alfie staring with a curious look I'd seen before.

"What?"

He handed me a beer and opened his own while I filled my plate.

"I was thinking about something my karate instructor said: 'Every time we learn something about someone, we add a new brick to our relationship, strengthening the foundation.' "

"That's cool." The visual made me think of building houses in *Minecraft*.

"For instance, do you prefer dogs or cats?"

"I couldn't have pets growing up, and Aida's allergic. But I always wanted a dog. You? Dog person, right?"

"Oh, I like them both. We always had barn cats and a couple of dogs."

"Barn cats? What are those?"

He laughed. "Cats. That live in the barn."

"You had a *barn*? Did you grow up on a farm?"

"Yeah, actually."

"No shit. So those boots you had on the other day weren't just for show?"

"You noticed my boots?"

I blushed and tried to change the subject a bit. "So did you study agriculture at Auburn?"

He shook his head. "Engineering."

"Yeah? So how does a farm boy with an engineering degree end up running a bar?"

"Well, I had an engineering job. I didn't like it, so I quit." He cracked another pair of beers and handed one over to me.

"Wasn't it a scary risk?"

"Actually, no." He gave me an appraising look. Then he sighed. "I had an inheritance to invest."

"An inheritance." The implications hit me. "Oh, Alfie." I reached over and squeezed his hand.

"I realized I was going to die miserable and alone, so I tried to think of a job where I'd always be surrounded by people."

"That's . . ." I couldn't imagine wanting to deal with people constantly. "Wow."

"What?"

"You're like my polar opposite."

"Am I?"

"An extrovert and an introvert walked into a bar."

He snorted. "You think I'm an extrovert?"

"You like being around people."

"I thought I would." His thumb traced mine, and it sent a shiver down my spine. "It's why I wanted to make this contest a continuing event. I thought maybe if I got some regulars, I'd start to make friends."

"Is it working?"

"I'm here with you, aren't I?" The shiver turned into an electric current.

"We got here from asking if I like dogs or cats?"

He waggled his eyebrows. "Imagine what would happen if we asked bigger questions."

"Example?"

He sucked on his teeth. "What would you do if you knew you couldn't fail?"

"Right now?" That was pretty easy. "Go to Germany to present our demo."

Jasper returned the ball, and Alfie rubbed the dog's head before rolling it out again. "So, what's stopping you?"

"Reynold. And my own brain."

"I have confidence you'll make it happen." When he smiled, it made all my anxieties seem so far away. I never felt like I had to pretend or perform for him.

I may have stared a bit too long, and he tilted his head, his smile fading into something softer, more serious. My eyes settled on his lips, and I had a deep desire to touch him.

I shook my head to regain control. "What would *you* do if you knew you couldn't fail?"

He chuckled. "I guess I set myself up for that."

"Well?" I nudged his foot with mine.

"If I knew I couldn't fail?" He scooted closer. "I'd kiss you."

My stomach flipped so hard, I thought the park had tilted. I wondered if he'd set the whole conversation up to lead us here. The way he gazed into my eyes, he could have hypnotized me with the endless worlds I saw in his. The electric current converted to a gravitational force.

I leaned closer. "I have confidence you'll make it happen." My voice sounded smoky. I placed my hand on his cheek where I'd been wanting to feel his skin, so soft. He closed his eyes, and I traced my finger down to his chin. "What's stopping you?"

He wove a hand into my hair, his fingers tangling in the loose strands, tentatively, willing me toward him, and when our lips brushed, it felt so right, so natural—inevitable, even. It was like we'd kissed a thousand times before, a thousand years ago, and yet it also felt like our first kiss. He didn't rush it, and I loved that he took the time to explore how we fit together, how we felt together. Our mouths touched, then broke apart, only to find each other anew, stronger, more urgent, then gentle. My pulse increased along with my desire for him, and I wanted more, so much more.

He drew away, breathless. "I've been wanting to do that for a while."

His hand slid around to the back of my neck. I shivered. Tentatively, I mirrored him. He had the softest, floppiest, loosest curls. Boy-band hair. "I've been dying to muss your hair since I first saw you."

My fingers spread out, explored, and without meaning to, I'd grasped hold with both my fists and pulled him back to me. I didn't ask if I could kiss him. And he didn't say no.

Encouraged, I knocked him onto his back and laughed at his surprise, as my face hovered over his. His pretty eyes sparkled with anticipation, and he said, "I didn't see this coming."

"Nor me." I ran my thumb over his lower lip.

He pulled me back down to him, lips parting now as his

tongue met mine, and I nearly forgot where we were until a woman cleared her throat.

Alfie started to laugh, and that chilled the moment. Jasper ran up and dropped a ball by his head. We sat up, fixing our disheveled clothes. I looked at Alfie, and that smile that had always been so open and friendly turned into something I'd never seen before, slightly wicked and knowing. It sent a fire burning in my thighs, and I wondered how long we had to stay at the park—and where he lived.

He had other ideas and suggested we take a walk along the boardwalk with Jasper, at least over to the lake for a bit.

The rest of the day at the park made for one of those memories I'd store in vignettes rather than words. Alfie taking my hand in his, without comment. Me laying my head against his shoulder as we sat by the lake, hearing his heart beat in his chest. Laughing over our funny running commentary. Jasper lazing in the sun beside us. Alfie taking pictures of our bare feet as the sun sparkled on the water beyond.

For the first time in my life, I was grateful for the fears I'd always cursed because if I hadn't lost my voice, I never would have found Alfie. In my quest to rebuild my confidence, he'd been waiting there at level one, like a mentor, to propel me farther in the game than I'd ever believed possible. As I continued to grow, he'd become my ally. And now, today, he proved he could be so much more.

Like Alfie, I hadn't seen this coming, and I was going to need time to process what it would mean.

This was no longer just a game.

Chapter 21

I blinked, and then it was Monday.

The only proof that magical day had even happened was the picture Alfie tagged me in. Thankfully, I'd taken the time to paint my toes since they were now on display for the whole world to see, but being a creep I also memorized every inch of Alfie's feet.

I opened a section of code I needed to walk through, but my brain didn't want to focus. I wanted to daydream.

When had I first noticed Alfie? He'd always been right there, and my brain hadn't caught up. I used to love this puzzle-based video game, *Myst*, but I could never solve the last big mystery. When I finally Googled a walk-through, I wanted to punch my own face because the answer was so simple. The key was recognizing context-specific sounds, but I'd been so geared toward the visual, I completely overlooked the obvious. It was like that with Alfie. Somehow my soul had been picking up on clues my brain hadn't deciphered yet. Thankfully, Alfie had read the signs correctly.

I looked at my computer screen again. I couldn't even remember what I was about to do. What was I working on?

Programming was normally an escape for me. I loved designing, storyboarding with the artists, and building the architecture with the developers. I even loved hammering out defects, which were little mysteries to resolve. But today, I wanted to go home.

No, actually, I wanted to hang out with Alfie and see what he was doing. I wanted to keep talking to him. I wanted to keep kissing him.

My Slack icon flashed in the task bar while I was staring at a block of code without processing it. Maybe I needed a break. I clicked on the notification, and the box popped up on Reynold's channel.

yt?

Ah, the universal chat acronym for *you there?*

Yes.

Come to my office.

Reynold had an office, even though he was rarely ever here. When I tapped on his doorframe, he looked up from his computer like he didn't remember he'd just asked me to drop in.

"You wanted to see me?"

He waved me in. "I don't want to get your hopes up, but you're currently back in the running for Gamescon."

"In the running?"

He ran his finger and thumb over either side of his mustache as if it was taped on. "Look. I'll be honest. I've considered everyone else here. I'm still considering hiring an outside salesperson for the position, but Aida's convinced me the logistics favor someone like you. What I've seen lately at that club shows promise."

I took a deep breath. This was what I wanted. "So what do I need to do to get the final yes from you?"

He tapped a finger on the desk a couple of times, then finished with one final palm slap. "I want you to wow me."

"How?"

"When does your contest end?"

"In a couple of weeks. Unless I get cut."

His soul patch moved to the left as he scrunched his mouth up, and his mustache winked at me. "Use those presentations to work out whatever's plaguing your performances. Practice as well. Then if you can come in here and nail it, the trip is yours."

That was incredible. "Thank you, Reynold. I won't disappoint."

"I honestly hope not. If you can pull it off, I'll send you off with my blessing. But I won't hesitate to go with an outside resource if I don't think you can do it. It's too important."

"Understood."

What would I do if I knew I couldn't fail? I suddenly understood the genius in Alfie's question. It wasn't about what I wanted, but about what I could be if I didn't let fear stand in my way. It was about reaching my potential. Aida and I had started our business with that kind of gumption.

I needed to face this challenge head-on in the same way.

"I won't fail," I promised because Reynold had made it clear that, if I wanted this, I *couldn't* fail.

I asked Marco to let me off by Alfie's bar. The OPEN sign was lit, welcoming anybody from off the street. The place felt extra dark after I'd been out in full daylight, and it was so cavernously empty, the bass from the song playing on the stereo seemed to dominate the space.

Nobody waited behind the bar.

Nobody sat at the tables.

Miranda came out from the kitchen. "Hey, Sierra? You looking for Alfie?"

"Yeah."

"Follow me."

She led me through the kitchen and up a set of stairs. At the top landing, she knuckle-rapped on the door. "Alfie, company!"

The locks turned. When Alfie saw me, he flung the door open wide. "Thanks, Miranda."

Miranda disappeared downstairs, and I entered. Alfie reached out his hand and reeled me in for a kiss. "You're here."

"I have news to share. I wanted to tell you in person." Sure, it was a pretext, but not exactly a lie.

Alfie led me in, saying, "Down, boy," as his dog pawed my legs.

I crouched to pet Jasper. Soft light filtered in through French doors. A half bar separated the dining area from a kitchenette. Across the room, a set of stairs led up toward a loft.

"What's up there?"

He held out a hand to indicate I should take a look. Upstairs, I discovered his large unmade bed, a dresser, and a closet in disarray.

He stood back and watched me with a patient look of expectation on his face, as if he was waiting for a verdict.

"You're messy," I said.

He chuckled. "Is that a deal breaker?"

"Not hardly. Just one more thing I've learned about you."

"I'm an open book."

I sat on the edge of his bed by a side table and picked up a framed photo. Three kids and two adults posed with a chocolate lab. It was winter, and they wore coats but weren't entirely bundled up.

"This is your family?"

He sat beside me. "Yeah. This was my parents' anniversary. We had a surprise party for them."

"I thought you had five siblings."

"Right." He pointed at each person in the picture. "My brother Will. My sister Lydia. Jasper was her dog. This is me. I was sixteen. Mom and Dad. And that was our dog, Cadbury. My older sister, Emma, and the twins, Harry and Oliver, were off at college."

"Wow. That's"—I absorbed all that—"a lot of British names."

"Yeah. Did you know Alfie is one of the most common names in England?"

"Is it?" I remembered how he'd bemoaned it in his journal. "I really love it."

"Well, I've grown to appreciate it."

"I can't imagine having such a big family."

"I'm closest to my brother Will."

"Where is he, now?"

"Atlanta. You might meet him if you hang around long enough."

I scanned the photo. In the background, I thought I made out a field but no signs of a street or other houses or even cars. "This is the farm where you grew up?"

"Yeah. It's gone now."

I put the frame back on the table and took his hand. "What happened?"

He looked at the floor and exhaled sharply. "My dad died four years ago."

I squeezed his hand and waited.

"Massive coronary." He swallowed. "He passed away, and then my mom couldn't take care of everything. Since the kids had all left anyway, she sold the farm and bought a small place in Athens."

"So the inheritance?"

"Yeah. Divided amongst us, it wasn't a massive windfall, but it was enough to let me take a step back and think about what I might do if I could do anything I wanted."

"If you couldn't fail."

"Exactly. When Dad died, I kept hearing him say things like 'Nobody gets out of this world alive,' and I realized I might as well do something I love."

I gave him a side hug. "So you bought the bar."

"Yeah, I went from being practically alone to having a hundred acquaintances. Then you came along, and I realized what I'd been missing all along."

How was it he could make me swoon when I'd been on the verge of crying a moment before?

The sun played in his hair, and I reached up to touch a reddish-brown curl. "You know what I'm missing right now?"

"What's that?"

I pressed my lips to his, so soft and warm, so delicious. When I drew back, the look he gave me was one I'd never seen before on any man. Was it desire? Gratitude? Hope?

He leaned in for a deeper kiss. His tongue gently scraped along my lower lip, and I wanted to bite him, suck on him, rip his shirt open.

But my stomach growled. Traitorous body.

He stood. "Do you like Indian? I can order some from down the street."

"God, yes."

My phone buzzed.

"Fuck." Tristan's name displayed on the ID. I opened the message.

Correction, messages plural. I'd missed a couple at some point earlier.

That guy from the bar tagged you in a picture yesterday.

I thought you were with me.

Are you ignoring me?

Shit.

The newest message, sent about an hour after the first five, read: *Fine. See you Friday, I guess.*

I scratched my head. We'd never made promises to each other. Was I supposed to explicitly break up with someone I wasn't explicitly dating?

"Important?" Alfie paused halfway to the stairs. "Can you still stay for dinner?"

"It's not important." I put my phone in my bag. "It's just Tristan trying to mess with my head."

He dropped on the bed next to me. "Are you . . . ?" He shook his head. "We haven't talked about what's happening here between us."

He was right. If only I'd had this conversation with both of them.

"What do you think is happening, Alfie?"

"I don't really know. Are you going out with Tristan?"

"Tristan who?"

He laughed, but his smile faded and he sighed. "Sorry. I don't want to sound like an asshole, but I feel like I've played this game once before and lost."

"In college? I never went out with him then."

"No, but you wanted to, right?"

I obviously couldn't deny that. I shrugged one shoulder as if that were a satisfactory answer. My past crushes shouldn't count against me now.

His skin flushed. "Yeah. I know. It was a long time ago. It just sucked to be overlooked."

I didn't know what to say. All I could do was acknowledge him. "I wish things had been different."

He nodded, and I thought that might be the end of it, but he gazed into my eyes, like he was trying to read my mind before going on. "I guess it still feels like I'm invisible."

Urgh.

Alfie had no reason to trust me yet, but I could reassure him at least with regard to Tristan.

I slipped my hand into his. "I admit I got caught up in the idea of Tristan, but I only want to be right here. Next to you."

"Yeah?" His shoulders relaxed.

"Truth." I touched his cheek. "I see you, Alfie Jordan."

"I have always seen you, Sierra Reid."

His hand slid around the back of my neck, and he looked so mischievously adorable, I wanted to do wicked things with him. When he kissed me this time, I swung a leg over him so I could face him straight on, and something grew between us.

Physically.

He moaned and shifted to adjust himself. And suddenly, I was completely zeroed in on the connection between us at a much more primordial level. I had the overwhelming urge to pull off his clothes and ride him like a mechanical love bull.

My fingers gripped his hair, and his palms flattened against my arching back, drawing me in for a kiss that went beyond romantic into purely erotic. It was messy and needy and wild. He sucked on my lower lip, and I nudged his head to the side so I could drag my teeth down his neck. I couldn't fight my desire to suck on his skin, unbutton his shirt, and run kisses along his collarbone.

He smelled so clean with the barest hint of something I couldn't place. Cedar? Sandalwood, maybe? I inhaled him and lost my mind for wanting him.

Dying to find out what his chest looked like under all that fabric, I popped the first button. Alfie took my hand and pressed his mouth to my palm, breathing heavily. "Sierra, hold up."

My eyes regained their focus as I took in the situation. I was straddling Alfie on his bed in his loft while his family stared at us from the picture frame. And he was hard as a rod between my thighs. A thick rod.

I wanted him in me immediately. My hips moved of their own accord, and he let out a ragged breath. I wished I could pull up an inventory screen and remove our clothes with a click of the mouse. Other than that barrier, we were in a perfect position to get instant relief.

He swallowed. Hard. "Let's slow down." His hands on my waist pegged me in place. "I don't want to make assumptions about this, but I don't want to just hook up with you. I want to go out with you. Like date you for real."

I exhaled all my disappointment. I could tell he still wanted me, right through my pants. It took everything in me not to grind against him again, but he was right; we weren't remotely prepared for this. We weren't even properly dating yet.

"That's what I want, too."

My stomach growled again.

He held out his hand. "Let's get something to eat."

When the food arrived, we sat at his kitchen table, sharing tikka masala, and he reminded me why I came by.

"You said you had news?"

"Oh, right. Reynold is going to let me audition for the demo again."

He sat up straighter. "Then we need to form a plan."

"We?"

"Of course. I make a good audience if you want to practice." He rubbed his chin. "I have an idea. Why don't you come do karaoke?"

That caught me off guard, and dizziness hit me. "And now I'm anxious again."

"You know how they say let your success be your motivation? If you really want to level up, come do karaoke at my bar."

"I want to puke."

He raised his eyebrows, coaxing. "I promise it's fun."

I breathed in and exhaled. I wanted to face new challenges and opportunities with his calm and his curiosity.

"When is it?"

"Saturday night."

That gave me days to wrap my head around it. "We'll see."

Dating Alfie was going to be like an interpretive dance: When I was getting off work, Alfie was just starting.

Tuesday evening, I hung out at the bar while he made drinks for other people, but Wednesday, I went straight home from work and fell asleep on the sofa after a long day. When I woke up around two, I flipped on my *Mario Kart* to find Alfie racing. I was no longer satisfied talking via the presets, so I FaceTimed him.

When he answered, I said, "Go easy on me."

He laughed, "You're kidding. You've been crushing me."

"I've been crushing *on* you. I wish you were here."

The light behind him went out. "Talk to me for a bit."

"What do you want to talk about?"

"Tell me about growing up an only child."

I stretched and set the controller down. "That is super boring. I had my own room, my own imaginary friends, but I never got a pony."

"Oh, funny, 'cause I did." His face nearly disappeared, and only a pair of black eyes, like an alien's, bobbed in the screen.

"Aida was an only child, too. We kind of glommed onto each other like the sisters we'd always wanted."

"When did you two move here?" His breathing sounded labored.

"As soon as we both had jobs after college. Hold on." I got up and fetched a bottle of water from the kitchen.

On my way back to the sofa, I heard a tapping on the door.

"Did you walk over here?" I opened the door, melting at the ruffled reality of him.

"Ran. I wanted to see you."

I spider-walked my fingers up his still-heaving chest and tugged his open collar forward. "Kiss me."

He pushed a strand of hair behind my ear. A shiver broke down my spine when his lips met mine. I slipped my hands under his shirt. His soft moan did dirty things to my insides. My heart pulsed in all my erogenous zones.

"You want to come inside?" Now I was breathing heavy. "My futon awaits."

"You are killing me." He pulled himself away. With obvious effort.

"You don't want to come in?"

He dragged his hand through his hair. "Maybe we should talk about expectations. Figure out where we're going."

Right. He didn't want to act on an urge, but I was nothing but urges. I stepped over and settled in a rocking chair. "Tell me where you want to go."

He sat beside me. "Would you take it the wrong way if I said, 'All the way'?"

"Mmm. That's more like it."

He chuckled and took my hand. "Is it crazy to want to make sure we're solid before acting on physical attraction?"

"Too late."

"You know what I mean. I find sex really confusing. It messes with my mind and my heart, and so I just want to know if this is real."

"*Eros* and *Agape*."

"What?"

"There are three kinds of love: *Eros*, *Philia*, and *Agape*. You confuse sex with real love?"

He smiled. "I hate to do this, but according to the Greeks, there are seven kinds of love."

"Really? I only ever learned about three. What are they?"

"You got the first three: *Eros*—love of the body; *Philia* or *Phileo*—love of the mind; and *Agape*—love of the soul. The other four are like self-love, flirtation, devotion, and effortless love."

"Where did you learn all this?"

"Honestly? In a bible study class on First Corinthians—you know, 'Love is patient. Love is kind'?"

" 'Love does not envy.' "

"Right. You know it?"

"Raised Presbyterian. So this class taught you you were confusing *Eros* with *Agape*?"

"That's another thing. *Agape* is more like altruism. *Eros* and romance are intertwined. I guess I confuse *Eros* with every other kind of love."

"Have you never had a one-night stand?"

He tilted his head. "Are we having this conversation already?"

"Oh. I . . ." I hadn't meant to pry into his sexual history so blatantly. I felt so comfortable talking to him, and what he'd confessed led me to wonder how he'd managed to navigate casual sex, if he ever had. While he might confuse sex with love, I was busy using sex in place of intimacy. I hadn't had a lot of experience with men, but I'd come to think they all preferred to fuck first, ask questions later.

This was new.

"Look." He leaned toward me, taking both my hands now. "I want to spend time with you and get to know you, okay?"

"You're nothing like what I expected. And I want to know you, too, but is this a wait-until-marriage thing?" He did say he went to church. What if—

"No. Not at all." He laughed with an adorable wince. "Maybe I want to see where we stand after we've survived our first fight. What happens when you're no longer charmed by the newness of me? When I do something to piss you off? I just want to trust each other first. You deserve that. I don't even know your favorite color."

"My favorite color's blue. My favorite *Zelda* game is *Majora's Mask*. I prefer autumn to spring."

He fell back farther into his chair, eyes closed. "Keep going."

"I thought you were cute the first night I saw you at the bar a couple of weeks ago, and you're the first boy I've ever known who made me feel calm instead of anxious."

His eyes popped open. "Is that right?"

"Your turn."

"I like blue. *Ocarina of Time* is my favorite *Zelda* game. I like autumn *and* spring."

I watched his lips while he spoke. He had this tendency to half smile most of the time, like the universe was a gentle, funny place, and nothing rattled him. Maybe it was his innate calm that placated me.

"What else?" I bit my lip, wanting to know everything about this guy I'd somehow managed to overlook once before.

"I thought you were cute the first time I saw you, but you know that because of my diary."

"And now?" I scooted closer so our knees touched.

His little smile grew into a full grin. "Now? I think you're here." He lifted my hand and pressed his lips to my palm. "You're beautiful, and you make me feel seen."

I wanted him to pull me onto his lap. I wanted to pick up where we'd stopped before. "So now we know all our favorite things."

"Some of our favorite things."

I hesitated. I'd never talked so openly about the physical aspect of a relationship. Nature usually dictated every move. Usually a look led to a touch, a touch led to a fuck, and a fuck led to an awkward goodbye and a silence that went on forever.

"Can I touch you now?"

He sighed, but not in exasperation, more like in anticipation. "Touch me where?"

I placed my finger on the side of his neck at the opening of his collar. I'd developed a fetish for his hidden neck, the tempting cord disappearing beneath the fabric of his shirt. "Right here. You have a beautiful neck, Alfie."

Dragging my fingernail along his skin, I teased his collarbone, and he let his head fall to one side.

"That feels nice," he whispered.

"Yes. You do."

I somehow refrained from tearing off his shirt and running my tongue down his chest, but he lifted his hand and placed his thumb in the exact same spot on my neck, and I thought I might burn from the contact.

"Who knew a neck could be so damn tempting?" He licked his lips.

My restraint broke and I pressed my luck, unbuttoning his top button. When he didn't object, I opened the next and moved my hand down another couple of inches. He had hair on his chest, dark but not abundant. He watched me as I explored a part of his body that shouldn't have felt so forbidden. How could a guy's chest turn me on like some hard-core Internet porn?

I looked into his eyes. "Would you kiss me at least?"

We both leaned in, and he gently pressed his lips to mine. "Always."

But always didn't last forever, and soon we broke apart, breathing heavily. I wished we'd already reached a point of trust he needed to come into my house and stay the night, but I knew he was right. I hated it, but because Alfie was taking such care of our emotions, I knew I wouldn't wake up in the morning filled with shame, regret, and anxiety. I wouldn't wake up asking if our relationship was based on nothing but sex. I wouldn't worry our friendship wouldn't outlive an orgasm.

And that added a brick to a wall I hadn't known I was building. It was a wall to a house where I might one day unpack my bags and settle in with a boy who'd known how to coax me to alight, like a skittish butterfly.

Chapter 22

Friday morning was merciless. I'd need to demand flextime hours to date a guy who was only available when I wasn't. The coffee in the break room wouldn't cut this exhaustion, so I went around the corner to a local coffee shop and ordered a latte with an extra shot of espresso. Bleary-eyed, I scrolled through social media and clicked a notification that popped up, saying I'd been tagged on Instagram.

My screen filled with my smiling face, touched by sunset orange—and Tristan's lips on my cheek—with a comment that read, *Spent an evening with my girl.* Jesus, Tristan.

He had to know Alfie would see this and jump to conclusions. I hadn't seen him since Wednesday.

I sent Tristan a text.

Would you please indicate that photo was taken last week?

My phone rang a minute later.

"Hi, Tristan."

"I finally got your attention." He sounded sulky. "Are you worried I'll make your boyfriend mad?"

I didn't acknowledge his question. "It's misleading, and you know it."

"Why? He posted pictures of the two of you enjoying a romantic afternoon."

My fist clenched around my coffee cup until it dented. I thought about hanging up. I thought about telling him we weren't an item, but I needed his help to fix this. "We took his dog to the park. Would you please just do me this one favor?"

Silence for a few ticks of my heart. Then, "I will, but on one condition."

I listened to his request and considered telling him to fuck right off, but I cared enough about Alfie's opinion to agree.

I pitched my empty coffee cup and went back to work on a weird defect that allowed one player to turn another's inventory against them through alchemy. The documentation read, *Mistakes may create poison.*

Indeed. This was proving true in my current predicament.

Tristan's knock at the door jarred me into reality. I messaged Marco. *Got a minute to stop by?*

Be there in a sec.

Tristan slipped his messenger bag off his shoulder and unzipped it. When Marco arrived, without waiting for an invitation, he opened his laptop. "I wanted to share a couple of drawings I did recently."

Marco shifted. I could tell he felt ambushed. And yet, he took a long look at the drawing and said, "Yeah, that's impressive, man."

"I was hoping you might have some openings."

Marco glanced at me so quickly it was like nothing, but I knew he wasn't happy with me for putting him in this spot. "So, yeah. If and when we get the green light for another project."

Tristan placed his laptop back in his bag. "Sure. I'd love you to keep me in mind."

I actually felt a bit sorry for him. Still, if we didn't have a place for him, there was nothing any of us could do.

As soon as Marco made his excuses and left, I turned to Tristan. "I did what you extorted. Now will you please—"

"You kissed me. Did you know that?" He moved closer, and my office shrank.

"Once. A couple of weeks ago."

"No, before."

I rubbed my eyes with the heels of my palms. "What are you even talking about, Tristan?"

He pulled his journal from his messenger bag and thumbed through the pages. A loose sheet slipped out, but he caught it and jammed it back in. He found what he was looking for and turned it to me. I scanned the first line.

Thirteen girls have come on to me since this morning.

Typical.

"Am I one of these nameless girls?"

"No. Read here." He pointed halfway down the page.

The brown-haired girl from my writing class was at the bar, shooting tequila. I asked if she was okay. She put her hand on my shirt and pulled me toward her. I was surprised and grabbed her shoulders to make sure she didn't fall. And then she kissed me. And not like a peck. We could have been in the back of a car with a kiss like that. She backed off and apologized, but it was hot. I said, "You can do that again if you want."

I stopped reading and looked up. "Is that supposed to be me? I have no recollection of that."

"You think I'd make that up?"

"If that had happened, I would have written it in my journal."

"So check it."

"I will. What was the date?" He told me, and I jotted it down. "Why are you even bringing this up?"

"Fair warning. I thought you might want to know I'm planning to read this tonight."

I considered how Alfie would feel hearing that. But it was a decade ago, and probably all lies anyway. "Fine. Be my guest."

He gave me a villainous smile, and I wondered how I'd ever found him attractive. I glared at him as he gathered his things. "Game on," he said as he left, and I stood there blinking, wondering what the hell he'd meant.

Everything in me demanded I withdraw from the contest to

avoid whatever conflict Tristan wanted to create. Maybe that was his intention. He'd proved once before he was willing to salt the earth if it meant winning, and he had a huge motivation to win this contest.

But he'd left a bad taste in my mouth, and I didn't want to concede the contest to him. I wanted to knock him out. But how?

I walked down to Aida's office for advice. After I explained everything to her, I asked, "What am I going to do? I'm certain he's planning to embarrass me with his journal, but what if he means to make Alfie jealous? This is why I avoid relationship drama."

"Why don't you just talk to Alfie before the contest? Surely he'll understand you can't control Tristan. You've already incriminated your past self. It's not like Alfie's going to be shocked if you kissed Tristan."

"True." I tried to remember that kiss, but I drew a blank. "I never went to parties. Can you remember any time I'd gone out and gotten drunk?"

"Maybe your journal has a clue?"

Taking her advice, as soon as I got home, I flipped pages. About halfway through, I noticed a triangular remnant stuck to the notebook's spiral coil. A page was definitely missing—on the date Tristan had given me.

Why would I have torn it out? I read the next entry, and a creepy chill crawled up my neck. I'd documented a hangover from drunken escapades. The missing page might have revealed exactly what I'd done under the influence. Maybe what I'd written had been too incriminating or embarrassing to save.

In the next passage, I came across confessions I'd never want to share at the bar. Not after Alfie had admitted how he'd felt about Tristan.

My phone is littered with unanswered texts to Tristan.

I returned to the corner of the missing page, wondering what had happened. I read through more entries for clues on how to thwart Tristan.

The first yellow star I'd won fell loose, and I caught it. In *Mario Kart*, when you activate a yellow star, you get temporary immunity. Nothing can hurt you. You can fly through obstacles, and weapons lobbed your way have no effect.

You can't fail.

I stroked the star. What would I do if I knew I couldn't fail?

I'd bested some of the most difficult strategy games using only resources available to me. Surely, I could outsmart Tristan. I stared at the notebook, imagining what the missing page might have held. If everyone else neglected to accurately report the past, why was I holding myself to that standard?

Like Tristan said, this was entertainment, not the nightly news. I could beat him at his own game.

I flipped to the back and ripped out a blank page, then tore off a corner to make it match the missing page somewhat. With my plausible prop created, I started scribbling down a tale so ridiculous I cackled.

When I stepped out my front door, I found Tristan waiting.

"Thought you could use an escort."

I gritted my teeth and hiked my backpack up on my shoulder. I figured he was trying to give truth to the Instagram lie he'd fabricated by showing up with me, but he underestimated me. He underestimated Alfie. Some battles weren't worth waging. "Thanks. I guess."

As we headed up the sidewalk, he said, "Are you mad at me?"

"Don't worry." I shot him a sideways glance, and he returned a crooked half smile that would have made my knees buckle a week ago. "I can hold my own."

"I'm sure you can." He shot out his hand. "May the best man win?"

I straightened my back as I gave him my most challenging stare. I reached out to take his outstretched hand but amended, "May the best *woman* win."

He laughed as we shook. "Sure. But I plan to win it all."

Once inside, I found Alfie in the kitchen, rinsing lemons. I snuck up and poked him. His hand flew up as he spun around, and he bobbled a lemon but recovered it. "You startled me."

He leaned forward, and I met him halfway. It was so nice to greet him with a kiss. "Hi."

"Hi. I guess it's getting late. You ready for tonight?"

I blew out a breath. "I have to talk to you about that."

I gave him the highlight reel of what had happened. "I honestly don't recall any of that night, and the page is missing from my journal. My entry from the next day proves I'd been drinking, and I know I had a crush on Tristan back then. So I have to assume that it happened, that I kissed him."

"I don't understand. Is he going to claim you kissed him without his consent?"

"No. He said he liked it."

"So what then?"

"I was worried about what you might think."

"You thought I'd be jealous of your past?"

"Well, you did say—"

He shook his head. "No. I'm not jealous of Tristan. I was. And yeah, if you ran off with him, it would suck a lot. But I don't think you'd do that."

"Never. Promise." I bit my lip. "That picture he posted on Instagram was old."

"I know." He rubbed my back. "So what are you going to do?"

"I have a plan of my own." I squinted one eye as I confessed, "I *may* have fabricated an entry."

He laughed. "I won't tell on you."

It was a relief knowing Tristan's machinations wouldn't blow things up with Alfie or make me quit the contest. "Thank you, Alfie. I needed your support."

"You got it."

"I'm gonna go sit down and prepare."

"See ya out there."

Zane and Bryce joined me as I frantically rewrote the last few lines. I glanced up. "Hey."

"Hey." Zane slapped his Get Out of Jail Free card on the table. "See if they can eliminate me tonight."

I hadn't even thought about whether I'd get eliminated. All I'd wanted to do was neutralize Tristan, and maybe even make him lose for once. He'd stolen my thunder often enough. Turnabout was fair play.

I wasn't gonna give up without a fight.

Alfie set a club soda next to me and leaned down to whisper in my ear. "Give him hell."

Miranda was already up on the stage, and Alfie headed over to wait for her to announce the start of the contest. The bar was packed. I took a sip of my drink, wishing for once I'd ordered something stronger. Then again, I was about to mount a defense against another night when I'd had too much. Probably best to keep my wits.

Miranda said, "Welcome to the fourth round of our increasingly popular Chagrin Challenge. Word must have gotten out because we're at standing room only tonight. Once again, we want to thank our contestants who have entertained us each week. We're down to seven." The room erupted in hoots and applause. Zane, Bryce, and I all smiled at one another. I felt like I was a part of an inner circle. I hadn't had that experience since my cross-country days. Even if I lost tonight, I'd be proud I'd come this far.

Miranda handed the mic off, and Alfie pulled out his smaller notebook, not the one from Ms. Maxwell's class. "Apologies to everyone who came out for the belly laughs. You'll have to make do with uncomfortable snickers because I have another embarrassing poem tonight. This one is called 'Crushing.' "

He inhaled, exhaled, and said, "This is for someone special."

I imagined he looked out at me, but I knew he couldn't see me in the dark.

"Seeing her, not seeing me
My heart crushed

With longing
Until her eyes found mine,
Seeing me, seeing her
And she's crushed
With my crush
Until our hearts align."

Claps followed his reading, but they applauded like he'd just read the back of a menu. Swine.

As he walked past my table, he winked at me, and I reached my hand out to grab his. I roped him over until we were face-to-face. I whispered in his ear, "That made me want to kiss you, right here, right now."

"Yeah?"

"Can I get a rain check?"

"What are you doing after the show?"

I smiled. "Can I get another tour of your place?"

He squeezed my shoulder. "Will this night never end?"

My pulse quickened. Had I stumbled upon the key to the treasure I'd been unable to secure? Could I unlock his forbidden chamber before the night was over?

Miranda called Bryce up, and Zane popped his ass as he passed. Maybe I should have stolen a kiss after all.

Bryce took the mic and dove right in. "I texted Danny this weekend and told him I loved him. I told him dirty things I wanted to do to him. So many things.

"And that would have been fine, except I wasn't texting Danny at all. Somehow I'd clicked on a message chain for Mr. Hart's biology class. The only reason I noticed this was that Sandra McIntyre replied with a dancing banana emoji. I scrolled back through my comments, wishing for some way to recall them all. Oh, my God, the things I'd written.

"So Monday morning, I got to class . . ."

As Bryce continued his tale, I caught a glimpse of Tristan, sitting with Shannon and Heather. He must have felt my gaze on him because his head swiveled around, and we locked eyes. I narrowed mine. He smirked and held up a loose piece of paper.

The corner was missing.

The corner was missing in the same shape as the corner in my notebook.

How had he gotten that?

Oh, my God. The things I might have written. Bryce had nothing on my potential embarrassment.

Tristan had been flipping through my notebook the week before. Had he stolen a page? Surely, he'd be disqualified for reading from someone else's diary. Would I be disqualified if I tackled him and wrenched that page free? What if I just punched the smug look off his face?

What in the hell had I written?

I clenched my fists and took a breath. He was just trying to scare me so I'd panic. Everything else I'd written in my notebook so far hadn't been that bad. Even if he had my journal entry, it was useless to him.

I drank the rest of my club soda, then got up and went to the bathroom to read through my planned presentation. Leaning on the knowledge that Alfie wouldn't hold what I'd written against me, I repeated it to myself, quietly, until my nerves settled. I re-entered the bar as Shannon was getting up to present.

Shannon started out, "So it's graduation day, and I got my period. Of course it wasn't one of those times when I got a little warning in advance. Nope. I was sitting in the crowd of two hundred seniors, middle of the aisle, as the principal called our names, and I thought, 'What's that?' 'Cause it could have been sweat or, God forbid, pee. They'd started on the names one row up, so I couldn't run to the bathroom, and I sat there as something indescribable happened to me. It wasn't until our row stood, and we filed out to stand in line by the stage, that the definite trickle of something wet—and thick—ran down the inside of my thigh."

I was giggling at Shannon's story, but as I looked around at the patrons, the look of stark horror among the men made me realize there were lines too far to cross at this particular venue, and I felt renewed pity for Shannon because she was reliving this embarrassment once again, and there was a good chance she'd get eliminated for it. Maybe the women would save her, but this might be too real to be funny.

She climbed down the steps to polite applause, grimacing like she'd started her period in the middle of her presentation, and I wanted to go up and hug her.

But I couldn't. Because then it was my turn.

Chapter 23

Tonight, I had to take things to a whole new level, but I felt ready for the battle, like I'd collected enough hit points to sustain the impact of this particular dungeon boss. My stamina meter was at full capacity. I was locked and loaded. Tristan was going down.

My stomach didn't even flutter with nerves. All I could think of was strategy and damage.

When I got in front of the mic, I closed my eyes and took a deep meditative breath. Once I found my center, I opened the journal to the entry I'd invented out of thin air.

The audience stilled, and I began.

"I kissed a prince, and he turned into a frog."

The laugh from the audience encouraged me. I needed to win them over before Tristan could. No pressure.

"I may have had too much to drink tonight, and my inhibitions were low. Very low.

"I took my last midterm today, thank God. Everyone was out on the town, bar hopping, celebrating, blowing off steam, and I joined the crowd. I accepted many a free shot. More than I should have.

"I lost track of time and place, but then I saw him. Tristan Spencer at the same bar as me. I walked right up to him, high on confidence—and tequila—and I cranked my flirting into overdrive. And by flirting, I mean I grabbed his shirt and pulled him in for a kiss. I've been imagining that kiss for weeks. Whenever I daydreamed about it, I pictured lovebirds perched on a nearby branch, chirping with happiness. I expected the sky to explode in fireworks. I at least expected the kiss to curl my toes. But instead, it curdled my stomach.

"Now, maybe it was my fault. I'd been drinking, after all. First, he tasted like cheap beer, which I may have as well, let's be fair. We both had an empty glass of . . . something . . . at our elbows. Second, the whole thing was a sloppy affair. His lips were too soft on mine—and too wet. It was like kissing a dishrag. Maybe his looks make it so easy to get girls he's never had to work for it. Maybe he didn't put much effort into that kiss because he knew I liked him."

I was hamming up this whole episode. From the crowd's giggles, I knew I'd nailed it. I wanted to sheathe my imaginary sword, but I had one last kill shot to make.

"When I managed to free myself from his lip lock, he grinned at me and said, 'You're welcome.'

"I guess I *should* have thanked him because he did something I wouldn't have thought possible until tonight. He finally cured me of an unwanted crush."

When I stepped back, miming a mic drop, the crowd applauded, and I accepted the yellow star from Miranda. I clutched it like a talisman of good fortune. I'd successfully navigated a potential minefield, and I was still standing.

Good luck defeating me now, Tristan.

As I stepped down, I caught Alfie's eye and raised my hand, palm forward. From across the bar, he didn't leave me hanging, and we connected in a long-distance high five.

Miranda called for Tristan, who shot me a glare. Yup. I'd weakened my opponent. I sat beside Zane, and he whispered, "Damn. That was an autopsy."

Bryce said, "You can stop murdering the boy. He's already dead."

I might have felt a little bad about how I'd annihilated him, but not after he'd raised the challenge. He didn't know who he was dealing with if he thought I'd take it lying down.

As Tristan climbed onto the stage, there was an uncomfortable shifting in the audience. The spotlight hit him, and his cheeks flamed. I could have sworn he was embarrassed for once in his life. He leaned into the mic, and silence blanketed the entire room, as we anticipated his response. My hands shook a little from residual adrenaline, and I steeled myself for what was to come. I didn't think for a moment he wouldn't return fire.

Tristan cleared his throat.

"That was an Oscar-worthy performance." He nodded my way. "Or maybe we should give her a Pulitzer."

He seemed awkward, and a small part of me took pity on him. But then he said, "Because that was a complete work of fiction."

He raised an eyebrow with a sly grin. "You may wonder how I know that."

My missing page slid out of the notebook, and he held it up.

"Because I have Sierra's actual journal entry right here."

Whispers and gasps rippled across the room.

"It's true. She lent me her notebook last week, and I found this entry. It was so flattering, it warmed my heart, and I confess I stole it to remind myself how she once felt about me. I wasn't planning to share it, but considering she's decided to malign me, slander me, what choice do I have but to set the record straight with her own words?"

Fuck me.

It was a trap, and I'd walked right into it.

What had he shown me this morning? Had he made up that whole journal entry to trick me into confessing to the crime before he produced the evidence? Not that I believed whatever he planned to read would be any truer than my own words.

Had we ever even kissed? Or was this all a setup and a hit job?

It didn't matter. He held the audience in his grip, and they believed him. The truth no longer mattered. I rolled my eyes and settled in for the ride.

"Shall I read on?"

I'd so viciously taken him down, nobody was going to tell him to show me any mercy. In any case, he didn't wait for any response but snapped the paper open and, in a voice I presumed was mine, he began.

"I kissed Tristan Spencer."

The audience erupted in hilarity at his preposterous high-pitched teen girl affectation. Honestly, I might have laughed myself if it weren't aimed at me. Instead, I crossed my arms and sucked on my teeth.

"I probably shouldn't have kissed him, but I did. He showed up at the bar where I'd been drinking, and he looked as beautiful as always. He came right over to me. Oh, my God. I said, 'Hi,' like it was the cleverest thing in the world. And he said, 'Hi.' "

The laughter had changed. It was harsher, more mocking. He was imitating me, and the audience could smell blood. My blood. The bar had become an arena, and someone was going to die. Tristan's eyes gleamed with power, and I trembled.

"Tristan Spencer was right there. I told him, 'If you come a little closer, I'll tell you a secret.' He came a little closer, and I grabbed his shirt and kissed him. Just like that.

"Oh, my God. I thought I might die.

"I said, 'Oh, my God, I kissed you. You're Tristan Spencer.' "

This whole thing was so dumb and over the top, I didn't think anyone could possibly believe I'd actually written it, but even Zane and Bryce were spellbound. Traitors. Everyone was dead to me.

"He said, 'I thought you were with that guy.'

"I said, 'What guy?'

"He pointed across the room at that dweeby guy Alfie from our class, and I said, 'That guy?'

"He said, 'Yeah.'

"I said, 'Ew. That guy creeps me out. He's always following me around.' Then I got a brilliant idea. I said, 'You could help me brush him off.'

"Tristan Spencer said, 'How?'

"And I said, 'Kiss me again. Like you mean it.'

"He said, 'If you want to prove you're not into him, you should kiss me.'

"Well, that made total sense, and I wanted to kiss Tristan Spencer again, so I stood on my toes and my dreams came true.

"Kissing Tristan Spencer was better than anything I'd ever imagined. I knew I'd never get the chance again, so I went for it. It was like magic. He must be the best kisser in the whole world.

"When I looked back, Alfie had left, and Tristan Spencer said, 'Well, mission accomplished, I guess.'

"I started to ask him if he'd walk me home. I wanted him to take me to bed. I wanted him. I opened my mouth to speak and threw up all over his shirt. He went to clean up, and I ran out of the bar so embarrassed. I think I might actually die. Oh, my God."

The room was quiet.

I hated him.

I wanted the earth to swallow me, but if I got up and fled, it would only draw more attention to me. Zane rubbed my shoulder. "Hang in there."

Miranda gave Tristan a yellow star, and he held it up like the bloody head of a foe he'd vanquished. Even Miranda seemed stunned, like she didn't know what had just happened. The applause was muted. A couple of people started to clap, but they must have realized they were outnumbered.

Everyone started chattering, and it sounded like a thousand bees. Zane and Bryce consulted with each other, then rose together and flanked Miranda, whispering to her passionately. Heather and Quinn joined the powwow.

I stayed in my seat, fingers twisted together in my lap. Bryce returned with a look of concern, but he leaned over and said, "Everything will be fine."

Miranda stepped up to the mic. "Quiet. Can everyone quiet down?" When the room stilled, she went on. "We don't exactly have any rules in place against fabricating stories told here, nor have we thought out how to handle a situation like this tonight where one contestant has apparently used another contestant's journal entry. The other contestants have made it clear they don't want to participate in a contest where admitted theft is involved, and so it has been determined that any votes cast for Tristan tonight will not be counted. Since he can't receive any votes, Tristan is effectively eliminated."

The volume increased immediately, and it took a minute to gain enough control back to allow Zane to take his turn. I sat paralyzed through his presentation, and I wondered if anyone gave him proper attention. But when he finished, Miranda sorted through the vote slips and announced, "Continuing on to next week will be Heather, Quinn, Sierra, and Zane. And Sierra, congrats. You've won the Get Out of Jail Free card."

I whooped and wanted to point at Tristan with an *in your face* gesture, but when I looked at him, he was smiling. He reached into his pocket and produced his own Get Out of Jail Free card. He lifted one eyebrow, like he knew something I didn't. What was he up to?

Miranda handed me my card, and I waved it above my head, like I was Link from *Zelda* collecting a prize. At least I'd bought myself an extra week, maybe even catapulted myself to the final night of the contest. And Tristan would have to burn his card to move on. Still, I didn't like that he seemed to think tonight had gone according to his plans.

I walked over to his table and leaned into his space. "You play dirty."

He stood up. "You made it necessary."

We were inches apart, and the virtual sorceress I played online came to life. I dared him to touch me. I had enough power surging through me, I could summon a magical ball of electrical wrath and torch him where he stood.

My wagging finger would have to suffice. "This is just like what you did to me during that other contest."

He shook his head. "I've told you, that wasn't me."

I snorted. "Yeah, like I'm going to believe that after tonight. You clearly have no qualms about cheating."

"Cheating? How can you cheat when there aren't any rules?"

"You knew you were crossing a line." My hands clenched into fists. "But you miscalculated. I didn't drop out. I won."

"You think I wanted you to drop out?" He tilted his head, and the room spun.

"What are you talking about?"

"This wasn't about the contest."

I narrowed my eyes. "What did you do?"

"I took out a different competitor." Never had a smug face needed so much smiting. "When I said, 'Let the best man win,' I wasn't talking about *you*."

"You . . ." I was at a loss. "What?"

"Last week, I thought you and I had something going on, some momentum. Without any warning, I'm suddenly in competition with this guy you've never looked at twice."

I was still catching up. "You're jealous?"

"Pssh. Why would I be jealous of him? Besides, he's ceded the field of battle." He grinned like he'd just unlocked a new level of *Candy Crush*. "It's just me, now."

I tried to piece together the shrapnel of my world exploding. My heart clenched tight in my chest at the possibility he might have succeeded in his diabolical plan.

I swung around to scan the room. "Alfie."

I'd been so mired in my own humiliation, I hadn't remembered he'd been thrown under Tristan's bus, too.

I abandoned Tristan and pushed past huddled merrymakers until I got to the bar, but Alfie wasn't there. I poked my head in the kitchen and only found a cook I'd never met.

Maybe Alfie hadn't heard Tristan's bullshit. I continued through to the back stairs, panic spurring me faster. Alfie didn't deserve the kind of bullshit Tristan had manufactured. I took the steps two at a time and pounded on his door until he cracked it.

"Sierra." He looked down but didn't open the door any wider.

"Are you okay?"

"Yeah. I'm fine. But can you give me some space? I just want to be alone right now."

"No, Alfie." I leaned my head on the doorjamb. "Please. Let me in."

I must have been certain he'd turn me away because a sob escaped me when he stepped away from the door, leaving it open behind him, like it didn't matter either way.

I wasn't about to let slip the chance, and I followed him in to the dark apartment to where he sat on the sofa, a bottle of scotch on the coffee table.

He poured a finger of scotch into a tumbler. "This is probably a bad idea." He swilled the liquid and took a sip, grimacing.

I sat beside him. "Are you mad at me?"

He frowned. "Of course not. But Tristan pisses me off, and I needed to leave. It's not a great idea to punch a patron."

When his eyes met mine, I saw the hurt his casual tone was covering. "Alfie. I don't know what Tristan is up to, but he basically admitted he wants to put a wrench between us. He's *lying*. He set this whole thing up to get just this effect. He made up that entire incident."

He snorted and shot me a devastating look. "No, Sierra. He didn't."

"How would you—?" I gasped when it hit me. "You were there? We really kissed?"

He pressed his thumb and forefinger into his eyelids for a moment before he responded. "Everyone went out that night, just like you said. I ran into you, and we hung out for a while. Do you remember that?" I shook my head. "It was one of those nights when you move from one group to another, so I'm not surprised if I don't stick out in your memory."

"I'd also been drinking, Alfie."

He looked into his scotch glass. "When I saw you kissing Tristan . . ."

"You can't think—"

"I don't care about that. It's your right to kiss whoever you want, and I know you never gave me that look. But he did, always finding ways to crush me." His fist clenched. "He knew I liked you, and that if I saw you kissing him, it would be a dagger."

"Alfie."

"Tristan might be embellishing his journals, but there's an element of truth, and I can't shake how small he made me feel. I thought I'd gotten over that."

"That was so long ago. You have to know it has nothing to do with who we are now."

"I know. I do. It's a whole bunch of shit I need to sort through, which is why I wanted to be alone right now." He pierced me with his galactic eyes. He picked up his drink and took a sip. "It's funny because I honestly hadn't actively thought about that night in ages. It's not your fault, but I think my body recorded that feeling in my muscles somehow, which might be why I've had a hard time feeling like I could trust this." He pointed between us.

I understood too well how the body could hold on to emotions the mind had reconciled, but I hated that an ancient pain that had no bearing on us now was coming between us.

"Are you repulsed by me?"

He looked at me like I was crazy. "Never. That's not at all what I meant. I'm just . . ." He sank into the sofa and closed his eyes. "I'm not good company tonight. Thanks for coming to check on me, but could you give me a little time? I hate that you're seeing me like this."

My throat hurt from the scream I was repressing. There was nothing more I could say right now. I wanted to yell at him to fight whatever demon he'd summoned, fight for me, but this was his battle. "Sure." I picked up my bag to go. "I'll see you tomorrow?"

"Maybe." He gave me a sad smile, but this was clearly the best he could do.

I left Alfie to his self-imposed grief and took the stairs two at a time, nurturing my own mounting rage. I was going to murder Tristan for detonating a buried land mine that could have slumbered on forever without hurting anyone.

The place was still fairly busy, and I located Tristan hanging out near the bar. I walked straight up to him and poked his shoulder. "You're a complete douchebag. You know that?" I crossed my arms. "You ended up hurting the one person here who doesn't deserve it."

He scoffed. "Me? You're the one who wrote everything I said."

"Are you shitting me, you liar? You have no right to be sabotaging my relationships. No. Right."

"I'm doing you a favor. The guy's a joke. You know you deserve better than him." His smile made me wish my backpack contained an arsenal of weaponry. What I wouldn't have given for a doom hammer right about then.

"You think you're better than him?" I laughed derisively.

"Obviously." He sipped his bottle of pretentious beer. "You and I are the same, Sierra. We're warriors. Where's your boyfriend right now? Why isn't he down here standing by you?"

It bothered me that he echoed my own doubts, but it didn't make him right.

"You're a jerk." I slung my backpack higher on my shoulder.

"Just winnowing the competition."

"I'm not a prize!" I threw my hands out and yelled, "Argh! You haven't changed one bit in the past ten years. Is winning all you care about?"

He threw up his hands like I'd physically threatened him. "Whoa. It's just a game. You gave as good as you got."

"You know, it's not a game. You're messing with my real life. And you *hurt* someone."

He snorted. "Like you just tried to hurt me?"

I started to say, *"Well, you started it,"* and realized we sounded like a couple of bratty children. Talking to him was pointless. "I'm going home."

He slid off the barstool. "At least let me walk you home."

I glared at him. "I don't need an escort, thank you very much."

"Whatever." He turned halfway around. "When you come to your senses, you know where to find me."

"The next time I see you, it will be to bury you."

"You can try." He grinned. "You can fail."

"Next week, I'll show everyone who you really are." I gave him that same exact smug grin he was so fond of.

He laughed like I'd said the punch line to a hilarious joke we were both in on. "Next week is going to be interesting, then."

"Why?"

He cocked a brow, and it annoyed me that he thought he was so amusing. "What? And ruin the suspense?"

He skipped away, swallowed up by the other patrons until all I could see was the blond top of his head as he settled himself back at the bar.

I needed to find a magic spell I could utter to bring him down. And I thought I might have just the one.

Chapter 24

One minute into Child pose, my brain caught up to my emotions.

My yoga moms had all asked me whether Alfie would be joining us. I didn't want to tell them I hadn't heard from him since the night before. I was a little miffed at him for sulking over the past, considering things had obviously been so good between us this past week.

Sitting perfectly still, focusing on releasing the stress in each muscle, calmed the raging currents and brought clarity.

Ten things I knew to be true:

One: Tristan had stolen a page from my journal.

Two: The entry he'd read had been rooted in truth.

Three: I'd kissed Tristan even if I didn't remember it.

Four: Tristan and I had both hurt Alfie.

Five: Alfie's hurt was valid. There was no moratorium on psychological scars. I mean, I still held a grudge against Tristan for what he'd done to me so long ago.

Six: Alfie hadn't acted out on his feelings other than to take a time-out.

Seven: Tristan *had* acted out on his feelings, recklessly.

Eight: I missed Alfie.

Nine: I needed to convince him he could trust me, rewrite his muscle memory.

Ten: I was going to destroy Tristan.

I left yoga resolved in my goals. I showered and changed into a pair of boyfriend jeans and a simple scoop-neck T-shirt. I left my hair down and fixed my makeup, only because I'd be on-stage again, and this time—shudder—I'd be singing.

When I came upstairs to grab a quick dinner, Aida took one look at me and said, "Where are you going?"

I shoved a plate of leftover lasagna in the microwave and punched the timer. "Karaoke."

"You?"

While my dinner heated, I joined her at the kitchen table. "Alfie invited me."

She snorted. "Oh, so all along, all you've needed was a magic penis?"

"Excuse me?"

"Some guy comes along and asks you nicely, and you're ready to jump up and sing in front of strangers?"

"It's time I leveled up."

She blinked rapidly. I'd actually managed to shock her. "Really? You think karaoke was the obstacle we were missing all this time?"

"I'm not talking about the demo right now. I fucked up, and I need to go make amends."

"What happened?"

I filled her in on my current debacle, her eyes widening at each new revelation. "And so, I'm going over to fix things, if it's not too late."

"How are you feeling about the demo, now?"

I got up to pour a drink, thinking about everything that had happened in the past few weeks.

"You were right to push me to do the contest. Since everyone is trying to out-shock each other, I've become more comfort-able."

She nodded. "I'm glad you're working it out."

"Reynold came to see the contest and said I had potential."

"You do." She pushed herself up and grabbed her side. "Shit. Ow."

"What is it? Should I call Marco?"

"I'm fine. Just ready for this demon to be out of me. Sorry, I mean, this beautiful, blessed demon. Who we love very much." She placed her hands on her back, like she had to physically hold her spine in place. "Good luck with Alfie. He's a good one."

I heard the *unlike Tristan* and didn't disagree.

The microwave beeped. I ate alone, then went to finish getting ready to go out. My phone buzzed and I grabbed it, thinking it would be Alfie, but Tristan's name popped up.

Can you meet me tonight?

I stared at it, furious and confused all at once. He didn't deserve a response, but I wanted to throw my entire arsenal at him.

What do you want?

I want to talk. I miscalculated, and I fucked up.

I'm busy tonight.

I want to apologize. In person. I want you to forgive me.

I considered all the things I could say to him, but suddenly I didn't care, and it would be easier to forgive him than have him texting me until I did.

Sure, Tristan. All is forgiven. Okay?

Then can I take you out tomorrow?

Did he really think he'd succeeded in wrecking things with Alfie? Then again, maybe he had.

Not interested, Tristan.

I muted my phone. I should have told him to fuck off. I didn't feel like I'd forgiven him at all.

When I went out for the night, the sun hadn't begun to set, so I enjoyed a pleasant stroll in the early summer warmth. I was worried Alfie would just decide to cool things off and go back to being friends. I had to hope he was the guy I'd started to trust, the guy I'd started to fall for.

Loud music met me inside the bar, and a cute black man I'd never met filled orders. He couldn't have been much older than twenty-one. I grabbed a stool and waved awkwardly to him, unsure if I should act like a patron, a regular, or as a friend of the owner.

"What'll you have?" he asked.

Dilemma. I didn't want to go on a liquor-fueled bender before talking to Alfie.

"Club soda with lime?" I sounded as unsure as I was.

My indecision didn't cause him a moment's hesitation, and he flipped a glass as pretty as you please, then winked at me as he shot the soda from the hose.

After he set my drink before me, he leaned in and flashed a stunning smile. "So you're here for the karaoke?"

An arm draped over my shoulder, and Alfie slid around beside me. "I hope so. Isaac, I see you've met Sierra."

"*The* Sierra?" Isaac straightened, but his shoulders seemed to droop.

It amused me the way he made me sound like a legend in these here parts, and it flattered me that he seemed disappointed I was already kind of spoken for. "Does my reputation precede me?"

Alfie laughed. "Only in the nicest way."

Isaac gave me a curt nod. "Nice to meet you. You let me know if Alfie's not treating you right." Then he moved down the bar and busied himself with a rack of glasses.

Alfie leaned in. "I'm glad you came tonight."

"Yeah." I sighed. "Look, I want to apologize for whatever happened. It might have been ten years ago, but something obviously made you feel shitty, and I hate that. I hate that I might have done that to you."

"It's okay, Sierra."

"I'm worried I fucked everything up long ago, when I didn't even know . . . when I hadn't figured out who I was or what I wanted. Who I needed."

His eyes widened. "Who you needed?"

"Who I need." I touched his hand. "I don't know what I was thinking that night. I can't begin to fathom why I even liked Tristan when you were right there. I was missing out on an amazing person. But I can see that now. Alfie, I am so sorry."

He swallowed, and it occurred to me that the walls we build can be good or bad. We'd been adding new bricks to a faulty foundation, but I hoped I'd knocked one of the rotten blocks from deep down free of its roots. Maybe I could replace it with something solid.

"Thank you, Sierra."

I wrapped my arms around him, hugging him tight until Miranda passed by and said, "Come on. Let's kick off the karaoke!"

Alfie grabbed my hand, and we followed her over to the stage. At least he joined me, so we'd look stupid together.

"Relax, okay? You'll be great."

"What are we singing?" My throat was constricting, and I had a mustache of perspiration. My pits were going full-tilt, too. Had I put on deodorant? Oh, God, I hadn't. Was I dizzy, or were the lights messing with my vision?

The monitor lit up with the title of the song: "Don't Go Breaking My Heart."

I clutched Alfie's arm. "I don't know this song!"

How could I sing a song I didn't know? I started to panic.

Alfie looked surprised. "Miranda, wrong song."

The title blipped off, followed by "Don't You Want Me."

I knew that one, but I'd never paid attention to the lyrics. My stomach was doing the flying trapeze. Lasagna was about to become airborne.

"Nope. Still wrong." He went over to the computer and futzed. After a second, the familiar synth of "Don't Stop Believing" started up.

I smiled. "I know this one!"

"You better. You're singing first."

This one was easy. I'd heard it a million times on car trips to visit the grandparents in Birmingham. I sang the first verse a little wobbly. Alfie came in on the second verse, and then we shouted the chorus together, poorly, but laughing. The fact that we sucked made it even funnier. Whatever shyness I'd had was replaced with a weird thrill. This was fun. When the song faded out, Alfie punched our linked hands up, like we'd just won a contest together. I wanted to look through the songbook and find something else to sing.

Instead, we had to cede our place to the next couple in line, and Alfie got back to work. Shortest date of my life.

The bar filled up as the night wore on. The patrons were way more raucous than on Friday nights. While I observed this microcosm of humanity, Alfie helped Isaac behind the bar, but whenever he could, he'd come hang out with me for a few minutes. Mostly we'd just chat or sing along with whatever song was being butchered.

And I kept my eyes on him throughout it all. He moved like a whirlwind until he stopped to deal with a customer. When he'd glance my way, his smile would tilt a little higher at one corner, and his eyes seemed to twinkle with mischief.

Alfie was straight-up adorable.

How had I overlooked him so easily? I'd clearly missed him in college when we crossed paths multiple times. And I'd failed to notice him as more than the bartender when I'd come to the first diary reading. More than once in my life, I'd let Tristan's flashy good looks distract me from Alfie's more subtle light. Tristan was like the sun blotting out the north star that was Alfie. But the north star was constant, and the sun would always set.

There was no denying Tristan had been and still was model gorgeous. He had that chiseled jaw, penetrating blue eyes, and perfectly styled blond hair. But like a photograph of the ocean, he was pretty to look at, but everything stopped at the surface.

I was quickly learning I preferred solid to superficial any day of the week.

Alfie promised depths. In him, I could glimpse a hidden world few people ever experienced. And of course I liked everything about the way he looked, but what I saw in him went beyond appearances. I saw a soul I wanted to know. We were friends, and I desperately wanted us to be lovers.

Next thing I knew, it was last call and people were leaving. Once the bar had emptied of patrons, the lights came on, and Miranda began clearing off tables. Alfie emerged from the kitchen and said, "Miranda, Isaac, leave it. I'll get it all tomorrow. Go on home. Thanks for everything."

Miranda nodded but went from table to table collecting tips before she flipped off the overhead lights and disappeared out the back door. Isaac came around and told me good night. And then it was just me and Alfie.

Only the soft, diffuse lights behind the bar remained on, and his face was shrouded in shadows. "Did you have a good time?"

"I actually did."

"Do you know what I think?" He held out his hand as if I needed help climbing down from the stool. I didn't, but I wouldn't pass an opportunity to touch him.

"Tell me." I hoped he was thinking we should call an end to our celibacy.

"I think I know how you can overcome your performance anxiety."

I stifled my initial grumble. "I'm all ears."

"Tonight, when you thought we were going to sing a song you didn't know, you panicked."

"Yeah, well, wouldn't you?" Surely anyone would have heart palpitations about flailing around unprepared onstage.

"Probably, but once you knew the song, you were perfectly at home on that stage."

"So you think I won't freak out if I know the material? It's a good theory, but I know my video game really well. I still blow every demo."

He held up a finger. "Ah. You know how to *play* the game really well. Playing and pitching are two different skills."

I tapped my index finger against my lower lip. "True."

He nodded, like he was adding pieces of evidence to prove some hypothesis. "So here's my theory: If you walk through your presentation until you know it cold, you'll crush it."

"I did practice before, though."

"But did you? Did you really memorize it?"

Had I? I'd practiced reading notecards, mostly in my head with my lips moving silently.

"Holy shit. Can it be that simple?"

He grinned like he'd solved a difficult puzzle, and in a way he had. "Come on. I'll walk you back."

While he locked the front door, I leaned against the glossy, over-painted wall. The silver moonlight made him look preternatural. He could have been a sexy vampire, and I would've happily let him bite me.

"God, you're beautiful," I said.

He moved closer, eclipsing the night sky behind him, darkness drenching him now. I closed my eyes, conjuring his face in my mind. I could picture the hint of a smile he always wore.

I wanted to hook my fingers around his collar and drag him to my lair. Instead he'd probably walk me home and kiss me good night. After all, we'd had a rough twenty-four hours.

My eyes flew open at the realization. "Hey, did we just have our first fight?"

"When did we fight?" His breath tickled my cheek.

"Last night. Did we just make up?"

"I would love if all fights were that easy."

"Is that a yes?"

"Is that what you want?"

I touched his cheek, needing him to hear the revelations I'd had, how much I'd come to appreciate him. "I know you want to wait, but my body feels like I've known you for years. Does that make sense? I'm drawn to you like . . ." I looked into his dark eyes to make sure I wasn't freaking him out. "You feel right."

His lips met mine, and all the stress in my shoulders and legs flowed out of me. I thought my knees might collapse from the sheer pleasure of knowing this kiss was for me alone. How I'd missed him. His finger gingerly tickled my neck as his weight shifted, as his lips parted. He told me everything he never had to say with the most sensual kiss I'd ever experienced in my life.

I sucked on his lower lip, and his moan nearly undid me.

Eros took control. I knew he wanted me as badly as I needed him. I tugged at the hem of his shirt and worked my hands under the fabric, loving the feel of goose bumps as my fingers traced his back.

"Alfie, take me home tonight. Please." I held my breath, waiting for him to tell me no, waiting for him to put an end to this before it could go too far.

He backed up, and I feared he was going to turn toward my

house and another lonely night, but he held out a hand. "Come with me."

I followed him as he led me to his apartment, and then to the loft where his bed glowed like a newly discovered shrine. He lifted my wrist to his lips and trailed kisses up my forearm, sending thundering aftershocks through my core. When he peeled the edge of my sleeve back, baring my shoulder, my goose bumps had goose bumps from my elbow clear up to my hairline.

I was in uncharted waters with him, which was what we'd discussed before. I didn't want to kill the mood, but I needed to know. "Alfie, do you want to talk about this?"

"Do you trust me?" he asked. I nodded. "Can I trust you?"

It felt like a bigger question when he turned it on me. Yes, I trusted him not to hurt me. I trusted he wanted something that would last beyond tonight.

Could he trust me?

I could promise him I wouldn't hurt him, not on purpose. I couldn't promise forever, but I could promise I wanted to. I could promise him more than a hookup.

He dropped his hands to his sides. "What do you want, Sierra? I'm all yours."

I let my eyes fall down the length of him. "I want you."

He grasped the hem of my shirt and lifted it up. I reached for the buttons on his as he unsnapped my bra. I'd barely traced the trail of hair leading into his pants before he laid me down on his bed. I groaned when his lips brushed my nipple, and my hips lifted in search of relief from pulsating need, craving his touch. He unfastened my jeans, fingers toying with the lace on my panties, driving me to desperation.

I shoved his shoulder to force him onto his back, stripping off his shirt in the process. I ran my fingers down his abs, mesmerized by the way his muscles contracted. He'd been hiding a world of beauty from me.

I might have lingered on every place his skin vibrated when I tickled him, but his pants were straining, and my patience ran out. He sighed an airy *ahhhh* when I popped his fly and slid my hands over the top of his boxer briefs. The sound of his bliss nearly devastated me.

His cock grew even harder as I stroked him, and I throbbed at the thought of his need satisfying my own. I kissed him while I worked him free so I could feel the smooth length of him.

"Do you have a condom?" I rasped.

He swallowed. "Are you sure?"

"I'm sure."

He rolled over and stretched his arm to a side table, jostling the furniture so hard it knocked his family's picture over. He abandoned that attempt and crawled over to open the drawer. I took advantage of his position to peel his jeans down his hips. He laughed but let me finish the job. On his knees, on his bed, stark naked in the moonlight, he was the most beautiful thing I'd ever seen. "You." I exhaled. "You are amazing."

That smile. It was going to kill me. He held the condom packet up, like a treasure, and I snatched it from him. He worked my pants off while I extracted the rubber, and then he ran fingers up my inner thigh and against my pleasure zone.

Unf.

Such a dilemma. I was slick from wanting him inside me, but I never wanted him to stop touching me, either. He kissed my neck, then whispered, "Feel good?"

I whimpered in response. He shifted, and his lips passed over my breasts, then tickled my stomach. I giggled and clenched.

He lifted his head. "Ticklish?"

"A little."

"How about here?" He kissed my hip, then crawled between my knees. "Or here?" He kissed my thigh.

"No. Not ticklish there."

His finger circled once before he bent forward and ran his tongue straight down from the one point of desire to another.

"That feels so damn good."

"Mmm," was all he said. He sucked on me as his finger slid inside, pushing me to a place beyond pleasure. My breathing grew ragged. I was lost in another dimension. My body had become a drug factory, and I was high on endorphins. Without warning, the intensity overwhelmed me, and waves of relief and happiness washed over me.

For a moment, I touched the doors of heaven.

Then I plummeted, and my body shuddered.

Either Alfie was a sex wizard or else our emotional connection amplified my senses.

Alfie read my body's signals and kissed me once, then rested his head on my stomach. "You are delicious."

My arms had turned into noodles. I laid a hand on his shoulder, desultory, satisfied but still wanting. "Come here."

He inched back up me, and I worried he might be chivalrous and call it a night. But then he took the condom from me and rolled it on with one hand. The moment that sucker was on, I hooked a leg around his butt and pulled him to me like a tractor beam.

He bent down for a kiss, and as he sucked on my lip, he slid in. I gasped, and he sighed. He moved slowly until we were hip to hip, and just the knowledge that he was deep inside me tripped a chemical reaction in my brain, and I understood what Alfie had meant about confusing sex and love, as an emotion broke over me like I'd never known, nearly bringing me to tears.

The only love I knew how to express was *Eros*, so I grasped his shoulders tight and rolled my hips back to encourage him to rock his in that motion so familiar, so intimate, but always such a surprise.

He started slow, as if he could make the feeling last forever, as if he could restrain the drive of his own body. I wrapped my legs around his lower back, and he lost control. Watching him take his own pleasure was about the sexiest thing I'd ever seen. Somehow knowing my body could affect his so powerfully redoubled my own body's response. We fed off each other, and instead of one and one making two, we were like facing mirrors. We were multitudes.

The orgasm hit me hard, and I rode the emotional tumult with a groan that started low and grew louder as I crested. I moaned his name, and he whispered mine, kissing me frantically until he cried, "Ah!" Sweat dripped from his forehead and hit my cheek, like a tear. He dropped down, stopping himself from crushing me with his full weight.

"Stay the night?"

I pressed my thumb into his delicious lower lip. "I'm never going to be able to leave this bed."

We twined together in the deceptive belief that forever was granted to mere mortals and drifted into a quiet place between the real world and some alternate reality of our own creation, where Mondays didn't exist and where Alfie's poor neglected dog didn't start whining before we'd slipped off to sleep.

Chapter 25

Alfie jumped out of bed, hopping around to pull his pants back on. "Crap. I'll be back."

He left me alone to go walk Jasper, and when he returned, he snuggled up next to me. I loved my skin on his. I loved his laughter rumbling deep inside me as we talked before we eventually fell back asleep.

I woke during the night to find his arm draped across my stomach. As I threaded my fingers into his, he stirred, and in the quiet of the early morning light, we made love without a word, slowly but relentlessly, settling into a rhythm that matched the beating of my heart. The night before we'd been churning waves crashing against each other, but at dawn we became the tranquil water that seeps into deep and hidden reaches of undiscovered inlets, languidly exploring every inch of our bodies.

When my phone's alarm went off, and *forever* came to its inevitable end, I kissed his forehead. "I need to go home and change clothes."

He got up and pulled on a pair of boxer briefs, and I nearly drooled at the sight of those abs in the sunlight. God, he was sexy as fuck in just his underwear.

"Stop looking like that, would you?" I bit my lip, rethinking my need for clean clothes. For any clothes, really.

"Me? Have you seen yourself?" He tossed a clean T-shirt in my lap.

I pulled it on, breathing in the smell of him, then hunted for the rest of my clothes. "What are you doing today?"

"You want to take Jasper to the BeltLine after you go home?"

I didn't care if we were dropped in the middle of a field as long as I got to spend more time with Alfie.

It was new, having a guy want to hang out with me. Other than Howard, I'd never been good at actual dating, the kind dating apps promised but never yielded. What I was good at was landing in a guy's bed. Granted, seducing a man with sex was like shooting fish in a barrel, but like fish, those relationships didn't last too long in daylight.

And here was Alfie wanting to spend time with me after a torrid night.

He put on some sweatpants that hung from his hips enough to make my body pulse again. I pouted when his shirt went on, but his messy bed head made up for the loss of torso. Somewhat.

"You're so cute after I've had my way with you."

He knelt on the bed and pinned my arm behind my back as he leaned in for a kiss.

Somehow, we got dressed, ate breakfast, and headed out. I was surprised for a second when he led me to a black Volvo. No, it wasn't as flashy as a vintage Mustang, but it felt safe and reliable and cozy, like Alfie.

We stopped by my town house so I could run in. While I was shoving notecards and anything else I might need into my backpack, Aida knocked on the doorframe. "Hey."

I paused where I was. "What's up?"

"Did you come home last night?"

"Uh . . ."

She slowly lowered herself down to sit on the bottom step. "I think I'm going to burst. This kid is pressing against organs I couldn't even name. How are you?"

"Good." I may have grinned a bit too much. Her eyebrow shot up.

"You're glowing. Did you know that?"

I put a hand to my cheek reflexively. "It's just the light."

"You live in a dungeon."

"Then how can you see me?"

She narrowed her eyes. "Were you with Alfie last night?"

"Yeah."

"Good. I like him. Marco and I thought you might, too, if you could get to know him."

I froze, hands buried in my backpack. "What do you mean?"

"Well, you know Marco met him a while back at the bar. When he mentioned the contest—"

I held up a finger. "Wait a second. You said you'd seen the contest in a Facebook group."

"He did post about it in there as well. He seemed cute and decent, so I stalked him a bit."

My mind was spinning. "Was this about the demo or about setting me up with some guy?"

"Two birds."

"Seriously? You planned this?"

"Was I wrong?" She grabbed the railing and heaved herself up.

I wanted to bitch her out for manipulating me, but she wasn't wrong. "No. Alfie's great."

"Took you long enough to get there, especially when Tristan arrived like a douche lord ex machina to grab your attention again. I still don't know why you gave him the time of day. After what he did?"

"Well, I've had a long time to let it go, and I thought he might have changed. But he hasn't." I sighed out my frustration. "He tried to sabotage me again Friday night."

"See? Stick with the nice boy. Once an asshole, always an asshole." She had a way with words.

I grabbed my bag. "I need to go. Alfie's waiting out in his car with his dog."

"Go. Be nice to that boy."

I was very nice to Alfie while we walked Jasper along the BeltLine. But he was nicer to me.

He listened while I recited the demo. I repeated phrases like, "*Castle Capture* is a first-person medieval realistic RPG similar to *Skyrim* or *Final Fantasy*."

"This was a dumb idea," I told him. "I can't remember all this."

He kissed me. "Let's start from the top."

On Monday morning, I moved into the conference room to practice the demo in the environment where I'd be auditioning. As soon as the video came on-screen, I paused. Tristan had used multimedia to screw me over at my presentation ten years earlier, and I imagined all the ways this could go wrong. My stomach hurt.

Maybe I should quit and try again tomorrow.

Aida peeked in. "Can I watch?"

My heart rate increased, but the accountability was well timed. "If you promise not to laugh. This is going to be rough."

"You've got this. Pretend you're talking about your vagina in front of a crowd of strangers."

"Not helping."

"Isn't that what you guys do at the diary contest?"

"Ha-fucking-ha. Maybe if you shut off the lights, I can pretend you're not here."

She *tsk*ed. "Gonna have to learn to do it with the lights on."

"That's what *she* said."

The video rolled behind me, but its power over my adrenal glands had dissipated. Aida had reminded me this wasn't close to how embarrassing the diary readings were.

After I finished, Aida bobbed her head from side to side. "Not bad." She got up, though it was more like seesawing into a standing position. "Keep practicing. I'm gonna—"

She made a face of disgust. "Oh, God. I think my water broke."

"Oh, shit! What do I do?" I rushed to her side.

Her light-blue jeans were turning navy. "Call Marco. Please."

I fumbled for my phone and nearly dropped it before I hit the Call button.

When Marco answered, I blurted, "Aida's in labor!"

After that, everything became a mad scramble. We helped Aida to the car, and then Marco drove like some bizarre combination of a New York City cabdriver and my great-aunt Ruby—fast, yet incredibly careful. Luckily, the hospital was only blocks away from our office.

Once we got into the hospital, an intense flurry of activity gave way to brutal inactivity. Aida was admitted into her room. And then, I was alone in the waiting room. I'd never paced in my life, and suddenly I understood the attraction.

Alfie arrived thirty minutes later with a couple of sandwiches and a bag of chips.

While we waited, I pulled out the notecards from my presentation.

Alfie said, "You should do this here."

"You're kidding me."

There were families huddling together, uncontrolled kids running free, people in wheelchairs either due to age or ailment, and enough ambient noise I could maybe talk low and not feel like a dork.

"You want to get good at doing this outside your comfort zone. This is definitely outside your comfort zone. Come on. When will you ever see these people again?"

I cringed but took a breath and spoke loud enough to be heard at least a row away. "*Castle Capture* is a medieval multiplayer online role-playing game in the style of *Final Fantasy*."

A teenager turned around. "*Final Fantasy*? I love that game." He had the look of our target demographic. "Do you play it, too?"

"Actually, I'm a developer. I've designed a game similar to *Final Fantasy*, but it's set in a medieval kingdom." I knew this cold. My memorization had cemented all this info in my head. Not to mention, I actually did design the game. "It has an arsenal of weapons, including a trebuchet."

His eyes lit up. "No way. I freaking love those things."

I described the landscape, the battlefields, the levels, the characters and skill sets, the game play, but in my own words, not based on the notecards. I was feeding off his interest. Knowing he wanted to hear the details allowed me to share the game with him with an authenticity I'd been lacking.

He was so enthusiastic it was infectious. If I could present to someone like him, it would be so much easier than Reynold. And it suddenly dawned on me, I *would* be presenting to someone like him. A whole lot of someones like him. The entire Gamescon was a magnet for true fans of gaming. How had I forgotten that?

Marco appeared. "You can come back now."

Marco looked changed somehow—exhausted, older, like he'd seen things that weren't available to low-level players like us. He'd been given access to the secrets of the universe.

He led us to a quiet, dimly lit room, where Aida propped against a pillow, holding a blanket with a wee face sticking out. She also looked tired and splotchy and incredibly happy.

She waved us in. "Wook at how pwecious him is."

I looked at Marco. "What have they done with Aida?"

She glared at me. "Shut up."

"There she is." I peeled back a bit of blanket to get a better look. "He's so tiny."

Aida stroked the baby's arm. "Meet my son, Kamal."

"He's beautiful, Aida," Alfie said. "Congratulations."

He really was, and despite obvious exhaustion, Aida glowed with love. I couldn't help envision myself in her shoes. Maybe when Alfie had asked me to share my life goals, I'd set my sights too low. Maybe I wanted what Aida already had.

Some day. I wasn't crazy.

I choked back a lump in my throat. I was so, so happy for my friends. "Good job, you two. You did it."

"Aida did it." Marco fell into a chair and yawned. "At least the hard part's over."

We all turned and stared at him, like he was crazy if he

thought life had just gotten easier, but his eyes closed and his breathing evened out. So we let him sleep, knowing full well it might be the last chance he got for a long time.

Soon Aida shooed us out, saying, "Go. Be free while you still can. I'm going to enlist your babysitting help when I get home."

Chapter 26

Alfie had the night off, so the plan was to go out on a real date. Dinner, dancing, and romance. I went home to shower and dress up, excited to finally go out in public together.

We did make it to a nice restaurant. He looked so gorgeous in a black button-down I wanted to rip it off him. The scruff had made a comeback, too, hallelujah. He was seriously cute with or without facial hair, but the scruff made me all silly inside.

Halfway through dessert, all the emotions and exertion of the day hit me hard, and I just wanted to be alone with him. Not to mention, with the wicked looks he was giving me while I licked the chocolate mousse off my spoon, I didn't trust myself around other people.

When I finished the mousse, I picked at Alfie's apple torte. "Can we skip the dancing?"

He pushed the plate closer. "What? You don't like dancing?"

"Think about it. If you and I get on a dance floor, our bodies will be pressed together. My hands will slide up around your neck. I'll sway against you, and my dress will begin to rise—"

"And we'll end up in the hallway, copulating like monkeys in heat, with no regard for anyone passing by?"

"In the hallway? I'd have my legs wrapped around you in the center of the dance floor."

His cheeks turned red, and he called for the check. "I have a better idea."

We drove back to his place. Once inside, he fiddled with his phone, and the room filled with music, from Bluetooth speakers.

As Ed Sheeran sang about finding a love, about dancing in the dark, Alfie pulled me toward him, and I lay my head on his shoulder, swaying with the music. He sang into my ear about finding a woman stronger than anyone he'd ever known, who shared his dreams, and one day our home.

I kicked off my shoes and danced against him barefoot. When I drew back, I saw the future in his eyes.

It was perfect.

The sweetness of that song transitioned into the sexy grind of "Make It Rain," and our gentle rocking became more deliberate. My fingers tightened around his neck, and he pressed his lips to my forehead. Our thighs slipped between each other's so we could get as close as possible, and our hips rolled in time with the slow desire of the music. Inexorably, our mouths met, gentle at first, like a question, but then urgent, answering each other's need.

My hands were on the knot of his tie as he worked the zipper of my dress. We would have been a sight on the dance floor. I peeled off his shirt and clawed his back until I could slip my hands around his torso to undo his pants. He helped slide off the rest of his clothes, while I let my dress and undergarments fall to the floor. As promised, I hooked one leg around his upper thigh, and his erection pressed between us. Our dance became a stumble, off balance and ungraceful. He lifted me and carried me until my back touched a wall.

"I've never done this before," he said.

"I've never wanted to try something so badly. Condom?"

Miraculously, he'd plucked one from somewhere before we'd begun this waltz of lust, and somehow, using the wall, my legs, and his left hand, he managed to roll it on. He let his eyes trail from where our hips met along my body until he reached my face. "God, you're perfect."

"Alfie, please."

Before, when he'd wanted to hold off on the sex, I'd worried maybe he didn't have much experience. Our first night together had blown my mind. But this? I'd never expected. He slid into me with the sexiest groan imaginable, and mine may have matched it when he pressed his thumb on my clit as he drove into me.

"Oh, God."

Then he leaned in and kissed me. It was a crazy combination of sensations that pushed me over the edge sooner than I'd ever gotten there before, and he grunted, "I'm gonna—" just as a scream ripped from my throat. I'd never been a screamer in my life.

We definitely had the *Eros* part down.

He slowed and laid his forehead against the wall, beside my ear, and whispered, "Never in my life."

He'd done all the work, but for some reason, I was panting. "Never."

He kissed me and set me down. "You were right. We should never go dancing in public."

I waggled my eyebrows. "Maybe you should restart that playlist."

I'd never hear Ed Sheeran the same again.

On Wednesday, Aida came back home, and as we expected, everything changed. I was blessedly two floors away from the crying for most of the night, but where I used to fight insomnia by playing video games in the living room, I found that was no longer going to be a viable option.

The television made a loud *bling-bloong* sound when it turned on or off, so even if I kept the volume down on the game, just starting to play might wake the baby. And our new game was *Don't wake the baby*.

And because I was no longer the only one awake in the middle of the night, when Aida or Marco caught sight of me, they immediately enlisted my help, so instead of gaming, I was on rocker duty or diaper duty.

We all took turns through the night. Even Alfie came by after the bar closed Thursday night—or Friday morning—to see if he could be of any help. Once the house was at peace, he and I ended up passed out on the sofa, barely holding hands. It wasn't my ideal life, but my biological needs were at war, and extreme exhaustion beat horniness every time.

We were all going to need to figure out new schedules, not just for the baby. Arranging my work schedule to match Alfie's would also give me more quality time with him. He and I could live a weird twilight existence where five a.m. was dinnertime, and we went to bed at sunrise. *La vida vampire.*

As if the baby didn't take enough of our energy, I had to schedule remote meetings with the rest of the developers to troubleshoot and put out these last-minute fires.

To top it off, I was tired, crampy, and cranky from PMS.

Friday morning, before heading to the office for the first time since the baby had arrived, I checked on Aida, sitting on the sofa nursing Kamal. "Don't forget I've got the contest after work. I'll try to come home for a bit first."

She waved her hand. "We're fine. Go win that contest."

I grabbed my backpack and drove myself to Midtown. Once in the car, I began to feel human again. I hadn't realized how much of a bubble we'd created for ourselves in a short time. The incessant world of baby was a microcosm with its own ecosystem and time measurement. It felt like we'd been isolated on a deserted island for weeks, and I'd managed to break free to rejoin civilization.

When I was finally all alone, peacefully settled at my desk, I struggled to stay awake. Instead of diving into a complicated defect, fearing I might introduce more problems than I would solve in my current state, I thumbed through my journal until I found the day I'd been trying to forget. The entry wasn't as long as I would have expected, considering how huge an impact that incident had had on my life. It was written in black ink, not the bloodred of my imagination. And the handwriting was legible and didn't betray an emotional whirlwind.

Yet I trembled to read it.

That day had wrecked me in a way I was still battling today. That day, my worst fears were realized. And it was all Tristan's fault.

As much as I dreaded delving into this episode in my life, I knew I had to. Not only was it sure to catapult me to the final round of the contest because, my God, the embarrassment was so visceral, my cheeks heated at the memory. More to the point, if I could present this in front of that audience, I could do anything. I'd be ready to face my boss the following week and defeat my final challenge.

And hopefully, it would bury Tristan once and for all.

But I was going to need to do a bit of embellishment, as Tristan would say, to make the words on the page come closer to the reality of what had happened.

Chapter 27

At the end of the workday, I wanted to take a power nap, but instead I ended up spending some quality time with a baby snuggled on my shoulder, patting his little back after he had eaten. Aida begged me to give her a breather to shower and close her eyes, so Kamal and I hung out together on the sofa with my legs propped up on the coffee table. He wanted to suck on my neck, and it made me giggle. I was nowhere near ready to have kids of my own, but I could understand how mankind continued to propagate based on how easy it was to fall in love with a vulnerable little creature.

Storge was the name I'd found for this kind of unilateral, unconditional, endless love.

When Aida came downstairs with damp hair and bags under her eyes, I offered to stay home. It was only partly altruistic on my part. I was bone tired, as I knew she was. I was also dealing with menstrual cramps, which I no longer confused with preperformance jitters. I wanted to curl up in a fetal position, like Kamal.

But Aida shooed me off, making me promise to crush it, so I finally got myself ready to go out. Makeup was my saving grace. I looked exponentially better than I felt.

I didn't put as much care into my clothes as I had in the past.

Something clean sufficed, so I grabbed recently washed jeans out of the laundry basket and dug out my *Zelda* MAKE IT RAIN T-shirt because it now had bonus significance after private dancing with Alfie to a song with the same name.

When I arrived at the bar, running late, Miranda waved and offered me a club soda. I nodded and headed to the table where Bryce and Zane had already taken up residence. Bryce had been eliminated, but he'd come to support his boyfriend.

There were only five of us left in the running, so assuming three people would be cut tonight, we'd be down to the final two—or final three if I got knocked out since I had a free life. Zane had used his card, and Tristan would presumably play his tonight. Nobody besides the three of us had won one.

My best shot at winning the whole contest would be to knock out either Zane or Tristan tonight, though I wanted Zane to win it all if I didn't.

"I'm gunning for Tristan," I said.

"Good." Bryce pressed his lips together in smug disgust. "He deserves it after what he did last week."

"Thank you." It was nice to have someone on my side. I was ready for this to all be over with. "Good luck, Zane."

"Oh, I don't need luck. I've got the bird-poop story from hell to share."

I guffawed. "For real?"

"Totally true."

"I can't wait."

Alfie came out from the kitchen. When I waved, he smiled and made a beeline for me. I tilted my head back as he leaned down for a quick kiss.

Bryce said, "Y'all need to get a room or something."

I saw Tristan at a table behind him, watching me. He looked away immediately, as if he hadn't been spying. Whatever. He could stare all he wanted.

Beyond him, Reynold leaned against the wall. I caught his eye and he jerked his chin up in acknowledgment. What would he make of the presentation I had planned?

Finally the show got started.

Alfie started us out with a quick limerick.

> "There once was a boy with a bar
> Who picked a girl up in a car
> They kissed in the park
> Exclamation mark
> Now guess who's a rock star?"

I giggled and slapped palms with him as he made his way to the bar.

Heather and Quinn went on next, but neither of them wowed the audience. Maybe everyone was running out of ammunition.

When Miranda called me up, I couldn't help but cast a glance at Tristan, unaware of what I was about to unload on him. If he'd been public enemy number one the week before, this would cement him as the bad guy nobody would vote for. I was about to cost him a thousand dollars, and he'd surely never forgive me for it.

But he deserved to hear how he'd hurt me since he didn't seem to understand the consequences of his actions. While I'd tweaked the details of my journal, the whole story was true.

Once in front of the mic, I remembered how easy it had been to talk to that video game fan at the hospital. I looked out to where I knew Zane and Bryce sat and imagined I was speaking only to them.

I cleared my throat and opened my journal to the entry from hell. Then I began.

"Today, my entire class saw my ass.

"My speech about the impact of violent video games finaled in the competition for my comm class. All I had to do was read it one last time for the win. This was supposed to be a cakewalk. Writing the essay had been the hard part, after all.

"The contest came down to six students: Me, Alexis, Dmitri, Jedidiah, Romi, and Tristan. I knew I had the best presentation. It was *TED Talks* good."

This was all true, though I'd added some context for the benefit of the current audience. I'd actually bragged about my stellar presentation skills, like a fool begging for karma to laugh at my arrogance. That confidence was about to be lost forever, but I didn't know that at the time.

"I'd come dressed in a professional suit—knee-length navy blue skirt, three-inch heels, the works.

"This final round was held in the conference center, on a real stage, four to five hundred students in attendance. A monitor hung behind the podium, and a slideshow cycled through images of the university, mixed in with scheduling information.

"I took my seat with the other finalists in the front row, scanning the program that listed the order we'd be reading. Tristan was first. I'd be following him. Or so that was the official plan.

"But Tristan arrived and sat beside me, urgently whispering, 'I'm gonna be sick. Can you go first? Please?' He made baby eyes at me and added flattery. 'You're so much better at this than I am.'

"I was better at it, but going first was suicidal. He leaned over and said, 'I'll love you forever.'

"Gah. Why'd he have to be so cute? 'Fine,' I said, like it made no difference to me. At least I'd get it out of the way faster and then sit back and relax.

"I should have been leery, though, because Tristan never had a problem presenting his stuff to the class. In fact, he relished the attention. Everyone always laughed at his jokes.

"Maybe he really was sick. 'You should ask to be excused if you aren't well,' I said.

"He scoffed. 'And lose?'

"Typical. I should have challenged him and made him take his place back, but the program began. Ms. Maxwell gave a brief introduction about the speech competition and what it had taken for the six of us to end up on that final stage. I felt giddy with pride as she complimented us on the quality of our work. Then she called Tristan up.

"When I stood and communicated to her with silent body

language that we'd changed things around, she corrected the names, and I climbed the steps onto the stage.

" 'Good morning,' I began, smiling and projecting my confidence. My speech would take no more than ten minutes, and then I'd be done. I stepped across the stage, with a raised hand. 'Violence begets violence,' I said bringing the invisible hammer down, dramatically glaring at the upturned faces of the audience, expecting them to return looks of awe or fear or at worst glassy-eyed boredom.

"The laughter that followed didn't match my content at all.

"I pressed on, talking about the perceived connection between video games and the uptick of violence in society, but the energy from the audience changed, grew disruptive, rowdy. A couple of people pointed toward me and whispered. Others took out their cell phones and snapped pictures or shot video, like we were at a rock concert. The chatter and laughter continued to rise. I stopped talking and looked around to figure out what was going on.

"Behind me, on the monitor, images of Tristan flickered by. Dumbstruck, I watched as he made a face, tongue sticking out, rawker hands framing his head. The slide dissolved. A new Tristan appeared, red-eyed, sitting by a pool, a bottle of beer in one hand and a cigar in the other. In the next, he stood on a beach with a bunch of barely clad girls laughing around him.

"I shot a glance at the real Tristan sitting in the front row, fake confusion on his face. I glared at him.

"I looked at the screen, then back at the crowd, who were now laughing at Tristan in a bathrobe and funny slippers.

"Then a picture I'd never seen of him with his arm around my shoulder, both of us holding a shot of tequila, my eyes so bloodshot, I looked like a laboratory experiment.

"My head was burning from anger or embarrassment. My heart raced with a fight-or-flight urgency. I wanted to tear Tristan's head from his shoulders. Instead, I stomped off to go hide my face forever, but when I hit the top step in those fucking three-inch heels, my ankle twisted, and I missed the step. Just like earlier in the semester, I fell, but this time face-first, with my feet pointed up the stairs, skirt flipped to reveal my ass, while my ankle screamed in pain. So much pain.

"The audience broke out in pandemonium as everyone gawked at my ass now flashing the conference hall, only my bright pink thong giving me any privacy. I needed to get myself upright, but both my wrist and ankle burned. I had to roll over like a human-shaped Slinky down several steps until I'd managed to get my head above my knees.

"Ms. Maxwell, bless her, rushed over to help me up.

"When I finally got on my feet, I pushed the agony out of my mind and hobbled out of the room, completely horrified."

I paused.

Nobody was laughing. I'd started reading this in a fun voice, intended it to be that comedy of tragedy plus time, recalling something that no longer mattered, but my fists were clenched, and I'd nearly snarled as I repeated this event. I couldn't help but add one more piece of information for the jury.

"This might seem small on paper, but all the ease I used to have speaking in front of people evaporated that day. Every public appearance thereafter has been a battle. Whenever I stand at a microphone or on a stage, I will always hear an auditorium full of my peers laughing at me.

"The sole reason I started this contest was to gain that confidence back, and thanks to you all, I think I finally have. Thank you."

I set the microphone back on the stand and took a breath. I'd intentionally left out the horrible aftermath. The fractured ankle that had me on crutches for weeks. The fact that my running career ended that day. The Internet memes students made from one ass-baring photo for months after.

I stepped down from the stage, shaking, pissed, and wondering what Tristan would have to say. Would I finally get a sincere apology? Would he admit what he'd done to me in the quest for victory?

Burning in my rage anew, I thought about Aida asking me

how I'd ever forgiven him. I'd forgiven him because it had been convenient, because I didn't want it between us, but I'd never truly forgotten. Maybe I'd never truly forgiven.

I sat down, surprised steam didn't shoot from my ears. Zane reached over and rubbed my shoulder. I twisted around, looking for Alfie. His was the only hand I wanted comforting me right then.

When Miranda called Tristan up next, I was almost shocked he had the nerve to get up onstage.

Chapter 28

"Bummer," Tristan said into the mic. "I was hoping Sierra wouldn't go there. You should know Sierra has thrown this accusation at me several times in the past few weeks, so out of curiosity I dug up my own entry to compare notes. I had to flip through my entire notebook to find it. But find it I did."

He held the journal aloft and displayed the page with the writing on it, as if it were state's evidence. "Note that this is right here in my notebook. It's even surrounded by other entries. This is what I wrote that same day. No revisions. No embellishments."

He looked out in my direction. "Cross my heart, Sierra."

Then he read.

"Today was completely fubar.

"I woke up feeling like a turd thanks to a massive hangover, but I had to go to some assembly thing because of my stupid essay on weed. I felt like I was going to yak, so I begged the girl who was supposed to go after me to switch places while I pulled my shit together.

"I have no clue what happened next. While she was reading, the display thing photobombed her. My head hurt like it might crack open, and I couldn't figure out why the pics were all of me. I spun around, looking for the source, and noticed an unattended laptop to the side of the stage.

"When the girl speaking saw what was happening, she completely freaked. She looked like she wanted to cry, and then she looked at me like she wanted to murder me, like I had anything to do with it. She was pissed. She stormed off and totally face-planted on the stairs. Man, that had to hurt.

"I started to get up, but Ms. Maxwell pointed a finger at me and told me to stay put.

"As soon as the girl had fled the auditorium, Ms. Maxwell came over and asked what I knew about the prank. I shook my head. I thought I might pass out from the pounding in my ears.

"She told me to get up onstage and continue, but she left the room, chasing after the other girl.

"There was nothing I could do but stand up, though I had to grab the back of the chair when the room spun.

"On my way to the stage, I saw a pale kid rush over to the laptop and mess with it. The monitor onstage went black. The kid fled when I looked back at him.

"One of the other teachers waved me onto the stage, and I made it that far before I puked on my own shoes. It splattered onto my pants and nearly hit the other teacher. I slipped and fell into my own vomit. It covered my hands and knees when I tried to stand. Totally disgusting. I'm pretty sure that will end up on YouTube tonight.

"The whole thing was like a bad nightmare.

"By then some other girl handed me a roll of paper towels and a bottle of Formula 409. Jesus."

Now people in the audience were laughing—with Tristan, not at him. Of course they were. He'd really sold the whole graphic, disgusting mess of his ordeal. And I was just "the girl" who'd had a couple of pictures to deal with.

He was right that a lot of it ended up on YouTube. I hadn't much cared about his problems because video of my own spectacular fall had been shared and reshared as well, and I blamed him for it all. I'd given him a chance to apologize, but he never did. He might have been sick, but I was sure he'd switched places with me to coordinate with the embarrassing pictures. I never knew how he'd pulled it off, but I never doubted he did.

And here he was trying to pin the blame on some mysterious stranger. Convenient.

Tristan hadn't finished talking.

"At the time, I couldn't think who might have wanted to sabotage me, but now that I have a fuller picture, I know perfectly well who that pale kid at the computer was."

He lifted a finger and pointed to the bar.

"It was Alfie Jordan."

I stood up. "Bullshit!"

He had no shame.

"Is it? What did I have to gain from showing pictures from my own Facebook profile? Did you ever doubt that I was legitimately sick that day? You know those pictures were intended to play out during the first presentation to embarrass me, and your boyfriend didn't anticipate we'd change the order, so he couldn't correct it once you started. You were collateral damage."

"Why? Why would he do that? You had all the motive. You're the one who must win at any cost. You sabotaged me back then so you'd beat me just like you did a week ago. It's your M.O."

"You sure about that?" He smirked. "Why don't we ask Alfie why he did it?"

I'd had enough. "Why don't you—"

Before I could finish, the audience sort of gasped in unison as Alfie edged into the spotlight between me and Tristan. The look of shame on his face made my heart sink. His expression confessed it all.

"Alfie?"

"I've wanted to tell you, Sierra." A sigh escaped him like ten years of regret. "I'm so sorry. It was a prank gone wrong." He looked over at Tristan. "I've wanted to apologize to you since it happened, but so much time had passed."

"What?" I couldn't process this. "Why would you do that?"

"I wanted to bring him down." He stared at his feet. "I was angry with him."

Everyone in the bar was watching us like a tennis match. I didn't want to have this argument in public. I marched over and grabbed Alfie's elbow. "Come with me."

I turned back to Tristan. "You stay here."

"What?" He threw up his hands. "What did I do?"

I dragged Alfie through the crowd out the front door. It wasn't private enough, but it would have to do. "Explain."

"Tristan was that guy who always got everything. I wanted to knock him off his pedestal. I saw an opportunity to make a fool out of him and I took it. That whole prank was aimed at him, but then you switched places, and like Tristan said, by the time I realized you were going to present, it was too late to fix it. I never expected it could hurt anyone, and I was horrified by what happened. I'm so sorry. "

"You expected it would hurt Tristan, though."

"What?"

"You said you never expected it could hurt anyone. You meant to hurt Tristan."

He shook his head, his eyes focused on something beyond me. "I told you I was a mess back then, and I couldn't stand him."

My fists clenched. I'd never wanted to punch a wall so badly. "And you never thought to tell me?"

"Back then?" He swallowed. "I wanted to, but I knew you'd hate me forever."

"And now?"

His eyes slid back to mine, almost like he was afraid what he'd see there. "Believe me, I wanted to tell you. I knew it was weak to hide the truth from you, but it also felt sort of poetic that Tristan took the blame, because he might not have done that precise deed, but . . ." His lips pressed together like he was holding in a curse. "I knew if I told you what I'd done, you would have forgiven him, and that would have been fair in the narrowest way possible, but it would have exonerated how he treats people."

I traced through every memory of the past few weeks. There had been infinite opportunities for him to come clean, and he hadn't. Tristan had been warning me all along.

"Holy shit, Alfie, do you know what you did?" All that pain I'd suffered from that one single stupid day. "I've been trying to get my confidence back for ten years now."

"I know. When you came in here that first night, I could see how badly I'd hurt you. I thought I could make things right."

Alfie *had* been eager to help me overcome the damage he'd caused. Had this all been about compensating for his guilt?

"Is that the reason you've been so encouraging the past few weeks? Reparations?"

"No. I mean, yes, I did want to—"

"To fix a problem you created? Was I just a project to you?" The impact of his lie continued to reverberate.

"Sierra, I never intended—"

"It doesn't matter what you intended. You did." I was so disappointed. In him. In me.

"I told you I'm sorry. I made a mistake. Can't you forgive me?"

Like that was so easy. "I've wrongly accused Tristan for doing this for years."

Christ. There was no bottom to this pit of despair.

He narrowed his eyes. "But you forgave him easily enough, right?"

He had some nerve to throw that at me, like we could trade one crime for another.

I wanted to scream at him, but I moderated my tone to explain it to him. "Because I never really *cared* about Tristan!" I thought I had, but Alfie had shown me that I hadn't begun to tap into the vast reserves of love I might feel for the right person. "Not like I'd started to care about you. Can't you understand there's a difference?"

He shook his head. "I thought you said it was because it happened so long ago."

Why wasn't he getting it?

"*This* revelation is news to me, Alfie. You can't expect me to just get over it that easily." He'd taken a wrecking ball to the wall we were building, and the shrapnel kept hitting me. I backed away. "I'm not sure I even know who you are."

He stepped closer, bridging the gap I'd opened. "A week ago, you asked me to forgive you for something that happened years ago." He sounded angry and frustrated, but he had no right to try to box me in with precedent. "Why can't you forgive me?"

He was never going to understand.

I glared into those eyes that had hypnotized me and lured me in. "Fine. You're forgiven for what happened ten years ago." I was mad about it, but on some level, I knew I'd eventually let that go anyway. "But you hid the past from me until today. I don't know whether I can trust you anymore. You deceived me. On purpose, Alfie."

I wanted to talk to Aida to get a handle on this new reality. And Tristan. Shit, I needed to talk to him. He was a mess, but it was time I released him from my wrongful grudge. Dammit, now I owed him an apology.

Alfie crossed his arms and brooded, so I figured we were done talking.

A roar of laughter greeted me when I returned to the bar, and at first I panicked that it might be directed at me, but then I heard Zane's voice regaling the crowd with a story about riding his bike down the cul-de-sac where his crush lived.

The show must go on.

I went to the bar and ordered a gin and tonic, double. I drank it down while Zane described the nature of the bird poop that landed on his shoulder at the precise moment his crush was riding up the street behind him.

"Trapped," he said. "Between love and loss."

Preach, Zane. I was right there with him.

He was a natural-born storyteller, and for a minute, I forgot I was mad, but Alfie came back in and passed me on his way toward the kitchen, maybe toward his apartment, and I had a sour feeling in my stomach.

How could he be the same guy who'd so patiently waited for my attention? Tristan was far from perfect, and he'd been downright shitty the week before, but maybe his bad behavior never disappointed me because I didn't have high expectations of Tristan to begin with. If anyone had been put on a pedestal, it had been Alfie. And now he was laid low like the rest of us, and I didn't know what to do with that.

As Zane finished and the crowd chatter rose, Miranda collected the scorecards before getting up to announce the winners for the night. I no longer cared.

"Moving on to the final round will be . . . Can I get a drumroll, please?" Fingers and palms beat on the tables, and she said, "Tristan and Zane. Congrats, Zane, you won first place for the night."

Heather, Quinn, and I were eliminated. I felt nothing. No regret. Nothing but relief. I'd reached the end of the road. I planned to go home and sleep for days.

Miranda continued. "Next week the showdown finale will be between Tristan and Zane. And Sierra may use her Get Out of Jail Free card to return if she wishes."

No thanks. I was done.

Everyone applauded, and I wended my way through back pats and condolences until I found Tristan.

"We need to talk."

He met my eyes like we'd been fearsome competitors who'd earned each other's full respect. But all he said was, "Yeah."

I glanced over toward the kitchen and saw Alfie edging back into the room. Our eyes connected, and I could only guess what was going through his mind. I knew this was a replay of that long-ago night when he'd seen me kissing Tristan, but I didn't care.

I turned back to Tristan. "I owe you an apology for everything I said."

"I told you I was innocent." He could have been a little more humble.

"Congratulations," I said sarcastically. I wasn't happy with him, either. I grabbed my backpack.

"Let me walk you home." He followed me through the bar.

Once we got outside, I turned and said the things I'd held back in front of a wider audience. "You know, you could have told me your suspicions about Alfie in private."

"Oh, like you would have even listened. You never would have believed me. You were taken in by his whole nice-boy pretense."

"It's not a pretense, Tristan. He actually is nice."

"Then why are you out here with me?"

"Because I'm going home." I turned, but he hooked my elbow and spun me to face him.

"You're out here because what he did to you is unforgivable. You need to reevaluate your preconceptions, Sierra. Maybe I'm the nice one."

"You?" As if.

He grinned. "I'm the last man left."

"Not on Earth, Tristan. You're the last man I'd ever consider."

"Come on. Which one of us has been fighting for you? Which one of us is fighting for you now?"

I tilted my head. "Don't you think I have the autonomy to make decisions without manipulation?"

"At least give me another chance. Get to know me at least. You owe me that."

I disagreed that I owed him anything beyond an apology, but he was right that I'd never gotten to know him. "You know you really piss me off, Tristan."

He winced. "I deserve that."

I started to walk away, but I turned back. "You don't fight fair, and you are way too competitive."

"Nice to meet you, Kettle."

I snorted. The liquor combined with my exhaustion to make me feel more than drunk. Punch drunk. I sighed. "Look, I may have misjudged you."

"That's all I'm saying."

"But you haven't exactly gone out of your way to get to know me, either."

"You haven't exactly given me a chance."

He had a point. We'd been on the precipice of sleeping together one day, and the next, I was on a trajectory toward marriage and babies with another guy. I'd cut Tristan off with no warning.

Maybe I *had* been unfair to him, but I was too tired and

crampy to sort it out tonight. "Fine. Do you wanna come to my yoga class tomorrow at the YMCA?"

He wavered before he said, "The one right up the street here?"

"The very one."

He stepped forward and leaned in like he might kiss me. Instead, he stuck out his hand with a grin. "I will be there."

We shook hands like we'd made peace, but he still had a lot to prove.

Chapter 29

Saturday morning, my phone rang. I let it go to voice mail. A text followed, but I didn't open it.

Alfie wanted to talk, but I already suspected what he'd say. I needed time to process that and decide if and when I could live with it.

Until then I didn't want to see him, hear him, or read him.

Beyond the fact he'd done something so unthinkably cruel, even if it was aimed at Tristan, it was the lie that had me questioning his fundamental integrity. If he'd been willing to mislead me about something so obviously important to me, what else would he lie about? Had our entire relationship been based on his guilt for something he wished he could change?

Sure, he used to like me, but maybe his past feelings for me had turned out to be as flimsy as my feelings for Tristan. The worst thing I could imagine would be faking our way through a hollow relationship because it had the patina of a love I thought we'd found.

Tristan showed up for yoga ten minutes late. If it had been an aerobics class that might not have mattered, but there's an order to yoga, a serenity that comes from moving through each pose. When Tristan knocked on the door, I had to disrupt the flow to let him in and settle him on his own mat.

"Can you follow along?" I whispered.

He sighed. "How long is the class?"

It had taken five minutes to square him away. "Forty-five minutes more. Watch what I do. Do your best."

"How hard can it be?" I shot him eye daggers, and he had the sense to say, "Sorry. I've never done this."

"Exactly."

I apologized to the class and moved us on to the next pose.

Mrs. Shih and Mrs. Gupta exchanged glances. Tristan had managed to tick off my yoga moms.

To his credit, or maybe due to his sheer competitive nature, Tristan shut up and mastered each of the poses. He was more flexible than I would have expected, and his strength served him well. Mrs. Garrett watched him out of the corner of her eye, and no wonder. When he did the Side Crane pose, his leg and arm muscles contracted, showing off his beautiful body. He winked at me, and I couldn't tell if he was flirting or letting me know nothing challenged him.

An image of Alfie doing the same poses flashed through my memory. Comparing and contrasting Alfie and Tristan was like weighing an aged scotch against a light bubbly beer. It wasn't a fair fight. Alfie might take more time to appreciate, but he was complex and serious. And he left a wicked hangover.

When class ended, I expected the ladies to swarm Tristan like they had Alfie, but they all quietly put their things together and said goodbye, each patting me on the arm or giving me a strained smile.

Maybe they'd gotten a clue they shouldn't intrude so much in my life.

Fat chance.

Mrs. Martinez was the last to leave, and she leaned in for a hug, whispering in my ear, "I hope Alfie will come back again."

I turned my face away when she drew back so she wouldn't see the tears filling my eyes. Damn hormones. "See you next week."

Tristan waited by the door. "Can't I walk you home?"

I unlocked my bike while he fetched his Vespa, and together we pushed our cycles along the sidewalk, like we were rolling broken purchases away from a garage sale.

We passed right in front of Alfie's bar, and I glanced up at the French windows, wondering if he might be looking out. My stomach churned, but I'd been having cramps all morning.

Tristan and I turned onto the street he and I had once walked along in the moonlight. Alfie and I had walked it, too. I'd willed Tristan to kiss me that night, but he'd disappointed me. I chuckled at how easily I'd been disappointed at the loss of something I'd never had, something I'd never really wanted. It was a pale imitation of true heartache.

I'd always crushed on Tristan because he was pretty, therefore, I wanted to know him—the exact opposite of my relationship with Alfie. I got to know Alfie, and he'd become beautiful.

Ludus. That was the name for uncommitted flirtatious love—seduction, teasing, playing. All my adult life, I'd been mistaking *Ludus* for *Eros.* Keeping my relationships light and bubbly, I'd walked away unscathed.

Until now.

As we approached the town house, Tristan asked, "Can I come up?"

I hadn't realized I'd signed up for more time in his company, and I couldn't deal with him for another hour. "It's been a rough week."

"We could play video games again."

I thought about the last time we raced, then recalled Alfie laughing as he passed me at the last second. I swallowed the lump in my throat.

"Not today. I'm still trying to catch up on my sleep."

"Tomorrow?"

I pulled the elastic out of my ponytail and shook my hair free. I hadn't put on a lick of makeup earlier that morning. Maybe all I'd needed was to be an absolute asshole to Tristan and I would have had him wrapped around my finger.

"We'll see."

Aida sat on the front porch, rocking a wee bundle. I took that as my excuse to tell Tristan I'd talk to him later in the week and sent him on his way. I refrained from adding, "Scat."

Before he put on his helmet, he bumped my shoulder with his fist, like he might a little sister. "See ya soon."

As soon as he'd disappeared around the corner, I climbed the steps, and a sigh transformed into a sob. Then I began to ugly cry.

Aida said, "That's how I feel whenever I see Tristan, too."

I laughed through my blubbering. I took the other rocker and dropped my face into my hands, still suffering the aftershocks. My shoulders shook, and Aida reached over to rub my back. "It's okay, Sierra. It will be okay."

I wanted to believe her. I wanted to let go of this rage even yoga hadn't diffused. "I miss him."

"So go to him."

"It's not that easy."

"He's right down the street. What could be so hard?"

I twisted my head around to look at her. "The guy I fell in love with doesn't exist."

Her eyes rolled. It was subtle but I caught it. "Such drama. The guy you fell in love with is alive and well and probably waiting for you to go talk to him."

If she wasn't holding a baby, I might have been tempted to punch her. How dare she trivialize a serious character flaw? She'd hated on Tristan for the exact same crimes.

"The guy down the street is a liar. At least when I thought Tristan had pulled that prank, I'd believed he'd done it to beat me in a contest. It hadn't been so personal. But what Alfie did? How'd he even manage to pull it off?"

"Marco figures he set it up on a timer and couldn't stop it while you were onstage without you seeing him."

I stared at her, blinking. At least she'd made me stop crying. "You two are analyzing this like it's a common crime drama?"

"It's fascinating. Marco has this one theory—"

I held up a hand. "Enough." I couldn't believe she was casually discussing the literal trigger of my current trauma.

* * *

On Monday, Tristan showed up at my office, uncharacteristically sporting a business suit. He looked like the prettiest version of Link if *The Legend of Zelda* were set in a modern-day corporate America.

"To what do I owe the pleasure?" I asked.

He leaned against my desk. "I ran into that guy who works here at the bar the other night. He said I should come in."

Marco had invited him? "Do you need me to show you the way?"

"That would be great."

I led him down the hall. When I knocked on the doorframe, Marco startled awake.

"You wanted to see Tristan?"

"What?" He rubbed his eyes, then stood and held out his hand to shake. "Oh, hey."

I left them to talk, a little pissed off that neither had warned me in advance.

But I turned my focus to setting up the demo for my final chance to audition. In the conference room, as I loaded up the video, Reynold entered, trailed by Tristan.

"Um." I blinked, trying to understand what was happening. "Why is he here?"

Reynold tilted his head toward Tristan. "We were talking in my office when I got the reminder."

Tristan grimaced. "Sorry, you misunderstood. My meeting was with Reynold."

How? I recalled Reynold at the bar, praising Tristan's performance. Had he approached Tristan on Friday? What was happening?

As I returned to the podium, my thigh clipped the conference table, and I dropped the notecards in a fanned-out pile at Reynold's feet. Tristan knelt to pick them up and handed them to me in no order at all.

"Give me a minute," I said, sorting them. At least they were numbered.

Reynold moved to the other side of the conference table and leaned against the window.

The video started, and I said, "*Capture Castle* . . . I mean *Castle Capture* is a multimedia online . . . I mean a multi*player* online role-playing game."

Fuck.

I sighed. "Can I start that over? I'm a little frazzled."

Reynold lifted an eyebrow, and I realized he thought I was having a crisis of nerves again. It wasn't that at all.

I squeezed my fists together. "*Castle Capture* is a multiplayer online role-playing game in the style of *Final Fantasy.*"

There. This would be easy if I didn't overthink it. I just needed to get rolling.

Reynold stopped me. "Could you add a little more personality to it?"

"Personality?"

"Pizzazz." He lifted his shoulder from the wall and looked from me to Tristan. "I have an idea."

I didn't think I was going to like this.

"Let's see how Tristan does."

No. I hadn't spent weeks preparing to hand it over to fucking Tristan. "What? Reynold. You're supposed to be letting me do this."

"I'm just curious. Tristan tells me he has sales experience. I want to see him try it."

Sales experience? "I thought you worked in graphic design."

I glared at him but held the cards out, fighting back a childish urge to fling them in his face.

"Just read them?" Tristan shrugged. He didn't care. He hadn't been working toward this goal for the past six weeks. So of course he began right off with his charming charismatic smile even though he read exactly what I'd written, which was, "*Castle Capture* is a MMORPG."

I snorted when he tried to say the acronym as a word. But as he continued, I had to admit he sounded like a natural-born salesman. I'd worked so hard, and Tristan might waltz in here and take my dream away from me. How dare he even consider presenting my demo?

I got up. "Would you both excuse me?"

Reynold had the nerve to ask, "Don't you want to learn how to present yourself better?"

"Actually, I wanted you to have a bit more confidence in me."

"Suit yourself."

I headed to my office, feeling blindsided. Would Reynold hire him just to demo the game? It made me laugh to imagine Tristan's disappointment to get hired as a salesman rather than an artist after all that maneuvering.

As I passed by Reynold's office, I took a gander in, hoping to find the bag Tristan always had on him. It sat open on a chair, and I stared at it. It would be so wrong to snoop in his things, but then again, hadn't he done the same to me? Was turnabout fair play? And wasn't he betraying me right this minute in the conference room with Reynold? Even after I'd invited him to my yoga class? I was such an idiot.

Besides, I was only interested in one thing. Sure enough, his notebook was tucked inside.

I glanced behind me, my hands shaking at this invasion. I'd make a terrible spy. I slid it out and opened the cover.

My journal had an entire semester's worth of cramped writing. Page after page filled with stories and nonsense.

Tristan's journal, in contrast, had half-finished pages and places where the handwriting and ink color didn't match. Maybe where he'd been revising the past for laughs.

A loose page slipped out, missing a corner—the entry I'd come for. I grabbed it and left, not wanting to be caught in the act of stealing. Even if I was only taking back what was mine.

Back at my desk, I flattened the page, adrenaline in my mouth from the double tension of having committed a nefarious act of espionage and of anticipating the words Tristan had read, the words that had hurt Alfie.

But none of those words were there.

What I'd journaled was in a way so much worse.

Long day. I'm a wee bit woozy from all the festivities, but with all my tests and—

Something illegible.

Went downtown and ran into the twins, Thad and Perry, who bought me a round. Who would say no? Some other kids from comm class showed up. Daphne, Sean, Alfie, and I hit some of the bars on Toomer's Corner.

It was getting late, and my head was spinning, so maybe I dreamed the last thing that happened. Out of nowhere Tristan appeared. I practically swooned into him, and he caught me. I grabbed his shirt to steady myself, and next thing I knew, he was kissing me. Maybe he was drunk, too. Maybe I imagined it.

He's not answering my texts, so maybe I did.

I remember I fell backward into a chair and missed. I may have broken my tailbone from hitting the floor. I guess I'll know tomorrow.

It didn't exactly absolve me, but at least I hadn't been as evil as Tristan had painted me. Still, I'd chummed around with Alfie and then sailed on past him.

I turned the page over and there, in pencil, I found Tristan's version of events. He'd melded together two recollections into one fiction with enough truth woven in to wreak havoc.

Had Alfie's shared memory been real, or had Tristan made him recall things slightly differently?

I wanted to show it all to Alfie, but this was old news, letters from a battle we'd already waged. What I should have stolen were Tristan's actual journal pages to deconstruct his revisionist history.

I stepped down the hall, but as soon as I neared Reynold's doorway, Tristan swung around the corner.

"Hey, Sierra."

For a beat, I considered telling him what I'd discovered, but it seemed prudent to keep it to myself. "So, are you working here, now?"

"They're running the background check now. Reynold seems to like me."

He paused, but one foot continued to point away from me.

"Are you going to do the demo in Germany?"

"I don't know. I guess. If they asked me to, why wouldn't I?"

I tried to keep the panic out of my voice. "You know that's the whole reason I entered the contest. I needed to prove I could do that demo. It's my only chance to go to the con."

He shrugged. "Yeah, well, I entered the contest to win the money so I could seed my comic book, but you didn't seem to care."

"But you're getting a job here, right?"

"No thanks to you. I begged you to get me in here, and this guy Reynold had no trouble finding me a position."

He'd used me. He'd totally used me. I pointed from him to me. "So what was all this about?"

"I like you, Sierra. I really do." His earnest expression gave way to that competitive smirk I knew all too well from contest nights. "And I'll still like you when I win the contest, and when I start working here. And when I demo your game in Germany."

I had to get away before I punched him in the eye. How had I ever found him remotely attractive?

"Fuck you, Tristan."

"I'd still be open to that."

"You're never going to work here."

At least that wiped the smug smile off his face before I turned and stormed back to my office.

I stewed for an entire day, considering threatening to quit if Reynold hired Tristan, but after battling demonic hordes in *Diablo*, my anger began to dissipate. A cold plan began to form in its place.

I kept letting Tristan off the hook for everything he'd done. He'd behaved way worse than Alfie toward me since forever, so why had I kept forgiving him when I couldn't forgive Alfie for one misstep, literally the same transgression I'd given Tristan a pass on?

In a fit of rage, I'd told Alfie it was because I didn't care about Tristan—which nobody would have believed based on history. And yet it was true. I'd been fascinated by him, but how could I care about him when I never really knew him? He'd always been more like a computer simulation than a real person.

How could I get mad at artificial intelligence? Might as well hold a grudge against a computer-generated Donkey Kong.

Whenever he hurt me, I shook it off because it was the way the game had been programmed. His behavior was as predictable as code. I'd never truly cared for him because I knew he could never care for me.

Tristan had always done what was best for Tristan.

When Alfie hurt me, it was real. When Alfie hurt me, I bled.

By Wednesday, I knew what I needed to do, so I texted Reynold and asked him to meet me. As Marco and I drove in, I asked, "Who's running the background check on Tristan?"

"Actually"—he grinned—"Aida handed the reins over to me. She's registered her vote of no confidence. I'm assuming you're opposed. Reynold's got a bug up his ass about that boy for some reason. That leaves me to take a side."

"Put me out of my misery. Are we hiring him?"

A little smile played at his lips as he parked. "What do we look for in our employees?"

"The quest for the Holy Grail?" We sought talent, experience, and some indefinable quality that couldn't be captured on paper. A work ethic. A passion for the games. But above all, no assholes.

He nodded and slipped a paper out of his leather messenger bag. "Tell me what you see?"

I scanned down Tristan's work history and looked back at Marco. "He's a shoe salesman?"

"Yes. This paper doesn't reveal what an asshole he is, but I can prove Tristan lacks the experience to work in our graphic arts department."

"He really was a salesman." I started to laugh, but then realized what that meant. "Reynold may still hire him for the demo based on this."

Marco winced. "I guess that part is up to you."

An hour later, I tapped on Reynold's door. He waved me in. "What did you need, Sierra?"

"Another chance." I crossed the office to approach his desk, more confident than I felt. "You threw me off my game by bringing Tristan in."

He shrugged. "I did give you a chance, but you fumbled it."

"I know the game. I can do this. What would convince you, Reynold?"

He banged his fist into the desk. "Fire, Sierra. I need to see some passion. Sell. The. Game."

"I can do that." I wasn't sure I could, but I couldn't let him see me blink. "Please give me another chance."

I was so frustrated with everything. A week ago, I'd been content that my plans were going my way. I'd been making progress with the presentation, confident it would go well. And I'd been certain I was falling in love.

I thought I owed Tristan an apology for assuming he'd been a dick. And then he turned out to be a dick anyway. I kept forgiving him. And I kept scapegoating and hurting Alfie.

That was going to change. Starting now.

Chapter 30

On Friday after work, I crept up the stairs to Aida's room, where she lay on her side, nursing Kamal. I sat on the floor. "So despite everything, it looks like Tristan is going to be sent to Germany. And I feel super used."

"Yeah, well, you kind of suck at judging people."

"Uh, thanks."

"Have you decided what you're doing tonight?"

The contest. "I've been eliminated."

"Oh, well, that's too bad."

"But I won a Get Out of Jail Free card I could use to return for the last night."

Aida asked, "So? What are you going to do, Sierra?"

"I don't know."

I could just stay out and let Tristan have it. But dammit, I didn't want him to walk away with something else that could be mine without a challenge. He'd been playing dirty from the start, and I wanted to see him go down. I wanted to sabotage him or throw pies at him. I empathized with how Alfie had felt back in college.

Not that I could absolve his methods.

"Have you talked to Alfie?"

"What can I say to him? I wouldn't blame him if he didn't want to talk to me after how I've acted."

"There's something for you downstairs. Go see."

On the kitchen table, a vase held the most perfect yellow roses. The card read, *I don't deserve this (but I'd like a chance to try).*

He must have known I'd recognize the reference to the Ed Sheeran song we'd danced to alone in his apartment, when we were learning to trust in what we'd found in each other.

That was all I needed to know. Alfie wouldn't fight for me like Tristan had pretended to. No tricks or coercion. Just a simple act of hope. Alfie's way took so much more courage.

With that the waterworks started again. I dropped into the chair, hands folded, with my forehead resting on my wrists. I'd never cried so much in my life, but I was torn up.

The card slid out of my hand as Aida invaded my privacy. "These are from Alfie, right?"

"Who else?"

She took a chair beside me, Kamal wrapped snug against her. "Just making sure there isn't some third suitor you haven't mentioned."

I snorted. "Only one that matters."

"So what now?"

Trust and communication. I'd failed at both. I'd made such a hash of things.

Alfie was right. I'd been unfair, expecting him to be utterly perfect. Nobody was perfect.

I'd conveniently forgotten what *Corinthians* also taught: Love keeps no record of wrong.

It was time I let go of petty grievances and grew up. It's time I piloted my ship instead of trying to stay safe on shore.

"I'm going to the contest," I said.

She sat up. "Okay. I'm putting Marco on alert that he'll be on his own tonight. I need to get out of this house, anyway. I'll totally be there for you."

"But I'm going to lose."

She scowled. "Say what now?"

"I won't get any votes for what I intend to say."

"So why are you doing it?"

"Because there's a bigger prize."

Aida and I arrived at the bar together as we had six weeks earlier, except this time I wasn't nervous for the same reasons I had been. I was still scared of the microphone and standing in front of the crowd, but it had been a mountain I'd conquered repeatedly now. I was nervous for what I planned to say. I'd run out of funny journal entries that would put me over the top, but I'd adjusted my view on what it would mean to win. I'd probably lost the one thing I'd originally wanted—the trip to Germany. And I may have lost something I hadn't known I'd needed.

I was here to fight for what was important.

We were late, and the place was mobbed. I stood on my toes to peer over shoulders and see if Alfie might be tending bar. I made eye contact with Isaac, and he gave me an ominous look, one brow cocked as if he'd heard nasty rumors about me. Maybe Alfie had told him I'd been a jerk.

Tristan had already arrived and sat surrounded by some of the people who'd been eliminated in earlier rounds. It was like a grand reunion for a thing that hadn't lasted as long as a gallon of milk in my fridge. Zane and Bryce had a table, so I dragged Aida over and introduced her.

"You ready?" I asked Zane.

"Yup. You?"

"Not at all."

It wasn't long before Miranda called everyone to attention. Since the only people left were me, Tristan, and Zane, I'd be going first for once. My stomach flipped. I scanned the room for Alfie, hoping he wouldn't hide out in the back or upstairs during the contest, but he emerged from the kitchen in time to jump up on stage with his own words.

"Welcome to the grand finale of the Chagrin Challenge. Let's have a round of applause for all our contestants." He waited for the clapping to quiet. "It took courage to get up here and share the awkwardness and mortification, and we sincerely thank you for making us laugh or cringe. And I know how hard it was since I've been trying to participate in my own way. I'm not copping out tonight. I'm going to share one last poem before we bring up the real talent."

He held up a piece of paper.

"This is called Outsider.

"Brick by brick
A wall, then two
A solid floor
A window, a door
No key in the lock
Can we talk?
Knock, knock."

The audience laughed as though it was a big joke, and someone yelled, "Who's there?"

When it was clear Alfie was done, everyone applauded. He'd probably win his own contest if popularity were the only judge.

I watched him as he handed off the mic to Miranda, and it hurt how much I missed him. He had the kindest eyes and a courage he didn't realize. He'd lent me that courage for the past few weeks, and I hadn't even appreciated how much emotional labor he'd done for me. I'd only seen what he might cost me.

Miranda called me up, and I stood, pegging Alfie with my eyes, hoping he'd understand I needed him to stay. He headed toward the bar and took a stool.

I climbed up the steps to the platform into a spot that had become comfortable with familiarity. Alfie had been so right about that. I couldn't see him through the spotlight, but I looked in his direction. If my nerves took over now, I'd be doomed. I needed to remember everything I wanted to say. This was more important than any Gamescon demo.

I'd thought the room had been quiet before, but the silence

became deafening. I felt like I was alone, speaking into the muffled darkness.

But I wasn't alone. And I was speaking to one person.

My stomach didn't clench. I didn't want to run. I wasn't even reading from a piece of paper. This was from the heart.

"Embarrassment comes in many forms. A few weeks ago, standing right here, I knew I'd be setting myself up to be mortified a second time for the things that had been bad enough the first time around.

"I came here, scared, with no other goal than to prove I could do this. I nearly left before I spoke the first words, but Alfie stopped me and said the only thing that could have made me stay. He gave me permission to quit but also reminded me I could fake it, and so I stepped up here that first night, knees shaking. And I made it.

"The next week, I wasn't even going to come back, but Alfie called me. And again, he told me something I needed to hear, that quitting was the same as losing, and he was right. I came back and I didn't lose.

"So, thank you, Alfie. Week after week, you've breathed confidence into me when I thought I had none. You told me who I am, and I believed you because you believed in me.

"And while I've heard everything you said to me that helped me, I haven't been hearing you. I told you I see you. And I do. But I wasn't listening. And I'm sorry.

"You didn't just tell me who you are; you showed me. You are patient and kind. You don't envy or boast, nor are you proud or self-seeking. You're not easily angered, and you keep no record of wrongs. You always trust, always hope, always persevere. You are love, Alfie.

"I'm sorry I let a ten-year-old wound re-open and shake the foundation we were building. We'd barely begun to find our footing. I never told you I loved you. You never told me you loved me. But all that time, I was falling in love. Seven different ways. Because, Alfie, I see you, and I may not deserve you, but you are worth everything.

"I know I'm sacrificing my spot in the contest by baring my soul instead of sharing some funny anecdote, but you know what? For the first time since I've stood up here, I'm not embarrassed or ashamed of a word I'm saying.

"Alfie, I don't know if you'll ever forgive me for reacting so poorly, but know that I will regret it for the rest of my life if I broke the only relationship that will ever matter to me.

"I'm sorry.

"I love you, Alfie Jordan.

"Yes, we can talk."

I stepped back from the microphone, bowed my head once, then turned to walk off the stage.

The audience didn't seem to know how to respond. There was an errant clap, like someone took my exit as a signal to applaud, and that was followed by another couple of claps scattered about, but mostly, everyone watched me as I wended between the tables straight back to the bar, where I took one of his hands in mine. "Can you forgive me?"

"Forgive you?" He tilted his head. "Are you saying you forgive me?"

"All I wanted to tell you is that I've been an idiot for the past week, and I'm sorry. Everything else I thought I wanted was wrong. If I lost everything else but won you back, I'd be complete."

"Win me back? Did you think you could ever lose me? I thought I'd lost *you*. I didn't know what to do about it. You were so mad, and I just wanted to talk to you."

Miranda called Tristan up.

"We do need to talk," I said, wanting to drag Alfie anywhere else because Tristan had a history of ruining everything in a way I couldn't predict, and the easiest way to defeat him would be to avoid him altogether.

Tristan jumped up onstage and began with his usual arrogance. "That was indeed mortifying."

A couple of people chuckled. I shook my head and whispered

in Alfie's ear, "Can we leave?" He slipped off the stool, and we threaded our way through the crowd toward the kitchen door that would lead us to the safety of his loft.

Tristan's voice followed us.

"You know, the first time I ever saw Sierra, I thought, now there's a nerdy girl. It took me a while to realize she was pining for me. And oh boy, she had it bad. In college, I had a lot of girls interested in me, and the only reason Sierra stood out was that rack. For a nerd girl, she had it going on in the tits department."

His first words pegged me in place, just like he intended.

A couple of guys laughed. I crossed my arms. How could anyone encourage that? And shouldn't he be disqualified for inappropriate comments?

Alfie nudged me, and I clenched my fists tight, then released the tension and continued to push through people standing behind the tables.

"So, I have to confess my own mortification. Ten years have passed since I was that cool guy."

I slowed again, wondering if he'd show an ounce of humility.

"How's this for embarrassing? I asked Sierra out, and can you imagine that I couldn't even pick her up because I don't have a car? I only have a scooter. Me, the superstud from college, reduced to an average loser. The worst.

"I took her out to dinner. It wasn't a fancy restaurant because I only had forty-seven dollars in my bank account." He shook his head with a self-deprecating laugh. "Try making any kind of impression with forty-seven dollars."

Despite everything, my heart clenched. I had no idea he was struggling that badly.

"I humiliated myself asking her to help me find a better paying job where she works, but she refused. I managed to get an offer on my own, and man, I was so relieved. I'd finally be able to get out of this hole. But guess what? Sierra somehow had me blackballed."

His voice cracked, and I held my hand over my mouth, horrified by every new revelation.

"That's one reason I entered this contest. I told her I needed to win this so I could seed the idea I have for a comic book, but she said she didn't care. She planned to crush me for sport even though, as she just confessed, she never cared about the win. She's just trying to overcome some anxiety. Can you imagine being so entitled you enter a contest with a thousand-dollar cash prize even though you admit you don't care about the money? Wouldn't we say she's already gotten all she can out of it?"

I couldn't drag my eyes away or stop listening to Tristan's roast. If I hadn't already thrown away my chance, this character assassination would have knocked me out. He was making *me* wonder if I'd been too harsh on him. The crowd was going to hand him the money at this rate.

"It gets worse."

He licked his lips, and I stupidly waited to hear what would come next.

"You know, I really thought she liked me. Didn't you? Y'all heard how she waxed rhapsodic about me, right? I thought with that much adoration, I might get some action, but she's a tease. She'll bat her eyelashes, then stomp on your dick."

"Such a nice girl."

Alfie's hand crushed mine, tugging me out of my paralysis, and I knew he was fighting the urge to rush the stage and punch Tristan's lights out. But as the owner of the bar, he couldn't do that. His only recourse was to get the hell out of there.

"But that's not the worst part.

"The worst was that she threw me over in favor of that same dweeby guy who she'd ignored in college. Sadly, Sierra couldn't figure out where she fell on the food chain and neglected him then. Now ten years later, here she is begging for that loser's attention. Hilarious."

Sympathy forgotten, I let go of Alfie's hand and strode toward the stage. He could attack me all he wanted, but as soon as he started slagging Alfie, he summoned a hell beast.

Tristan couldn't see me coming.

"At first, I thought she was looking for an edge, since he runs this contest. There's no possible way she would prefer him to me, right? Look at the guy."

That was when I heard myself shouting, "Shut up! Shut up! Shut up!"

To my astonishment he did. He lifted an eyebrow and smiled so smugly, I couldn't hold it in any longer. I moved close enough to enter the sphere of spotlight, so he'd have to look me in the eyes when I unleashed my wrath.

"You!" My finger pointed at him like it could shoot lasers. "You troglodyte narcissistic sexist caveman asshole. You are so entitled to believe you could step up to that microphone and win automatically because . . . why? Because you were born with passing looks and average height? You think everyone else gets ahead by cheating or by taking a shortcut, and you bitterly believe that when your privilege is put in question it's because someone else is taking something from you. I thought maybe you'd changed since college, but I don't think you've had one introspective moment in your entire life that didn't lead to you believing your own self-written press. You tried to use me to get a job! And you know what's funny about that? You never bothered to find out that I founded the company you want to work at. Yes, *me*! I am part owner, and while I don't hire people, I can sure as fuck fire them."

Man, it felt good to get that off my chest.

"As for the person you refer to as a dweeb, Alfie is a grown man who looks out for others. Unlike you, he has bettered himself in the past ten years, and you aren't worthy to know him."

I took a deep breath to continue on before I remembered where we were. I looked over the faces of strangers all staring at me with popcorn-eating expressions, entertained by all the drama because they weren't a part of it. Then I saw Reynold leaning against the far wall, eyes wide.

Tristan opened his mouth, but I had something left to say. "And you're right. I didn't need to win the money. You and

Zane can duke it out. I got more out of this contest than I came for. I only hope I haven't lost what matters."

As if to answer that question, Alfie laid a hand on my shoulder, and I said, "Can we get out of here now? I have things to say to you."

"I'd like that."

"Vote for Zane!" I yelled and tugged Alfie after me through the kitchen and toward the back stairs.

Chapter 31

The sounds of the crowd faded as we climbed his stairs. He held my hand, and I followed behind him, no longer the least bit nervous. It was like I'd never known nerves in my life. The confidence I felt about Alfie was total, and I'd almost missed it because of an inability to let something go that I should have forgotten years ago.

He unlocked the door, and before it clicked shut behind us, he spun me and kissed me again. "Did you mean what you said? Do you really forgive me?"

"Yes." I laid a palm to his cheek, looking into his beautiful eyes. "We both hurt each other without meaning to. Tristan's been trying to drive a wedge between us, and I almost let him."

"No, I'm totally at fault. I should have come clean years ago. It's no excuse, but Tristan had been bullying me that whole semester, and I hated that he of all people had everything handed to him. I couldn't help it; I wanted to embarrass him.

"When Ms. Maxwell sent a few of us in early to set up the contest, and I saw the PowerPoint slideshow, I didn't even think. I started downloading every unflattering picture I could find of him from his public Facebook photos, and I built a second slideshow. It was easy to swap them out when Tristan was called to the stage, but when you went up . . ." He sighed. "I should have gone over and yanked the laptop plug from the wall, but I was afraid you'd see me, and that only made things worse."

I could envision the entire scene. "I have to confess I've come to understand why someone would want to murder Tristan."

He gave me a half smile. "It was the wrong way to go about it. I saw how I hurt you, but it was too late. I'm so sorry. It was wrong of me. I should have told you sooner."

I listened and couldn't disagree. "Yeah, it was wrong, Alfie, but you learned from your mistake and you changed. You went on to be a better person. You make me want to be a better person."

He brushed my hair off my forehead and pressed a kiss there. "I hope I've made myself into someone good enough for you."

"You are, Alfie." I thought about the past week and how stupid I'd been. "You asked me why I'd forgiven Tristan so easily, but then got so angry at you. The truth is, my disappointment with Tristan was baked in. Enough time had passed that his betrayal no longer surprised me, and I didn't expect a lot from him. The sad thing is that I don't expect a lot from most men. In my experience, every man will eventually let me down."

His shoulders dropped. "I never meant to—"

"And then I met you. You were everything I didn't know I was missing. It turns out there are princes among men. But the hope you gave me crumbled when I discovered you of all people had deceived me. It reinforced my worst expectations and fears."

"Sierra—"

"Shhh." I laid a finger over his lips. "I thought it proved you were too good to be true, especially since you *are* too good for me. But I was wrong, and I'm so sorry. I should have trusted you. I should have talked to you and given you a chance."

He kissed my finger, and I lifted it, permission to speak.

"You have nothing to apologize for." Of course, his first response would be to absolve me.

"Oh, Alfie. I love you. You've become like my best friend in such a short time." I laughed as his face dropped at the moniker. "Yes, my *friend*. And my lover. My soul mate. I love how you've learned to love yourself. I love how you've taught me to love myself."

He ran a thumb along my cheek, and I realized a tear had loosed itself. I didn't know when or why I'd started crying. Happiness? Maybe relief?

"Well, that is quite convenient since I fell in love with you a long time ago."

The power of those words broke something loose in my spirit, and I sobbed. "How could you have been in love with me? You barely know me."

"I know you, Sierra." He gazed into my eyes, connecting soul to soul. "I knew it wasn't real love at first. Just a fascination with a girl who intrigued me. When you came into my bar, I felt that spark again. I can't believe how lucky I am that you saw me."

"I see you, Alfie. I will always see you."

He touched my chin with his knuckle and tipped my face up for a kiss. "Do you realize we just had our first real fight?"

"And I'm still here. Does that mean we get to have sex now?"

His eyes widened. "That reminds me! I have something for you."

I waggled my eyebrows. "Is that a euphemism?"

He laughed. "Come with me."

"That's still sex talk."

He tugged my hand, and I followed him up the ladder stairs to his loft, where he opened what I considered the condom drawer and produced an envelope.

Inside, I found two printed pages. The first said *Gamescon*, and I eyed it curiously before flipping to the second that read *Lufthansa*. "You bought me a trip to the conference?"

He shrugged. "In case the flowers didn't work."

"This is too much, Alfie."

"I was afraid you'd say that, but I was so worried you'd drop out of the contest because of me, and then you might be rattled when you presented to Reynold, and I couldn't stand the thought of you losing out on the trip when it was all you wanted, and you've worked so hard. You deserve to go."

"Thank you." I didn't know if I could accept such an extravagant gift, but the care he'd shown in organizing it floored me. "I love you for doing this. I love you for making my dream come true. I love you, Alfie. But you're wrong."

His eyebrows knit together. "I am?"

"Yes. Because all I want is you."

I hugged him, and his arms wrapped around my back. It was just supposed to be a hug of gratitude, but I hadn't felt his body against mine in over a week, and the smell of him brought back a rush of desire and longing.

He kissed my cheek and whispered, "Did you say you love me?"

"Many times."

"Say it again."

I shoved him onto the bed. "I love you, Alfie."

"I've missed you." He leaned forward and claimed my mouth, but I needed more than kisses.

I worked the buttons on his shirt and stripped his torso bare. "Mmm. I've had dirty thoughts about your chest."

He worked my shirt over my head. "Same."

I ground into him, feeling him through his jeans. "You're still wearing too many clothes."

"Same."

I lifted up to open his fly, then stood to help him wiggle free. While I was up, I dug in his drawer for a condom, and finding it, ripped it open. I handed it to him to let him roll it on, then slid off my pants and straddled him, rubbing against him while I kissed him, until we were both panting. He was so hard against me, and I needed him, so I positioned him and slid down his shaft. He sucked in his breath and then whispered in my ear. "I love you, Sierra."

I kissed him long and hard as I rocked up and back down again.

"Let me make love to you." He knocked me over onto his bed and reentered me as his lips found mine. Then he began to move slowly, languorously, deliciously, his hands roaming across my body. He felt so good, so perfect, the pleasure grew until I thought I'd go right over the edge, but I hovered there with him, working my hips against his, both of us picking up the speed until we were breathing heavily and making the occasional outburst of moans and groans.

I wanted more than his body. I wanted everything that made him Alfie. I wished there was a way to bind our entire beings, souls or essences or whatever made us separate creatures. I wanted to slip into his skin and know him. I wanted our hearts to combine into one.

It all became too much, and I went over the edge, like rushing rapids at the precipice of a waterfall. I hit the bottom with a cry, just as he shuddered and dropped his head to my shoulder.

"Oh, shit," he said. "I couldn't hold back."

"Right there with you." I wrapped an arm around his back and pulled him to me, and we clung to each other in that bliss, exhausted, spent, completely one.

His phone rang, and he peeked at it. "It's Miranda. Do you want to know who won?"

"I couldn't care less."

He got up and started to dress. "Well, I have to go cut a check. Come on. We can't hide from the real world forever."

I couldn't understand why not, but I dressed and followed him back to the crowded bar where everyone waited for the announcement. Alfie climbed the stage, and Miranda handed him a giant envelope, like we were at the Oscars.

"And the winner is . . ." He fumbled with the seal then folded the card open. "Zane!"

I hooted, and the audience cheered. Zane bent and kissed Bryce, and I no longer envied them. I no longer felt any negative energy, not even toward Tristan, who walked out of the bar, hopefully never to return.

Just like that, I let it all go, ten years of pent-up hostilities, and I felt a peace like I'd never known.

I joined in the celebration for Zane, catching him in a hug to congratulate him while Miranda took pictures of us for the Instagram feed.

And through it all, Isaac sold drink after drink at the bar.

I found Reynold there, drinking his scotch. He appraised me

with his mustache tilted. "I've never seen you like that. Where did all that passion come from?"

"From fighting for what I believe in." This was true now.

He raised his glass. "That's what I've been waiting to see."

"So? What are you saying?"

"We begin work on Monday."

"But the trip is mine?"

"Looks like you're the only one left."

Aida slid in between us. "What did I tell you, Reynold? You should have just trusted me to begin with." She looked at me. "You, too."

I hugged her. "Thank you. I'll never doubt you again."

She held my shoulder and gave me a significant look. "Grab hold of that boy and never let go. It's not just that there are so few gems like him, but I can see how he makes you feel. And it's clearly mutual."

I looked over at Alfie, laughing as he chatted with Zane and Bryce, happy and in his element. "How I didn't notice him sooner will be the great mystery of my life. Maybe it's because he's so easy. He fits me so perfectly, it's like slipping into warm water."

"I don't think that's it, or you'd still be with Howard."

"Well, I can't explain it." In the seven types of love, I'd never found anything that described what I felt for Alfie.

"You don't have to. It's how things are with Marco. We were made for each other. It's not always perfect, but I wouldn't want to be without him."

That was it.

"I felt like something was missing all week. I couldn't figure out why, but the minute I saw him again, I knew. It was him."

"Are we losing our babysitter?" She slid her purse on her shoulder, getting ready to head out.

"I haven't moved out, Aida. But even if I do, I'll be right down the street. I can always come back."

"Nope. I'm going to start giving your things to Goodwill soon. Your space is going to make a great playroom."

"So is Alfie's." I couldn't resist a wicked smile, and she shook her head, but she was smiling, too.

When she and Reynold left, and Bryce and Zane packed it in, and the bar slowly emptied, and Miranda began closing out the register, and the lights went out section by section, and nobody remained but us, Alfie snuck up behind me, arms wrapped around my waist, and said, "You wanna go take a dog for a walk?"

I leaned back against his solid chest. "Take it easy on me, Parzival."

His laughter tickled my neck. "I'll get you next time."

"You've already got me."

I surveyed the bar as we left, remembering the first day I'd walked in, ready to puke from nerves, seeing Alfie's comforting smile. As it turned out, I'd never completely overlooked him. I'd only been playing the wrong game, focusing on my rivals, and neglecting to take inventory. Everything I'd ever wanted had been right here since level one. All I had to do was uncover the treasures hidden in plain sight.

Epilogue

As soon as the plane touched down in Cologne, I turned my WiFi back on. Text messages began coming in fast and furious from the hours we'd been in flight. While we taxied on the runway, I flipped through the pics of Kamal Aida had sent.

Alfie stretched and started scrolling through Instagram. "Reynold's really promoting the crap out of that comic book."

I glanced over. I still didn't care about comic books, but Reynold had decided to invest in Tristan's venture. Now that they'd gotten his first comic printed and in stores, Tristan's weekends were spent driving his actual car around Georgia to promote it. Bully for him.

A driver met us at luggage claim and whisked us through town. I wanted to get out at every street corner and walk around. Finally, we pulled up to the hotel and carried our bags in, looking around in awe.

Alfie's eyes were saucers. "This is incredible."

Because the hotel was near the convention center, we saw girls with colorful hair and guys in cosplay costumes from different games. The energy had me completely jazzed. "These are my people!"

In our room, we found a bottle of champagne chilling on ice with a note. *Knock 'em dead, kid. We all have full faith in you. Reynold.*

A lone butterfly loosed itself, but I took a deep breath and focused on Alfie, my north star. He took my hands. "Ready?"

"I am now. Thanks to you."

"Nope. It's all you, Sierra. You made this happen."

"I did, didn't I?"

We spent the rest of the day exploring the convention center. I found the room where I'd be presenting and Alfie sat back and listened as I said my words aloud several times. Then we took in a tour of the city. We ate food from street vendors and drank beer at a real German beer hall. It was all the better because I was able to share it with Alfie. He'd used the convention ticket he'd bought me for himself.

After we'd worn ourselves out, we strolled hand in hand back to the hotel. He kissed me in the elevator, and by the time we got back to our room, I'd opened the top buttons on his shirt. His neck hadn't stopped tempting me. I also loved his elbows, his earlobes, and the backs of his knees. I fetishized his entire body.

We made the most of a strange new bed and fell asleep perfectly content, talking about our day, about the presentation, and about our plans to fly to Paris to visit Emma the following week. Meeting his older sister made me more nervous than the demo.

Demo day, I woke up, showered, put on my favorite dress—the one covered in moons and stars and planets, some with smiling faces—and let my hair fall free with its new purple and pink unicorn colors. I wore the fun raspberry-colored lipstick I'd stolen off Aida. I felt confident. I felt like me.

Alfie and I walked together to the designated presentation hall. I was disappointed to find so few people there, and worried for the first time that instead of flopping I might not have anyone to present to.

I set up the laptop and asked Alfie if he could figure out how to cue the video. "No shenanigans this time."

He blushed. "No pranks. I'm rooting for you."

A man in a Link T-shirt peeked his head in. "Is this the demo for *Castle Capture*?"

"Yes."

"Awesome. It's in here, guys!" he hollered.

A group of guys in various pop-culture-themed clothes came in searching for seats. One of them, wearing an actual suit, broke free of the pack and asked Alfie to move.

I asked, "Are you the tech guy?"

He looked over at me. "Yup."

That made it official; the demo was about to happen. My hands began to shake as more gamers filled the room.

Alfie slipped behind me to rub my neck and whispered, "Do you know what you call a group of gamers?"

I laughed. "A gaggle of geeks?"

"Nope. A herd of nerds."

I snorted and relaxed. It reminded me these were my people. We were a drove of dorks.

The video screen lit up behind me but it was pure white. I breathed in and out. What if I forgot everything?

Alfie sat on the table before me and took my hands in his. "When we get home, why don't you move in with me."

"Huh?" My brain had started hinting at potential calamities. Why was he bringing this up now?

"Let's make it official. You'd still be close to Aida and Marco, but you all need your own space. I want you with me. Every night. I want to wake up with my arms wrapped around you. I want to come home at night to find you tangled in my sheets. Move in."

I could picture it, and I loved the idea. We'd been practically living together for the past six weeks. I still paid rent for my old room, and since my things were still there, I straddled two homes. My room in the basement was feeling smaller and smaller, more supplemental, emptier.

But my brain never failed me, and I could also picture a worst-case scenario. "What if we don't work out?"

He leaned his forehead against mine. "We're going to work out."

"What if we don't?"

"That would be a problem whether or not you moved in, right?"

"But it would be more complicated."

"It's always complicated. But I don't want to spend another night alone. Move in."

Like he said, I'd only be a few blocks from my old pad. I supposed I could move back in with Aida if things went south. But I wanted to be optimistic things wouldn't go bad between us. I'd discovered the other half of me, and I'd be crazy to spend another day alone.

"Yes." I squeezed his hands.

"Seriously?"

"Let's do it."

He gave me a chaste kiss, one that promised more heat in another hour. "I love you."

I checked the time and realized he'd tricked me into paying attention to him instead of the upcoming presentation, misdirecting my nerves from one battle to another. It had worked. I'd forgotten to panic, and I wasn't scared.

"I love you, too, but I need to start."

"You're going to do great."

Alfie took a seat in the crowd, smiling, encouraging, and I faced a packed room. My crowd. My people.

A family of fans.

The screen lit up behind me with the title sequence, and a roomful of nerdy geeks gasped at the beautiful art Marco had created. It was a gorgeous game. I couldn't wait to share it with our future gamers.

I spread my arms toward the imagery.

"Welcome to the next generation in RPG games. I'm excited to present to you the expansive world of *Castle Capture*."

Without referring to my notes, I launched into a presentation of the game I adored.

And I crushed it.

Connect with U s

Visit us online at
KensingtonBooks.com
to read more from your favorite authors, see books
by series, view reading group guides, and more.

for sneak peeks, chances to win books and prize packs,
and to share your thoughts with other readers.

facebook.com/kensingtonpublishing
twitter.com/kensingtonbooks

Tell us what you think!

To share your thoughts, submit a review,
or sign up for our eNewsletters, please visit:
KensingtonBooks.com/TellUs.